SONGS OF SILENCE

SONGS
OF
SILENCE

Patricia Barrie

HONNO MODERN FICTION

Published by Honno
'Ailsa Craig', Heol y Cawl, Dinas Powys
Bro Morgannwg CF6 4AH

First impression 1999
© Patricia Barrie

ISBN 1 870206 39 8

British Library Cataloguing in Publication Data
A catalogue record for this book is available from the British Library

**Published with the financial support
of the Arts Council of Wales**

Cover illustration: "Fan Hir 1989" by Megan Jones
(original painting in Brecknock Museum in Brecon)
Cover by Chris Lee Design

Printed in Wales by Dinefwr Press, Llandybïe

For Catherine Taylor, with love.
With grateful thanks to Mary Morgan for
her advice and encouragement.
Thanks also to the jolly hill farmers of the
Tai'r Bull, in Brecon.

AID TO WELSH PRONUNCIATION

Bach: small, little one; a general endearment but sometimes used sarcastically (*bach* – 'ch' as in loch).

Cariad: love (*kar-iad*).

Da iawn: very good (*da yown* – as in brown).

Diolch: thank you (*dee-olch* – 'ch' as in loch).

Diawl: devil, hell (*d-yowl*).

Duw: God (*dew*).

Einion Ddu: Black Anvil (*Ine-yon Thee*).

Gwragedd Annwn: dames of the dark regions (*Goo-rag-eth Anoon*).

Llyn: lake (*lin* – make an '1' with the tongue and blow through it).

Malen: girl's name (short 'a' as in talon).

Nos da: good night (*no star*).

Pen-y-Coed: place name, 'above the woods' (*Pen-uh-Coyd*).

Rhodri: man's name (*R-hodree*).

Sut ydych chi?: How are you? (*sit ud ichee* – 'ch' as in loch).

Twp: stupid, daft (*toop* – short 'oo' as in book).

Tŷ bach: little house, lavatory (*tea bach* – 'ch' as in loch).

Tŷ Mawr: big house (*tea mour* – as in sour).

Ydych chi eisiau coffi?: Do you want coffee? (*Ud ee-chee* ['ch' as in loch) *ice yie* [as in tie] *coffee*).

Star Song

What are words on another's tongue?
Glimpses through torn curtains,
Starlight through clouds.

Each of us is a world we travel alone,
Returning with tales only of moments:
River in flood,
Beggar at the door,
Sunrise over the sea.

Like stars clustering the night
We gather within rooms,
Spilling our radiance as if to touch,
To shine: my light upon your world,
Yours upon mine.

Yet all we see is the glimmer, the gleam,
The bright light of a star seen
Across aeons of space and time.

What are words on another's tongue?
The night's cry, the star's song.
The moan of the wind on the mountain.

CHAPTER ONE

They called it an eisteddfod. Jill, who'd looked it up, had said it meant, 'Sit down, shut up and listen'. Owen was sitting down, he was shutting up, but he wasn't listening. He hated music. Music dug too deep. It made him aware that beneath his crisply laundered linen he'd journeyed only evolutionary inches from the ape. It made him want to tear off his clothes, thump his chest, howl and run wild. But it wasn't done in general practice. The patients didn't like it.

Warm zephyrs of 'Myfanwy' fanned his ears. He scratched his temple, crossed his legs, searched the programme for the time of the interval and checked his watch to see how much longer he had to suffer. Forty more minutes. Christ, he'd die.

How could it touch you so when you didn't understand the words? How could it break your heart? *Dirion*. What did that mean? Dread? Doom? Despair? It sounded like rocks falling down a well, rousing up monsters that were best left alone. Sighing, he leafed through the programme again, searching for translations, rustling the pages. When that failed to divert him, he gazed up at the roof of the 'concert hall' – a clear cobalt sky, with house martins and swallows darting to their nests in ruined castle walls.

He could see it was beautiful: the ruins, the sky, the mountains in a circle all around. But it was all so strange, so far away. Even the weather seemed foreign. He should have stayed in London, where he belonged. Yet if Jill and Paul had left him there, alone . . . Grief turned his mouth downward like a tragedy mask and he covered it with his fingertips, furtively hiding the evidence.

He glanced left and right, seeking distractions. Across the grassy aisle two hundred rapt listeners gazed, misty-eyed, at the choir, as if this schmaltz, this borrowed sentiment, was the best thing that had ever happened to them. On his other side, Paul – with another two hundred suckers – gazed, misty-eyed, at the choir.

Jill leaned across Paul to pat Owen's hand. 'Are you all right?'

He nodded. Useless to tell the truth, that he was panicking and close to tears. He wanted to run: not just from the castle, but from Wales itself, where the mountains, like eavesdroppers, hung over his thoughts, listening with raised eyebrows, passing it on.

1

It had been a blistering day. Now the sun was lowering and would soon slide below the peaks, although it wouldn't set for an hour yet, far away. No one ever saw a sunset here.

Myfanwy breathed her last and was mourned with a sob and a fanfare of blowing noses. From the seat just behind him Owen heard someone say, 'They couldn't 've had better weather for it, could they? Remember last year?'

Owen remembered last year. Last year, the world had caved in. He'd lost his marriage and his children . . . Lost his marbles.

The choir sat down and a dark, busty girl, brightly blushing, ascended the platform. She stood at the microphone with feet apart, shoulders set square, her hands splayed like a gunfighter's, a few inches clear of her hips.

Owen clenched his fists and his teeth. He closed his eyes, waiting for the spiteful, soprano shriek which he felt sure would be his swan-song. Nothing happened. The silence lengthened. A low, moaning wind moved among the broken stones of the castle walls.

Freezing airs touched Owen's temples, making his hair stand on end. He opened his eyes. It was the girl! She was singing! Singing about the wind and the stars, her voice so deep, so low and controlled, it seemed scarcely human. There was no accompaniment. She was alone, her song changing from moan to melody, softer than the sheen on a black cat's back.

> *What are words on another's tongue?*
> *Glimpses through torn curtains,*
> *Starlight through clouds.*

Owen tipped back his head and took a deep, relieving breath, allowing his eyes to close again. The muscles in his shoulders and belly relaxed, his mind emptied of everything but the song, and even the song was an anxiety he could scarcely bear. He didn't want it to end.

> *Like stars clustering the night*
> *We gather within rooms,*
> *Spilling our radiance*
> *As if to touch . . .*

The other songs had touched him with hard, tearing hands, rough

2

fingers digging at unhealed wounds, making him bleed again. But this was comfort. This was ease. Her voice, the melody, the words . . . Their meanings.

With feet braced and shoulders squared, the singer had drawn out the deepest notes of her range, stretching her spine to reach the clearest and brightest. There was a curious effervescence in these brighter notes, a distant humming which conjured starlight without need for words, rendering the words almost redundant.

Yet he wanted to hear them. They had meanings he needed to understand. Frowning, he opened his eyes and stared at her mouth, searching for meanings and hearing only the harsh fricatives of an alien tongue.

Fear pierced his feet and bolted upwards to slam under his heart. She was singing in Welsh! He didn't *know* any Welsh! Yet he'd heard! He'd understood! And it was all gobbledegook, like everything else! He heard someone cry out and knew that the utterance was his own only when people whirled in their seats to stare at him, outraged. He leapt from his seat and ran, the moon-faces of strangers staring with hatred as he passed. But the voice followed, mocking him for imagining that he'd understood.

> *What are words on another's tongue?*
> *The night's cry, the star's song,*
> *The moan of the wind on the mountain.*

He fetched up on the far side of the car park feeling ashamed of himself and bitterly disappointed. He'd thought he was over the worst. He'd thought all he'd needed was a break from everything, a change of air. But he'd never been to Wales before this week and he *didn't* know the language. His understanding of that song had been a delusion, nothing less. But if it was a delusion it was the worst one he'd had yet. Poetry? Next thing you knew, he'd be getting messages from the saints, telling him he was Jesus.

Jill strolled towards him between two shimmering rows of cars, looking, as ever, about twenty years younger than she actually was. Beautiful hair. Wonderful figure. Face like the back of a bus. But you had to make yourself notice her face and even then it didn't matter. She was a beautiful woman: a cool, elegant, soothing woman, the perfect doctor's wife. Trouble was, she'd married the wrong doctor.

She tilted her head, gently chiding, 'What went wrong?'

3

'I don't know.'

She tilted her head the other way, back towards the castle. 'She's singing again. She has a fantastic voice, yes?'

'Yes.' He sighed. 'Go back to Paul will you? I'll walk home. I think I . . . I'll be better on my own for a while.'

'You aren't feeling too awful?'

'No. Really.' This was true, in a way. He never felt good, but if you measured 'awfulness' on a scale of ten, this scored about two, which was surprising. He knew where he was. He knew what his body was doing, knew where all the bits were and that they were behaving normally. The panic had gone.

'It's a long walk,' Jill warned.

'Do me good.' He smiled and turned away, but he'd grown accustomed to being watched over and, while he walked to the first bend in the High Street, his mind screamed, 'Stop me!' and collapsed in a grey little heap when she didn't. Yet why should she? Paul was her husband. They were happy together. He should count himself fortunate that they'd taken the trouble to support him this far. But they'd be going back to London on Sunday, leaving him here alone. To *relax*, Paul had said, evidently not guessing that if Owen relaxed he'd fall apart.

But he could manage a little walk on his own. He wasn't so far gone that he couldn't do that. He was forty years old. Forty was not the right age to be behaving like a child – eighty would be soon enough for that. He flung back his shoulders and marched like a soldier, swinging his arms: left, right, left, right. He caught sight of his reflection in Dixon's window, thought, Christ, I look like a lunatic, and slowed to a stroll, sliding his hands into his pockets and his gaze to another reflection of himself, in another window across the street. He looked fine from a distance, tall and spare, dark and well-dressed. No one would know, just by looking at him, that anything at all was wrong.

He had hated this town the first time he'd seen it. An airless maze, overshadowed by the hills, its narrow, sunless streets were built almost entirely of granite: a grim, remorseless grey which too closely matched his state of mind. He'd discovered since that it was a decent little place: clean within its limitations and remarkably prosperous, making its living out of tourism and the ubiquitous mountain sheep, which occasionally strayed into town to check on the profits. But the greyness still frightened and oppressed him. He couldn't wait to get out of it. Panicking, he began to run and almost immediately stopped, biting his lip. No, he mustn't run. He was over the worst. He could control it now. Count. Counting was calming. It focused the mind, kept it from straying into dark, uncharted territories where snakes and staring monkeys lurked. When he reached two hundred he'd be safe again.

He reached the war memorial at the foot of the hill at a hundred and thirty-three. The road was wider here, flat and straight, with corporation flower-beds at either side which, although they did little to relieve the dismal aspect of the granite, at least set its shade at one remove and opened a view of the sky.

His fear of the town left him and he was assailed by another. He hadn't reached two hundred and he'd forgotten his place. A hundred and thirty? Thirty-five? To be on the safe side, he went back to twenty-nine, matching his stride to the rhythm of the count, his count to the rhythm of his stride.

Now he'd be safe. He'd said he'd be safe when he reached two hundred, and it was unwise to short-circuit the process, to break the charm. You had to be careful with this sort of thing. Even when you knew you were being ridiculous, you had to be careful just in case there was something in it. One never knew. He'd once thought he knew everything it was needful to know. Since then, he'd learned only one more thing: that you *never* know.

CHAPTER TWO

It had rained all week. Now, suddenly, the wind turned and strengthened, blowing dry and cold from the north-east, clearing the sky. Tonight there'd be a star-white frost and ice crystals in the peat, crunching underfoot like spilled sugar.

'Look at that sky, Ness,' Rhodri stood at the door, his chest bared to the wind, naked toes cleaving the worn slate of the doorstep. 'Breathe it in. Make the most of it, girl. There won't be many more like this one, this side of lambing.'

It was good to see the world again after living in a raincloud for so long. It was good to see that the mountain hadn't floated away, that all the landmarks were still there: crags and gullies, walls and watercourses, the road looping down to the valley. About five miles over and half a mile down the town huddled under its own cloud of coal smoke which, back-lit by the sun, appeared as the steam from an enchanted cauldron. The trees down there still bore a few mists of gold-dust and bronze. The streams were like shards of blue enamel, broken from the sky.

It felt like spring: the day after the thaw when the mountain chuckles and forgives everything and the rills run free from the ice. But the ewes were down from the high tops and the rams – fat as butter when they first went a-tupping – had worn themselves thin on their lusty autumnal occupations.

Shivering, Rhodri ran to the fire where his shirt was airing. He called back over his shoulder, 'Don't you go wandering off now, Ness. It's Saturday, remember,' and saw her watching him with scorn in her milk-blue eyes. Of course she wouldn't wander. He'd changed the sheets and swabbed the floor, polished his boots and taken his tweeds from under the mattress: things which happened on Saturdays only. Now she was waiting for all the omens to be fulfilled: the dressing, the combing, the hunting for wallet and ration book. Finding the key.

He'd damped the fire earlier on, swept the grate, set the guard, made certain that no vagrant spark could burn him out of house and home while he was gone. But now he checked it again. He checked everything again, just in case. When you lived on a mountain, five miles from anywhere, forgetfulness was death – or at best a waste of shoe-leather.

By the time he'd finished, Nessa was heaving a sigh as she took to her bed on the mat by the fire. She made no fuss, but her eyes burned with a wronged woman's spite and, as he blew her a kiss, she closed them. *I am not too old, Rhodri Thomas*, she said.

She was, though. The last time he'd walked her into town he'd had to carry her back and he wasn't volunteering for that again in a hurry. She'd been ashamed of herself, too, poor thing, scarcely raising her eyes above his knees for the best part of a week afterwards. Then, when Saturday came again, she'd been full of it: yapping and capering, raring to go. She'd cried like a child when he'd left her.

It didn't do to get too fond of a dog. Nessa could almost speak, yet because she couldn't, quite, he filled the silences for her, crediting her with thoughts and feelings she couldn't possibly have: *his* thoughts, *his* feelings. It opened up false roads of sympathy and understanding which, when you came down to it, were pure narcissism. Nessa loved him because he loved himself and he loved her because she . . . No, it didn't do to get too fond of a dog. It was too confusing.

Walking down to the town was easy: five miles, quick march, do it in an hour. It was on the way back, with his face whipped raw by the wind and ice underfoot, that he sometimes longed for a motorbike. Or a quiet little farm in the valley. Both cost money, however, and Rhodri didn't have any. His sheep kept him solvent only if he lived like a sheep. His poems earned him a new pair of boots every other year, a pint of best bitter now and then and a few dozen books, second-hand. Not much of a life most would say, yet he was happy enough. Lonely, sometimes, but a man needn't live on a mountain to be lonely sometimes. He could read, write and sing, he could talk to his dogs, even to his sheep (although they didn't listen); and what is company, after all, but the occupation of the mind?

But he was twenty-eight, and the years since he was eighteen had flown on the wings of the wind, making him think tomorrow he'd be forty. When a man was alone at twenty-eight he was as free as a bird, yet he'd found the corpses of ravens on the mountain, seen their empty skulls bleached by the frost, heard the wind whispering through their eye-sockets like a dirge. There comes a time in the life of all things when freedom and desolation are the same.

'But not yet.' He spoke aloud and with a baring of teeth which might, had anyone seen him, be interpreted as anger, but he burst into song a moment later, hearing his fine Welsh tenor echoing from the hills and thinking, You could be on the wireless.

> *There was a jolly miller once*
> *Lived on the River Dee.*
> *He worked and sang from morn to night,*
> *No lark so blithe as he.*

Perhaps he would get a wireless. A wireless would be company. It lacked the three (the only three) things a wife might have offered – sex, children and edible pastry – but you could turn it off when it cried and complained; you could turn it off when it talked too much. You could turn the damn thing *off*.

> *And this the burden of his song*
> *Forever used to be,*
> *I'll care for nobody, no, not I,*
> *If nobody cares for me.*

With this sentiment made plain to the world, he squared his shoulders, filled his lungs and launched into the passion-torn melody of 'David of the White Rock'. He usually sang 'Men of Harlech' on the way back. It was exactly the right rhythm for gasping your lungs out, which he sometimes was if Young Sue Philips had taken pity on him.

'Ooh, love me, Rhodri; love me with your eyes wide open! Tell me I'm beautiful! Tell me I'm cute!'

He drew the line at cute. Beautiful was easier. Even a cabbage can be beautiful. With a blue bloom and a fresh dew and the light of the morning shining, a cabbage can be beautiful indeed.

He stopped singing about three miles down. People were always asking him, 'Not gone mad up there yet, then, Rhodri?' and he would give them no futher cause to wonder. He sometimes did feel a little crazy. When all the speech you hear in reply to your own is the bleating of sheep and the crying of buzzards, and the mists come down so thick even your own feet depart from view, there's a feeling comes over you so strange you'd be mad *not* to open your throat and howl like a loon. He had done so once or twice. Felt better for it, too. But they'd never understand that in the Co-op.

8

The first house on the left was the manse: a grey, neo-Gothic house, with green-painted window frames and brown lace blinds, which looked as if it had never had a fire in the grate. Rhodri put up his chin as he passed it, hardening his mouth, not just against Malen Price should she be watching him, but against whatever had burdened her that she would carry for the rest of her days. She had looked at him once, just as Nessa did, with all of her soul in her eyes, but a dog's soul and a young girl's are different things, and he hadn't dared hear what Malen's soul had to tell him.

His order at the Co-op was much the same every week: potatoes, carrots and onions, cheese and macaroni, his ration of shin-beef and bacon, five stale loaves (half price), porridge, tea, marge, soap and a tin of condensed milk. He allowed himself very little of what he liked, having discovered that an appetite served is an appetite raging, but sometimes his body lusted for juices even Young Sue Philips could not give him, and then he bought a tin of pineapple chunks and gave her back door the go-by.

'Here he is, then, lovely boy.' Mrs Cadog Evans, Co-op, always blushed when she saw him and pretended a profound interest in her bacon-slicer until the heat of her cheeks had cooled. She worried about him, up there on his own, with no one to call if he broke his leg and no one to find him until the ravens had stolen his eyes. She loved his eyes, had told him more than once when the shop was quiet, 'If I was thirty years younger, boy, I'd die for your eyes.'

She was not alone; yet Rhodri could value no one who would die for his eyes. He was not responsible for his eyes. They were a wealth he had inherited, like jewels, from father to son down the generations. There were other things more precious that were his alone: things nobody knew, let alone thought to die for.

'Not gone mad up there yet, then, Rhodri?'

'When I do I'll be the last to know it, Mrs Evans.' He smiled and reached for his wallet. 'How much do I owe you?'

It nearly always came to sixteen shillings, perhaps a few coppers more or less. Coal and paraffin took a similar sum, but the pain of handing over two green pounds and getting only a few coins in exchange never lessened. With his savings growing by scarcely a hundred pounds a year, he'd be sixty before he could afford to marry, and who'd have him then? When he was sixty, Young Sue Philips would be seventy-three, and if he wouldn't have her now, he'd be damned if he'd have her then.

'You haven't heard the news, then, Rhodri?'

'I heard the rain,' he said.

Mrs Evans narrowed her eyes and looked at him sideways. His dislike of gossip was well known and his eyes could look daggers as well as forget-me-nots if he was rubbed the wrong way.

'Mrs Roberts, Manse,' she said carefully. 'Took sudden, last Sunday. Heart attack. Post-mortem, too, poor woman. They only buried her yesterday.' She shook her head. 'The minister's breaking his heart, poor man, but what can he do?'

She darted him another look, but Rhodri, his heart thudding, pretended not to have understood.

Mrs Evans explained it. 'Well, he can't keep Malen with him, can he? Think of the talk! Even if she wasn't cracked—'

'I'll take a pound of apples,' Rhodri said stiffly.

'She's not his daughter, Rhodri. Be practical, *bach*. Just because you don't like talk doesn't mean there won't be any. Russets or Coxes?'

'Russets,' Rhodri said. 'And my change, please, Mrs Evans.'

'Oh, you're a funny one.' She slid the apples across the counter and counted his change into his palm. 'But I suppose it would be a better world if we were all as funny.'

He was opening the door when, to his annoyance, curiosity overcame him. He turned to find Mrs Evans gazing after him with love in her eyes. 'Forget something?' she said.

'I just wondered. What will Mr Roberts do? With Malen, I mean.'

Mrs Evans shrugged. 'I don't know, *bach*. But going by the talk . . .' She bit her lip. 'Well, what choice has he got? He'll have to put her away, won't he?'

Rhodri walked up towards the library, telling himself he was soft, telling himself to forget it, telling himself Malen was cracked and that the asylum would be the best place for her. But he was too soft to believe it.

He'd first noticed her about three years ago, when his love of music had overcome his hatred of chapel and taken him, struggling, to the Sunday School Anniversary. Never again. They'd welcomed him like the Prodigal and he, too embarrassed to know what he was doing, had dropped two florins into the plate, not realising until they'd left his hand that they were not the few coppers he'd put by. The shock of it had never left him. Ever afterwards, when he'd thought of Malen, he'd lost that four bob all over again and known sorrow. He should be glad they were putting her away. She'd been nothing but trouble to him from the first.

Alto, her voice had been: solid gold, with a spine-prickling shadow over the low notes. She'd sung Tchaikovsky's 'Crown of Roses', all by herself, her face a white parchment valentine, her hair a bolt of crimson satin, her hands like moths' wings flying from the night of her gown. Nervous, yes, but it had been a nervous song, full of thorns and blood and viciousness, and her voice hadn't faltered; there'd been strength in her soul, he was certain. Good girl, scholarship girl, full of promise. What had happened to her? What had they done to her that she should forsake it all for silence?

Without quite knowing where his feet were leading him, Rhodri ended up in the graveyard, beside a mound of raw earth heaped with the blood and rust of funeral chrysanths. He'd spoken to Mrs Roberts once in the Co-op, when she was still the widowed Mrs Iestyn Price and working in the office at the glove factory. A proud, sour-faced woman he'd thought her (English, of course), with a mouth pursed up like a cat's arse. Tight skirt, high heels, neat little waist with a green fitted jacket. Fancied herself something chronic. Later, when she'd married the minister, it was all pleats, woolly cardies and Jesus-bids-me-shine. Everyone had said she'd been happy – until Malen had cracked. Then Mrs Roberts had become herself: grey and grim, plodding drearily to the end of her sorrow.

'You knew, didn't you?' he murmured.

But it was too late, now. Had he wanted to turn busybody he should have done it last spring, when Malen had looked at him with her soul in her eyes, asking him, telling him . . . Nothing. She hadn't spoken for years. She hadn't made a sound except, when someone spoke to her, to scream and run away, feeding her mouth with her fists as though to silence herself entirely. Cracked. She was cracked and no one could help her. He shrugged and walked away, jingling his change in his pocket and wishing it would breed.

But everywhere he went, people spoke to him about Malen. And Enid Griffiths, Library, mourned for the girl she had been.

'Used to do her homework in here, she did, Rhodri, waiting for her mam to finish work. Shakespeare, geometry, the lot. Very tidy. She had ambitions.'

11

'What sort of ambitions?'

'Oh, I don't know. Same as mine were, I suppose. College. A tidy job. Anything to get away from this dump.' She gazed out into the narrow street with its greenish slime of cold chips and spittle. 'How do you bear it, Rhodri? You could have done anything; you needn't have come back here. You're brainy, good-looking . . .'

'I don't like people, Enid. They make me itch. Anyway, you came back, didn't you?'

'I had to. You can't leave your mam to die on her own.'

'I did.'

'That was different. You were in the Army.'

He sighed. 'It was different, I'll grant you.'

But he would never have come back, except to her funeral. He was sorry it had been so and yet had no regrets, no wish to turn the clock back and do it otherwise. She had made him what he was and, give or take a few weaknesses he would rather be without, he had accepted what he was and learned to like it. He had courage at least, and strength and honour. And a mind of his own. And Nessa.

Enid Griffiths stamped his books, flicking the covers to see what he'd chosen. 'Oh, you'll like Chekhov,' she said. 'He's very clean.'

'Clean?'

'Like standing on a mountain, with the wind in your face.'

He laughed. 'Oh, that'll make a change, then. Got anything dirty?'

CHAPTER THREE

'A hundred and ninety-nine, two hundred.'

Relieved, Owen sighed, closed his eyes for a moment and turned his face to the mountains. From the castle, their roots screened by the town, they had seemed to rise up like painted flats from the boards of a stage. Now, as he left the last of the town behind him, their vast third dimension became more obvious, more daunting. Once he crossed the river he'd walk no more than a few hundred yards before the road began to climb, yet the nearest of the peaks – Einion Ddu, the Black Anvil – was still more than eight miles distant. It looked very like an anvil now and as black as its name, thrown into gilt-edged silhouette as the sun slid behind it. Going, going . . . A blinding starburst of radiance, flying sparks shot from molten gold . . . Gone.

> Each of us is a world we travel alone,
> Returning with tales only of moments:
> River in flood,
> Beggar at the door . . .

Owen stopped counting, stopped walking. His face turned cold and he dragged a damp, trembling hand over his mouth. That song again. The Welsh song, sung in Welsh, the meaning of which he couldn't possibly have understood. So how could he remember it? He was a doctor, not a poet. It *couldn't* have sprung from his own mind! True, some pretty strange things had sprung from it just lately, but he'd seen most of them at the zoo in happier times and regurgitated them like vomit, crushed and fermented almost beyond recognition, but still recognisable. Aged monkeys, staring at him out of the darkness with dull, accusing eyes.

He reached the bridge just as a laughing group of girls began to cross it from the far side, half-naked in shorts and sleeveless vests, soft skin reddened by the heat of the day. Fear shrivelled his groin. Shame scorched his face and lowered his eyes to the narrow cinder path that led to the river bank.

The girls were coming closer, staring at him with wide, rapacious eyes, red mouths leering. They giggled and fell against one another, whispered (about him!) and shrieked with laughter, holding their bellies. Owen fled.

He had run no more than a few yards when the girls appeared again, not in reality but as a clear and cogent thought: a recognition. Not one of them (and there had been only three of them) had been a day over twelve. Since when had he been terrified of three little girls? A pack of them, perhaps. A hundred or so, screaming blood, death and vengeance. But *three*?

He closed his eyes and released his breath in a puff of weary laughter.

He knew his own anatomy as thoroughly as he knew anyone else's, but it had changed recently; changed from an organised, closely packed collection of working organs to a shadowed gallery of images culled from the paintings of Breughel and Bosch: little men with hammers beating at his heart, fat snakes with flickering tongues slithering through his guts, ants swarming the raw underside of his skin. At night, in the dark, there'd been the monkeys, whose only function had been to gaze at him, like judges, and know him to his soul.

Now, as he laughed, his body became something else: the wings of a bird, gently folding. He was calm.

He had been calm before: as silent and dull as if his skull had been sucked clean of his brains. Partly sedation. Partly a kind of emotional death, a dreadful death which had never been as dreadful as the thought of resurrection. But this was different. He was calm and alive, all seeing, all hearing.

He walked on, watching the river, listening to it, quite unafraid. The landscape resolved itself into something logical and deep, with layers of meaning he fully understood. He was now going north, and realised with a glow of satisfaction that he was taking a short cut. About a mile further on was an old ford road – he'd walked that way with Paul only yesterday – which, about half a mile up the mountain, forked into the lane where the cottage was. If he kept going at this rate, he'd be home before the others arrived in the car.

Although the sun had disappeared, the evening was still very warm and he a little overdressed in his concert-going outfit. Shirt and tie, linen jacket . . . He took off the jacket, loosened his tie. He sat on the river bank and smiled, thinking of Ratty and Mole, messing about in boats. He'd wanted to be a boat builder when he was a kid. They'd made them of wood in those days and it was more the wood than the boats he'd fallen in love with. At school, he'd made a garden seat for his mother and a document box for his father, the former of teak, the latter of holly, bound with brass. Since then, he'd done as much woodwork as there'd been time for, but there'd never been much time. He'd spent the past twenty years of his life chasing his tail. Now he seemed to have caught the bloody thing and disappeared up his own backside.

His was the sort of hardy, middle-class background most people would give their eyes for: dogs and ponies, public school, rowing, rugger, chilblains at every extremity. Yet even as a kid he'd viewed it more as an onlooker than an active participant. It was as if he hadn't belonged in his own life, as if he was acting it out for someone else, reading a script he'd never seen before. But it had never been as bad as this. *Never* as bad.

He closed his eyes and saw a Welsh kitchen dresser, with acorns and oak leaves carved into garlands. He opened his eyes and gazed at the trees. Willows for cricket bats, alders for clogs. He'd never thought himself an especially intelligent man, just a man with a phenomenal memory. He'd been given a list of woods and their uses when he was fourteen years old and he could still remember most of it. He could remember most of everything, especially the things he most wanted to forget.

It was that, he supposed, which had knocked him off his trolley. Remembering too much, the fine details of things, knowing how they all fitted together – like a piece of fine furniture – and thus being unable to comprehend how they could, so easily, have fallen apart.

Best not to think of it just now. Not now.

Carrying his jacket over his shoulder, he wandered on. The river bed was as wide as a road, the water a mere country lane meandering peacefully down the middle. The only boat you could sail here would be made of paper. He'd made paper boats with Jonty . . . No, best not to think of that. Count, that was best. Keep calm.

'One, two, three, four . . .'

But he couldn't go through the rest of his life just counting, not thinking. He had to begin some time. He had to work it out. Jonty and Em were his children, not some whore he'd propositioned, some money he'd stolen, some cruelty he'd committed and was too ashamed to remember. He'd done none of those things! He'd given life to two beautiful children, and that, goddammit, was *worth* remembering.

His heart began to thud, squeezing his lungs.

'Five, six, seven, eight . . .'

He came to the ford, where a line of stepping stones crossed the river beside the roadbed. Save for the murmurings of water and the humming of flies there was nothing to be heard, nothing to be seen that wasn't beautiful: trees and grass, bracken and foxgloves. He was too close to the foot of the mountain now to see its peak; the lower slopes on this side were covered with pine forests and huge expanses of bracken: extraordinary stuff which grew as high – and in places higher – than a man's shoulders.

Forgetting his count – forgetting he'd needed it – Owen laid his jacket on the bank and searched the ground for dry sticks. He hopped stepping stones to the middle of the river where, smiling, he bundled three sticks together and crouched to set them carefully on the breast of the stream. One for Jonty, one for Em, one for me.

They sailed off together, neck and neck, before tumbling down a miniature rapids and being separated – Jonty and Em one way, Owen another. Even this didn't disturb his calm. He felt sad, that was all: sad that the miseries of life should be made explicit even in an innocent game. Yet the moment Jonty and Em sailed out of sight, he became agitated and jumped into the dry margins of the river bed to chase them downstream. They hesitated for a moment to spin in a tiny whirlpool between two stones and, just as they broke free, the stick named Owen rushed to join them.

He laughed out loud, covering his mouth as the laugh changed to a sob of relief. It was going to be all right! *He* was going to be all right. This had been just an eddy in the stream, but he was through it, over it. Everything was going to be all right!

He felt marvellous. He ran back to the stepping stones and, in the mood for fun as he hadn't been for years, crossed them like a tightrope walker, outstretching his arms for balance, rocking his ankles as though about to fall. Even the way he retrieved his jacket from the bank was an expression of triumph and elation. He scooped it up, twirled it like a bullfighter's cape, flung it over his shoulder and suddenly froze, his lungs emptying, his heart slamming with shock.

He was being watched.

He thought immediately of the monkeys who had watched him in the dark. The man's face was not unlike them: craggy and brown, with deep channels of age and solemnity cut into his cheeks from nostril to jaw. But there the resemblance ended. His eyes were blue and friendly, his mouth faintly curved in a smile.

He was dressed like a hillwalker in stout boots and knee-breeches and was of a walker's skinny, wiry build; yet he looked as if he'd never moved from that spot; as if he'd been sitting on the bank since the dawn of time, watching grown men make bloody fools of themselves on the stepping stones. He was so still, so at ease with himself, it was impossible not to envy him. Although very clearly amused by Owen's antics, it was just as clear that he'd decided to be discreet about it and not say anything until Owen did.

The first cacophony of shock faded to a distant drumbeat and Owen could think again. He tilted his head to look at the sky. The sun – somewhere – had set and sent fronds of pink clouds to signal its departure: 'I am going to Australia. Taking the kids.'

Above the forests and the farewell fronds, the sky had changed to a pale, luminous green, set with a single star.

Each of us is a world . . .

'Lovely evening,' Owen said.

He sketched the old man a smile and turned away to cross the river again. As he turned, he noticed the preparatory movements of a reply: intake of breath, shoulders lifting, a sudden animation of head and hands which – subliminally – led Owen to expect a deep, cheerful voice of the 'hail-fellow-well-met' variety.

He was in mid-stride between one stepping stone and the next when the old man screamed: a passionate, terrified scream which seemed to herald the ending of the world. Staggering sideways into the dry river bed, Owen whirled around to see what dreadful danger had befallen them, how he would have to die; but the old man hadn't moved. He hadn't moved an inch. His posture was precisely as it had been before he'd screamed – relaxed and at ease, his mouth already closing in a smile.

It was worse than the monkeys, worse than the snakes, which had made Owen think only that he was *going* mad. Going, going, but not yet gone. He'd known he could survive them if he was careful. He couldn't survive this.

He ran, clutching his jacket to his chest, his heart slamming against his ribs like mortar fire. The world was exploding around him and all he could do, even knowing it was the last thing he would ever do, was to run until he died. On the far side of the river the ford road went up like a wall, snatching him against it. He scurried on all fours, stepped on his jacket and fell down, whimpering with terror. The old man screamed again: a cry of such anguish, rage and misery that it shattered the sky.

CHAPTER FOUR

It was growing dark by the time Rhodri walked back through the town. He was aware of tea being cooked and lavatories flushing, kids playing skipping in the streets, gossiping girls with folded arms who watched and whispered as he passed.

He walked past the manse very slowly, fighting a hypocritical urge to go in and give his condolences to the minister in hope of seeing Malen and saying . . . Well, what could he say? I'll visit you at the mental? I'll bring you harebells off the mountain lest you never see them again?

They would cut her lovely hair with a basin and dress her in grey, take her, shuffling, around the garden, three times a day.

The road was dark in the vale of the mountains, the sky still light, with a tissue-paper moon climbing to its watchtower above the peaks. As was his habit, Rhodri looked up towards his cottage, dreading to see the red tongue of flame which would mean that all was lost. Fire in his absence was the greatest of his terrors. The others were of getting lost in the mist or of freezing to death with his leg broken.

Just as his muscles tensed from downhill to up, he heard Malen screaming. It was a loud scream, broken off short, as if someone had cut her throat before she could finish.

He walked on, muttering 'Men of Harlech' through gritted teeth:

'Wele goelcerth wen yn fflamio,
A thafodau tân yn bloeddio—'

She was always screaming. It was all she could do. And why not tonight? Her mam was dead and she had nothing.

'Ar i'r dewrion ddod i daro,
Unwaith eto'n un!'

No one answered his knock. Embarrassed by the impulse that had brought him running back, he turned away and stood at the gate, staring up at the mountain. 'Think,' he told himself. 'Go home, good boy. Put one foot in front of the other and keep going until you get there.'

19

But she was still screaming: over and over, like a sick child whose only comfort is the rhythm of its misery. Rhodri turned again to face the manse. Then, holding his breath as if it was his last, he crept along the path to the rear of the house.

A bare electric bulb shone yellow through drab lace at the kitchen window. The house was built up high at the back, with steps to the door, and the window-sill just fitted under Rhodri's nose. But only for an instant. In the next he lost his temper and most of his reason, yet with the little he had left he could tell himself calmly, You will regret this for the rest of your days.

Having thrown open the door with unnecessary violence (he'd thought it would be locked), he said nothing and did nothing and kept his gaze fixed sternly on the minister's buttocks as he tried to pull up his trousers. His braces were hooked under his foot and, as fast as he laid claim to his decency, as fast it escaped him again. His face was like tallow, his mouth trembling. 'God help me, God help me,' he muttered, while Malen, discreetly ignored beyond the corner of Rhodri's eye, curled to her knees and sobbed herself to silence.

'Well, Mr Roberts,' Rhodri said, 'at last you have brought me to chapel.'

'No! No, look, Rhodri, it wasn't what you thought! It was . . .'

'It doesn't matter what I thought. It doesn't matter what I saw with my own two eyes. All that matters in this town is what I say of you when I address the congregation tomorrow.'

'They won't believe you!' He wailed it, like the wind.

'Oh, they'll believe me! I could tell them your prick is a stick of seaside rock, with "Malen" written right through it; and still they'd believe me! I will see you shamed, Mr Roberts; I will see you ruined; I will drive you through the streets with your backside bared, so that all may see the filth of you!' He flicked his gaze to the mantel over Malen's head. 'Malen, get up and dress yourself.'

He had been speaking in Welsh, forgetting she would know none except the little she'd learned at school. Now, still without looking at her, he said in English, 'Malen, get up and make yourself tidy, good girl.'

'She can't,' the minister whispered.

He'd trussed her like a chicken. He'd tied her elbows against her spine, lest she scratch out his eyes in the battle. But at least she was decent. She'd shaken her skirt down over her thighs and Rhodri was grateful for that, although the terror in her face disgusted him. She screamed when he cut her free and scuttled away, to shiver in the corner like a dog.

'Look,' the minister said. 'I'll give you anything you want. Money! Every penny I've got, if you'll only . . .'

'Ten thousand pounds,' Rhodri said. 'And your balls on a plate, fried in batter.'

'No, no, it wasn't my fault! She – she tempted me, Rhodri. She tempted me, you see, from the beginning. You're a man; you should understand. I couldn't help myself!'

'Oh, yes,' Rhodri said mildly. 'I understand.'

'You do?' The hope in his face was pitiful.

'Yes, because now I am tempted to kill you, and am not at all sure I can help myself.'

He stood six foot one in his boots. Mr Roberts was very much shorter, and large and loose in the belly. His teeth were made of pottery and his spine of yellow cheese and as Rhodri advanced on him he trembled and wept, 'Oh, please, oh, please, God, help me!'

'But I will restrain myself,' Rhodri went on. 'For as you said, I am a man. What are you? I've known tups with more decency, dry grass with more religion, *stones* with more pity!'

He had been speaking softly to keep Malen safe from his rage, but he was a man whose rage could rip out his guts by the roots, make him puke, make him faint, and he couldn't do that now. He had to think, and his thoughts had flown, leaving him in a panic, with only one thing certain: that he could not leave Malen here.

'Get your coat,' he told her. 'Put shoes on your feet.'

'You are taking her?' The minister jumped up from the chair where his shaking knees had thrown him. 'Good, good. That will be for the best. I didn't mean it, Rhodri, I swear!' He was wringing his hands. 'I will get her a coat and a muffler against . . . the cold. And – and her shoes. She will need gloves . . .'

'Tomorrow is Sunday,' Rhodri said. 'Will you meet me in chapel, Mr Roberts?'

The minister bowed his head. 'No,' he said.

21

CHAPTER FIVE

It was nearly dark by the time Owen arrived back at the cottage. He felt very weak and fragile, bemused, but no longer afraid. He hadn't met the old man at the ford. It hadn't happened. It had been another delusion. He *must* tell Paul he needed help. He couldn't go on like this, pretending it would all go away and leave him as he'd been before.

With barely a hundred yards still to walk, he saw the headlights of the car swinging into the drive. A few moments later, Paul came running down the lane to meet him. 'Christ, what happened? I've been back down to look for you . . .' He placed a hand on Owen's shoulder. 'Hey . . . You all right?'

'No. No, I'm not.'

He was surprised to hear the timbre of his own voice. It sounded like a horn: soft and low, gently humming.

The night's cry, the star's song . . .

'I walked,' he said, 'along the river, to the ford.'

'Good,' Paul said. 'Shorter that way.'

His arm slid behind Owen's back, shepherding him along as if to hasten him from the pursuing shadows of his madness. 'Come on. Let's go in, before Jill calls the cops. She's been worried sick. We got back ages ago, couldn't think what had happened, where you could have gone . . .'

They reached the gate. Owen stopped walking and shook Paul's arm from his shoulders. 'I met a man!' he wailed. 'I met an old man who – who *screamed* at me, Paul! It – *shit* – it was so *real*!'

There was silence. Owen heard the silence as a tense holding of breath. He filled the silence with Paul's thoughts, his firm, reasoned responses.

Well, I think that's enough, don't you, Owen? Take you back to London tomorrow, hmm? Find a decent clinic where you can have a good, long rest. Don't worry. We'll get you right. Just leave everything to me . . .

But it wasn't that easy. Nothing is that easy when your mind has cracked and it occurred to Owen that, cracked as he was, he

22

should have anticipated that Paul would not say anything in the least reasonable. That he would say nothing. That he would simply squeak.

It was a brief, tortured little sound, almost immediately followed by another squeak, more prolonged, more agonised, like a mouse caught in a trap.

Owen stared at him through the gloom, not even bothering to wonder what might happen next. It could be anything. Paul could sprout wings, explode in a puff of blue smoke, drop dead . . . Anything. Nervous breakdowns were like that. He'd met a woman during his psychiatric practice who'd thought she was a poached egg on toast and everyone else a salt cellar. 'Sprinkle me lightly,' she kept saying. 'Salt's bad for the heart.'

'I . . . er . . .' Paul murmured at last. 'I . . . umm. Look, I don't want to confuse you, Owen, but . . . Oh, dear. Look, come into the house, will you? Let's . . . er. Yes, let's do that, shall we?'

All the lights were on. Bruch's violin sobbed loudly from the sitting room. Paul bellowed, 'He's home, darling!' and Jill emerged from the kitchen, wringing her hands in a towel.

'Oh, thank God. Owen, where were you? We thought . . .'

'No, no, he was fine,' Paul interrupted briskly. 'He walked along the river, to the ford.'

He sounded strange. His voice was louder than usual and shaking a little. He said, 'Oh, turn that bloody fiddle off,' and strode into the sitting room to cut off the Bruch in mid-sob.

'Sadly,' He returned to the entrance hall, watching his feet. 'He met Gethin Morgan, and he's not . . . He's not certain . . . He thinks he *imagined* it!'

Paul covered his mouth, but the ploy failed and he abandoned it – and himself – to a snort of laughter.

'Swine.' Jill glared at him and ran to take Owen's hand. 'Take no notice. *He's* never met him . . .'

'I have!' Paul protested.

'Not before you knew about him. And it's dreadful, Owen, I know. I was with Lucy the first time – she was only twelve – and it was terrifying. In fact,' again she sent Paul a glare of disapproval, 'it's terrifying even when you *do* know him.'

Throughout most of this, Owen had passively stood and passively listened, observing Jill's distress and Paul's laughter more as symptoms of his own state of mind than of theirs. He didn't understand any of it, didn't think understanding could be expected of him any more. He was just waiting for them to take charge, make decisions, shove a needle in his arm and take him away to somewhere cool and very quiet with green venetian blinds.

Instead, Jill shook his arm. 'He's mute, Owen,' she said firmly. 'He's deaf.'

'Who?' He gazed blankly in Paul's direction.

'Gethin Morgan! The old man you met at the ford. He's mute. He can't *do* anything but scream, poor old thing.' She smiled, letting her shoulders droop in sympathy. 'Oh, *poor* Owen. This was the last thing you needed, wasn't it? But he's quite harmless. Really. He was just saying hello.'

Owen woke a little before seven, feeling surprisingly rested and easy of mind. He stood at the window for a while, thinking ordinary things about the weather. Another scorcher. Not a cloud to be seen. It had rained virtually without cease from Christmas right through to Wimbledon fortnight, yet now it seemed as if it would never rain again.

The cottage was on one of Einion Ddu's many foothills, scarcely more than six hundred feet above sea level and still about seven miles east of the summit. But the Anvil seemed much closer this morning, less awesome, its every stone sharply delineated and softly coloured by the morning sun. You could never say what colour – or even what shape – a mountain was. It changed with every change of the light: now pink, now green, now violet, black, or bright, burning gold. Last night – vast, dark and ominous against the lowering sun – Chris Bonnington would have had a hard job to climb it. This morning it was a quiet stroll before breakfast: ten minutes and you'd be there.

He showered and shaved, blinking a little as he recognised his face in the mirror. Funny, that. He'd been shaving at least once a day since he'd arrived here last Friday. Now it was Friday again, yet he had the idea he hadn't seen himself for months.

He looked much the same as ever. Disgustingly healthy, in fact, although he had that sort of complexion: roses, roses all the way – especially in the whites of his eyes. His hair had turned a little frosty over the temples and he'd developed, just recently, a badger-like streak of white just over the left eye. Also, his left eyebrow kept sprouting two wiry white hairs which grew at twice the rate of the black ones and tickled his eyelid. All that aside, he didn't really look like a man whose life wasn't worth living. A touch baggier around the eyes, perhaps; a shade grimmer about the mouth, but on the whole, not *bad*.

Tears filled his eyes and he stood and stared at them, wondering how they could have sprung from what had been – for him – a fairly optimistic train of thought. But he hadn't, really, been thinking about himself. He'd been thinking about the old mute at the ford.

Just saying hello? Yes, perhaps. The poor devil couldn't hear himself screaming, could have no idea that the cries he uttered were so terrible. Yet why would he cry out if there was nothing he needed to express? And what the hell *had* he expressed? Loneliness and desolation such as Owen could barely imagine, let alone claim to have shared.

But it was strange . . . He kept seeing little images of the life he'd lost – the busy, responsible, family man – spliced with a picture of the old mute sitting at his ease by the river. And the one looked so dark, the other so bright . . . There was something wrong with that. It should be the other way around, surely?

He tipped up his chin to shave his throat and found himself thinking of the girl at the eisteddfod. She'd been a contralto, he supposed, albeit a very unusual one. An unusually good-looking one, too. He liked women who wore their hair long. There was something generous about it: hide nothing, give all. Her breasts had been on the generous side, too. Thirty-six? Thirty-eight? When she lay flat on her back they'd spill sideways, not . . .

Christ, what was he thinking of now? *Sex*? That was a bit normal, wasn't it?

He'd been nuts last night and now he wasn't?

He gazed again at his reflection, levelling his eyes, telling the truth: that Gethin Morgan had screamed only once. Owen had been nurturing the second scream for more than a year and although its release had, for a short while, rendered him almost entirely witless, he now knew the precise meaning of the phrase 'better out than in'. He could almost wish he'd done it before, even knowing it wouldn't have helped. He'd needed to know . . . to feel . . . He'd needed to be told – as poor Gethin Morgan had seemed to tell him – that the end of the world was at hand and that there could be no purpose, any more, in keeping up pretences. Scream, sob, drum your heels, lie in the road and eat dirt. It doesn't matter any more.

25

He'd hit the bottom he supposed, and although 'having no further to fall' was not the most pleasant thing one could say of oneself, it was very much better than falling. It was restful, at least. One could think, examine one's wounds, ask oneself, 'So where do you go from here?' and know that 'up' was the only answer.

Up. Well, he was in the right place for it. He'd been here a week without attempting the mountains. It had been too hot. He'd been too tired, too scared. Mountains opened up views of things that were best kept hidden.

He leaned over the basin, pressing down with his fists until his knuckles turned white. He'd lived on the low ground all his life for fear of the view he might see from the top. Don't raise your voice, don't raise your fists, don't raise your hopes.

'And where the hell's it got you?' he muttered. 'Climb the fucking mountain!'

CHAPTER SIX

Malen seemed not to comprehend that she'd been rescued. She left the house quietly enough, but as soon as Rhodri touched her shoulder to guide her at the gate, she flung up her hands and screamed to raise the dead.

You will regret this for the rest of your days, he reminded himself. She's *crazy*. He had noticed, too, that she was as ugly as sin, and it was no comfort to tell himself that any girl would be ugly when her eyes were swollen with tears, her lip cracked, her face stone white on the one side and purple on the other where Roberts had hit her. Crazy, ugly and screaming, and before this night was out, there'd be two of them.

'All right,' he said. 'You go where you like, Malen. I'm going home.'

He knew the way like the back of his hand, knew the precise turn in the road where the backward view closed over. He walked to that place swiftly, wishing that Malen and her troubles were things of the past and home his only prospect, yet knowing also that if she did not follow he would take the town apart to find her.

The road glimmered with frost. A needle wind pierced Rhodri's ears like a gypsy's. He turned. Malen was foreshortened at the foot of the hill, a little black shadow creeping laboriously after him like a slug up a wall. He waited, slowly freezing, until she came to within a few yards of him. She was crying, sniffing, wheezing with the effort of the climb.

Rhodri raised his eyes to heaven. 'Only four miles to go,' he whispered.

He held out his hand to help her and she screamed and scuttled away, eating her gloves.

'I'll wait for you further up,' he said.

The madness of it all – his madness, not hers – came over him in nauseating waves as he walked on up the mountain. He had nothing to offer her. No blankets, no electric, scarcely any food (the Co-op delivered, but not until Monday) and no indoor lav. She had only the clothes she stood up in and, since she'd dressed beyond his gaze, he wasn't even certain she'd put her drawers on.

The minister had destroyed her and should rot for it, but Rhodri

27

had done all he could to ruin him. Roberts wouldn't dare go to chapel on the off-chance that Rhodri would not, and if he had any sense at all he'd pack up and leave before the hounds of rumour gave tongue. Innocent or guilty, pure or defiled, when those rumours ran you were finished.

Where is the minister?

No one knows.

Where is Malen?

With Rhodri, dirty swine that he is. You'd think he'd know better, wouldn't you? You'd think he'd have more sense. He always seemed so decent, but I could tell. I knew what he was up to, all along.

'Bloody hell,' he breathed. 'What have I done?'

He was asking himself the same question at dawn the next morning and the answer, that he'd dug himself into a dirty great pit, was no more comforting now than it had been the night before. He'd had no sleep at all. His skin felt like sandpaper and his thick coat no more substantial than gauze against the wind. Garth and Pen, his working dogs, trotted close at his heels, sensing the mood – although he'd said nothing about it – that forbade any silly antics. When he stood at his usual place to survey the flock lower down, the dogs sat one each side of him like kids in a schoolroom, heads up, feet together, tails banging the frozen ground as if to say, 'Look how good we are.'

'I don't know what to do,' he said. 'What the hell am I going to do?'

He'd gone all to pieces, like a torn feather pillow shaken on the wind. He hadn't felt so confused in years. He couldn't get a grip on his thoughts, couldn't sort them into order. He'd done the most stupid, irrational, pointless (probably illegal) thing he'd ever done in his life. They could lock him up for it. She was only sixteen. And she was mad. He could tell the judge, 'She followed me of her own free will,' until he was blue in the face and it would make no difference.

She was sleeping now – he'd thought she'd never go off – flopped in the corner of the settee with her mouth open and her neck at such an angle she'd howl with the pain of it when she woke. Howl, scream, sob. It was all she could do. She'd screamed even when he'd given her a cup of tea, and then she hadn't touched it; thought it was poisoned, probably.

In the night, he'd prayed she'd run away and lose herself on the

28

mountain – until he realised they'd blame him for it and do him for murder. Well, this was the last time he'd act on a chivalrous impulse. Sir bloody stupid bloody Galahad. He'd been right all along: keep yourself to yourself, mind your own business. Why the hell had he changed his mind for *her*, of all people? She was *terrible*.

As they walked back to the cottage, Garth grumbled in the back of his throat and stood for a moment looking up the mountain. The sun hadn't come up yet, and all of that flank was still in shadow. There was nothing to be seen. Fox, maybe. They usually lived lower down at this time of year, nearer the hen-houses, but even foxes could be crazy.

He tiptoed to the kitchen window and peeped in to see if Malen was still sleeping. She was, but had evidently been awake during his absence and had found a way to call Nessa to her side. Now the pair of them were cuddled up on the settee, Malen's arm cradling Nessa's neck, Nessa's head resting on Malen's knee. Ness wasn't sleeping, though. She had more sense. A guilty conscience too, for he'd told her to stand guard, not lie about in luxury, enjoying herself with the visitors. She flicked her eyebrows at him and twitched her tail. *It's not my fault*, she said. *She tempted me. I couldn't help myself.*

He crept in on tiptoe and closed the door with care, pressing the latch right down to keep it from clanging. As he turned, Nessa's guilty conscience got the better of her and she slid off the settee to creep to her mat by the fire. Malen woke and blinked, her face crumpling when she saw she'd been deserted.

'Go back, Ness,' Rhodri said softly. 'Malen wants you. Go back now, good girl.'

She went, looking warily at him over her shoulder: *You're quite sure about this, are you?*

'Yes, yes,' he said. 'You look after her, Ness. And if anyone comes near her, bite him.'

Malen didn't make a sound and, encouraged, Rhodri went on, 'I can tell you one thing, though, Ness. You won't have to protect her from me. You would if you had to, though, wouldn't you, girl?'

He flicked a glance at Malen, who was frowning into Nessa's face as if waiting for her to reply. Nessa never replied, and yet he'd always pretended she could, if only to keep his own train of thought running smoothly.

'What d'you mean, you'd bite my leg off?' he demanded indignantly. 'After all I've done for you?'

He turned away to fill a pot with water and oatmeal, his heart thudding with hope as Malen's silence continued. She'd screamed at every word he'd said to her so far, but now he was talking to Nessa, and she was silent. Perhaps she was just worn out.

'I'm making porridge,' he said softly. 'Will you eat some, Malen?' She screamed and bit her hands. She wasn't worn out.

'Remember when you first came here, Ness?' he went on quietly. 'I've never seen such a blizzard, and the wind rattling the door so hard it was a wonder I heard you. Frozen to the bone you were, and so thick with snow I thought you were a white dog: white all over, like a ghost. Remember that, Ness?'

He glanced across the room. Nessa had laid her head on her paws and was looking at him with one eyebrow cynically cocked. *I don't know what the hell you're talking about*, she said, but Malen was looking at Rhodri under her eyelashes, waiting for the rest.

Rhodri filled the kettle and put it on to boil. 'I never knew where you came from that night,' he said wonderingly, 'whether you came up the mountain or down it, or whether the fairies brought you. I think they must have, come to think, for I've never met a dog who could talk as much. Nag, nag, nag, morning to night. Worse than my mother, you are.'

He glanced once more in Malen's direction and she turned quickly away, but not before Rhodri caught sight of her smile.

Duw, he thought, I'm winning.

She had veiled her face with her hair, which, dull and matted after her night of suffering, was still a wonder to behold. Never had he seen such hair. The colour of blood on a copper plate, it fell rippling with deep waves and tiny ringlets almost to her waist. Her skin was white as milk, her eyes like silver shillings touched by shadow. And if she could smile, perhaps she was not mad. If she could smile, perhaps he could keep her.

Oh, I knew what he was up to, all along!

He stared into the porridge pot, biting his lip, listening to the talk, knowing it was true.

Duw, he thought, I'm lost.

CHAPTER SEVEN

Owen hadn't thought it possible to get lost on a Welsh mountain, in summer, in broad daylight. He'd thought he'd walk to the top, turn, see where he'd just come from and walk back again. But it hadn't worked out like that. He'd walked up, walked down, walked north, south, east and west – and now wasn't certain which was which – been lured into deep gullies where icy streamlets ran, up rocky slopes which hadn't led anywhere and now, amazingly, had even lost sight of the peak he'd been aiming for.

Rather more amazingly, he wasn't in the least scared. He was hot, that was all. His feet felt like char-grilled steaks, burned into stripes by the griddle of his trainers. That aside, he felt terrific, as if the effort of walking for hours in this stark, deserted landscape had cauterised all his wounds. He couldn't quite make it out. Last night, when Jill and Paul had gone back to London, he'd felt desolate, cut adrift in a sea of silence,

> *Like one, that on a lonesome road*
> *Doth walk in fear and dread . . .*

(Poetry again! Where the hell was it all coming from?)

He felt quite different now, strong and inspired, like a schoolboy pursuing the adventure of his life. Famous Five stuff. Bottled pop in his backpack, sandwiches and cake. No chocolate, sadly, and no shaggy dog panting at his heels, but one had to be practical in such matters. The chocolate would have melted, the dog chased the sheep.

He'd met a good many sheep up here: brave, brazen animals that stamped their hooves, stood their ground and stared straight through him with insolent, piss-green eyes. Their eyes made him think of the devil, so cold they were, so devoid of any character or feeling. He couldn't imagine why they were always associated with God, yet could think of few sounds more peaceful than the rasp of their endless grazing.

> *The mountain sheep are sweeter*
> *But the valley sheep are fatter,*

> *We therefore deemed it meeter*
> *To carry off the latter . . .*

Now, what was that one? The War Song of Someone or Other: some wild Welsh chieftain . . .

Owen was Welsh. He'd never confessed it to a living soul. Even Alison had never seen his adoption certificate, although he'd had to tell her his parents weren't his own. She'd quizzed him about it, of course, told him he had a right to find his real parents if he wanted to. 'I don't,' he'd said. 'Leave it.'

'Why? There's nothing to be ashamed of in being adopted.'

Try it yourself, he'd thought, but he hadn't said it, and she'd never mentioned it again. He'd been grateful for that, if only because shame hadn't been what he'd felt, and he hadn't known how to explain what he'd felt instead. He hadn't *wanted* to explain, and Alison . . . He'd thought she'd dropped the subject in respect for his feelings. Instead, she'd filed it away, to use later as ammunition.

'I never knew you, Owen. We've been married eight years and I still don't know you. But that's hardly surprising, is it? Even *you* don't know who you are.'

He was strong enough now to think of that as a cheap shot. It had hurt him badly at the time: not more than everything else, just . . . It was like having your arms and legs blown off and getting toothache at the same time. Too much.

He sat in the shadow of an outcrop of rock, drinking warm apple juice from a small green bottle, peeling a squashed sandwich from its partner. The cheese had melted to a consistency very like Evostik, but it tasted all right. Proper picnic fare. Jonty would have loved it. But Jonty would never have got this far, and even if he had it wouldn't have been the same. Owen had needed to do this alone, to be alone on the mountain.

It was vastly different from being alone in the cottage, where not just the walls but his own skin had seemed to rub against him, like a hungry cat which tripped him at every turn, yowling, 'Feed me, feed me!' And not even a bacon rind in the house to shut the damn thing up.

He wasn't hungry up here. The mountain had fed him, somehow, although it was hard to analyse the nutrients it had stirred into the soup. Oxygen, space, colour; a curious, minimalist beauty which struck you between the eyes and left you wondering,

'What beauty? Where?' The sky was blue, the mountain green. One might be forgiven for seeing nothing else, but it seemed the less the eye could see, the more it saw. What had been just a green mountain was now a riot of subtle colours: ochre and stone, black, grey and purple, bright patches of magenta where the heather bloomed, lemony lichens, orange and verdigris.

It was easy to understand why, in more dangerous weather, one might think the mountains were peopled by ghosts. The curves and angles of the land, sinking into hollows or rising up into crags, breathed with their own static life even on a day like this, when the air could scarcely stir itself for the heat. But the thing he would remember best, the thing he would remember for the rest of his life, were the lines. The swooping diagonals of the hills, the curves of the ridges against the sky, the sinuous blue thread of a stream far below. It was like being in the middle of a fantastic drawing, a miracle of draughtsmanship which made Cezanne a mere doodler and Picasso stone blind.

He didn't want to go down again. He didn't ever want to go down. He felt so good, so free. It had something to do with the heat, he supposed. There was safety in being warm. You could wander at will, find shade when you needed it, take a rest, do whatever you liked. There was time. The days were long.

But it was more than that. He'd set off soon after seven, wearing shorts under his jeans, a sweater over his shirt and forty years of himself draped like horse blankets around his shoulders. All that had gone. He had stripped to his shorts and his skin, to a man who had never learned, loved or suffered, who had never lived before. His life was like a film he had watched long ago. He could vaguely remember having been touched by it, touched enough even to shed a few tears at the end, but it hadn't mattered; it hadn't been real. It had had nothing to do with *him*.

This – this mountain – was the real Owen Read, the naked, ignorant, new-born Owen Read for whom life was not over but just beginning. He could do anything he liked with it. There was no one to say, 'Do this, be that, follow where I lead'. He was alone for the first time in his life, and – at least for the moment – he loved it. So why in hell's name was he grieving? For forty years wasted? For the torture of beginning all over again? Or simply because he'd eaten his provisions and would have to go down?

He could be in his surgery now, wondering when the list would end, whether he'd get any lunch, why Mrs Thing's bloodtests

33

hadn't come back and if he'd get a minute to fetch his suit from the cleaners. But he wasn't doing any of it. He was free. And just because freedom and loneliness felt very similar, it didn't mean they were the same. He'd rather be here than in London. He hated London. The very thought of it made his stomach swoop with nausea. So why *was* he grieving? He wasn't.

He walked on, climbing again – mostly on all fours – to the ridge of a massive scree. As soon as he reached the top he knew he'd come the wrong way. There was a small but unscaleable cliff to his left, a deep, rocky valley straight ahead and beyond that only more mountains, with the elusive Black Anvil nowhere to be seen.

'Come on,' he said. 'Be sensible. Give it up.'

He walked along the ridge, looking for a place to descend which would not involve tobogganing down on his backside. His calf muscles were beginning to ache and when he found a patch of grass roughly the size of his left buttock, he sat on it and massaged his legs until his hand went into cramp. He should have brought salt tablets. He should have brought more to drink. He should have brought a sleeping bag and a box of matches and a bag of firewood and a bow and arrow. Barbecued lamb chops and a night under the stars. Surely that would cure him?

'You have a brain the size of an oil tanker,' Alison had said, 'and a soul the size of a gnat. Oh, come *on*, Doctor! Haven't you any feelings at all? I'm leaving you, for Christ's sake! *Say* something, can't you?'

He couldn't. He'd been as mute as Gethin Morgan. He hadn't said a word, hadn't known where to begin and, had she insisted, might well have screamed as old Gethin had screamed, having feelings indeed, having feelings too many, but no means of expressing them which would make any sense. In the end, if only to prove to himself that he could still speak, he'd said goodbye.

She'd wept, then. Owen had been bewildered by her tears and still hadn't a clue what had engendered them. She was leaving him for a man she loved. She was taking the kids and at least half of everything else . . .

But he couldn't think of it now. Not for the usual reason – that he couldn't bear it – but because it seemed to have lost its importance. The mountain was bigger.

After a nasty moment at the top of the scree, when he lost his footing and began to slide, he went down the hill with care, having realised that if he broke his leg he'd be dead before anyone found him and, more surprisingly, that he had not the smallest desire to die.

God, if he could only live up here . . . If he could throw off the whole bloody lot of it and build a little hut, far away from everything except sheep and the buzzards which rode their blue, ecstatic thermals, high overhead. He'd always been interested in birds, but had never had time to make a study of them and now was appalled to think that he might have seen a rare red kite and mistaken it for a buzzard.

He knew so *little*. He knew – within limits – his profession, a fair chunk of English literature, the geography and general history of the Mediterranean, an extensive vocabulary in French and Italian (sod all of their grammar) and the basic rudiments of sailing. He could make a perfect dove-tail joint, sweep a chimney without making a mess on the carpet and tell the difference between a rose and a buttercup. That was about the sum of it and for a brain the size of an oil tanker it was – like his soul – a very small sum.

The many things he still wanted to know were things . . . Astronomy, for instance. How do you study astronomy without staying awake all night? He'd had enough of that in the call of duty – and fatherhood. Yet on the few occasions when he'd had a chance to lie, warm and sleepless, under the stars, they'd enchanted him, intoxicated him, called out to his puny gnat of a soul . . .

The night's cry, the star's song,
The moan of the wind on the mountain.

CHAPTER EIGHT

'That'll be two pound nine and six,' the woman said.

Rhodri leaned across the counter to check her arithmetic upside-down. He'd never seen her before and it was unwise to trust strangers with money.

'Seems a lot,' he murmured anxiously.

'Beautiful quality, though,' the woman said. 'Lovely and warm around her – um. She'll need that, just coming out of hospital, won't she?'

He'd walked twelve miles to find a shop where no one knew him. He'd told a crop of bare-faced lies to explain his purchases and made accusations of overcharging. Yet now the woman gazed at him with love in her eyes and whispered, 'Had a baby, has she?'

'What?'

'Your wife. Just had a baby, has she?'

'No! No, no. Appendix.'

'Oh, there's terrible. Very lowering. So that'll be two pound nine and six.'

It was like shooting a dog he liked, handing that money over. His fingers fumbled the trigger a dozen times before he could screw up his nerve to fire. Two whole pounds and a ten shilling note, and all he'd get back was coppers. Coppers, and a few bits of clothes for Malen. He'd grieved three days solid for all the clothes she must have at the manse. He'd gone down there to fetch them a dozen times in his mind, but every time he'd thought of it his rage had come back, worse each time, terrifying him with its intensity. He could kill Mr Roberts, break his neck without thinking. Crack, crunch, out like a light, and take my regards to the devil.

But he knew himself too well. He knew that at least half his rage – more than half – was aimed at himself, not the minister. He'd been a bloody fool. More fool than any other fool, for most fools don't *know* what they're doing; and Rhodri had known. He'd known for years, deep down, and now, too late, could see the pattern of his acts as clearly as if he'd written it in a poem. He should have written it. He should never have filed it away in that part of his mind labelled, 'Things Best Forgotten'.

He'd wanted Malen Price since he'd first set eyes on her: her blood-red hair, her milk-white face, her throat as slender as a flower-stalk.

Well, he'd got her, and already she'd cost him seven pounds. Clothes, sheets and blankets, a hairbrush, a toothbrush, a flannel. And he still had no idea how to get her to use any of them. She was filthy. She stank. It was partly his fault. Until she'd started hammering at the door with her legs crossed, he'd forgotten to tell her where the *tŷ bach* was, and that was nine hours after she'd arrived. God, what a bladder! But it must have leaked, and she'd been sitting in the same pair of drawers ever since. His only comfort was that she seemed almost as appalled by her condition as he was. She looked beaten and ashamed. She didn't dare move for the reek.

He left home at regular intervals, staying out until he was frozen to give her a chance to wash. But she wouldn't take her clothes off. He knew what she was afraid of and couldn't blame her for being afraid, but it was a nasty feeling, being tarred with the same brush as the minister. He felt almost as ashamed as if *he* had raped her, and as chastened as if his shame was no worse than he deserved. Yet barring that first guiding touch at the manse gate he hadn't laid a finger on her. Didn't want to, either.

He'd never been depressed before. Not like this. He'd been stricken by melancholy once or twice, but that was a different thing: a feeling that the world was too big and he too small ever to make his mark on it. What was his little mountain and his little brain, his tiny (though bilingual) vocabulary? There were jungles and deserts and apes out there, religions and cultures, snakes and insects, stars beyond the power of his eyes to see. He cured himself, usually, with the bitter truth: that he so often found himself struggling for words to describe snow, he'd give himself apoplexy trying to describe a jungle.

A man was as a man was made and he had no right to ask for anything other. A man took what a man was given and made the best of it that he could. Rhodri had done that. He'd recognised himself, his strengths and weaknesses, and lived accordingly. Malen Price had been one of his weaknesses and he'd put her behind him, like Satan, refusing to acknowledge she was there. But Satan has his ways of being noticed. A tap on the shoulder, *You want her* . . . A tap on the shoulder, *She needs you* . . . A tap on the shoulder and he was ruined.

When he looked at it from Malen's point of view he could tell himself he'd done right, that for her the hardships of the mountain were better, far, than being beaten, tied and raped. But she didn't know that, didn't believe it for a minute. She shrank from him when he came near her, flinched when he moved too fast, stared at his hands when, with a flick of his wrist, he tipped coal on the fire from a hod that weighed almost as much as she did. She was waiting for him to do to her as the minister had done and although he told himself he'd rather die, he wasn't certain of it any more. You could know your weaknesses as you knew the mountain: every stream, every stone, every treachery. Yet when the mists came down, you were as lost as the next fool, and be blowed if you could find your way home.

'Take her to the mental,' he told himself. 'You've done your best. You're not to blame. Take her to the mental and be shot of her. There's nothing more you can do.'

He knew immediately that he'd made the right decision. As soon as he'd made it he saw where he was and realised he'd been about to be as lost in the literal sense as he'd been in the figurative. He'd taken the wrong path over the mountain and was at least a mile out of his way.

'*Diawl!*' He paused for a moment, assessing his options, his heart thudding with the fright of a nasty moment. Another of his rules had gone by the board. You didn't dare take your eyes off the mountain in winter, although it could kill you at any time of year. He sometimes thought killing him was its only purpose and his only purpose to thwart its every attempt, yet he'd been walking blind for the past five miles, not seeing a thing. And why? Because of Malen.

She tempted me. I couldn't help myself . . .

God, that was so easy to say. So easy to believe. It was as easy as taking the wrong path over the mountain: keeping the contours at the corners of one's eye instead of looking, searching, identifying one stretch of heather from the next (which looked much the same) and choosing the way with a conscious will rather than leaving it all to nature. Nature was the mountain, which could destroy a man without moving an inch from its appointed place. It shifted only in mood, yet in its moods could change its shape in the time a man takes to wink an eye. All it needs is for the sun to go in. All it takes is for the clouds to come down . . . *She tempted me.*

No. He would not blame her for his own stupidity, his own, barely acknowledged, lusts. Lock her up, just because he couldn't bear the trouble he'd brought upon himself? If he did that, he'd be as bad as the minister, and he wouldn't, couldn't, be that bad.

'So what will you do instead?' He was gazing up at the mountain, changing places with it, as he'd often done in the past when he'd needed its strength to support him.

Have patience, it replied hoarsely. *What else is there?*

He wasn't the type to love buildings, but his own cottage was different. He'd built it himself or, rather, rebuilt it from the ruin it had been. Before the war – in fact, long before the war – it had had a two-roomed upper storey with a loft in the roof. Now it was just the one floor, with scraps of Rhodri's flesh embedded in the roof joists, smears of his blood staining every other nailhead, his cries of pain and frustration mixed in with the mortar. He'd completed it in a single summer, with no more idea of building than he'd had of embroidering a tray-cloth. It had been the first, agonised step on a road he had deliberately chosen. Now, with just as much agony and no deliberation at all, it seemed he had taken his last.

The first winter he'd spent here had been the worst in living memory. He'd been up to the neck in snow from November to the middle of April and had thought little of it, if only because much of the rest of the country had been in a similar plight. Since then, he'd discovered that he was a few hundred feet above the snow-line. When it rained on everyone lower down, it snowed on Rhodri. In milder winters it was rarely more than a greyish scum, resembling the foam at the edges of the sea, but where foam would hit the beach and disappear, the snow stayed, like a ragged-edged petticoat at the knees of a neglected child.

Strange how everything came back to Malen. She had besmirched everything, corrupted even his metaphors, rendered the very snow obscene.

'Bloody women.' He covered his mouth with his hand, struggling against tears of fury and disappointment. He'd had it all worked out. He'd known everything and thrown it all away on a moment's whim.

Oh, you knew everything, did you? the mountain murmured. *Smug bastard. I've stood here millions of years and can't say as much.*

'You haven't my intelligence,' Rhodri said nastily. 'Quick as a flash, I am. You noticed the ragged petticoat, did you? Pure genius, that was. Came out of nowhere, just like lightning.'

He sighed and tipped his face up to the sky which, having been as grey as an army blanket between dawn and sunset, had now cleared to a pale, duck-egg blue, warming to alabaster on the western horizon. The mountains were like pools of spilled ink on a painted table, the moon – waning now – a counterfeit shilling to pay for a worthless thought.

It was no good to talk about whims, as if they came from outside, like the snow. A whim was a choice you made, all by yourself. Stupid or otherwise, it had a purpose to serve.

'Yes,' he confessed humbly. 'I've done snow to death, haven't I?'

And rain, the mountain said. *And bloody sheep. And where's it got you? Where are your laurels, your Bard's chair, your fame? You needed a spot of anguish, see, and Malen's it. Be grateful.*

Shrugging, smiling, Rhodri turned from his thoughts to make the last weary climb to his cottage door. As soon as he turned, the door opened and Nessa ran out to meet him, twitching her rump like a trollop for a soldier. He didn't know how old she was. He knew only that when he'd first known her she'd come down the mountain like a waterfall, quick and brave and heedless. Now she came like a rug in the weaving, picking her way from side to side to ward off the twinges of rheumatism. Yet she could still jump to lay her muzzle in his hand. She could still run between his legs and nip cheekily at his bootlaces. 'Stupid bitch,' he said fondly. 'Get out of it, will you? Show a bit of consideration. I'm worn out.'

As fast as Malen had opened the door she'd shut it again, as though to remind him that his home was no longer his own. A spurt of rage prompted him to kick the door open, show her who was boss, but suddenly he heard his father shrieking, 'I'll be master in my own house, damn you, woman! I'll be master in my own house!'

Rhodri let himself in very quietly. Malen was not there, but the floor was damp, with a faint hint of Lifebouy still wafting up from the flags. The fire was strong and bright, the kettle simmering, the clothes rail draped neatly with Malen's laundered clothes.

'Oh, Ness . . .' he breathed.

He noticed that Malen had set the clothes rail too close to the grate, but he moved it automatically, acknowledging his fear of fire without even thinking about it. Thinking only of her. He wanted to run to her, hug her, kiss her, lift her up in his arms and swing her through the air for joy. But it wouldn't do.

40

He eased his pack from aching shoulders and set it carefully on the table. 'Well,' he said irritably. 'I'm back and no one to welcome me but you, Ness. I see you've put the kettle on, good girl. Oh! And you've washed the floor.' He crouched to fondle Nessa's ears, to drop a kiss on her brow. 'What a good dog you are.'

Nessa was a cheat. She took all the credit. Didn't deny a word of it.

'And that Malen,' he added sorrowfully. 'I've walked my legs down to stumps to buy her new clothes, and she can't even . . .'

He heard a movement in the passage which led to his bedroom: the soft scrape of her shoe on the cold stone floor. Rhodri turned away to make a pot of tea.

'Still, what can you expect? She doesn't trust me as far as she can spit and between you and me, Ness, I'm not sure she thinks as highly of *you* as she claims. Oh, she helped you, did she? Well, that's different. Credit where credit's due. Come back all I said.'

When he turned again she was there. She had on her overcoat, buttoned tightly to the throat. Her eyes were like flakes of soft coal glittering with silver, her skin wild roses, her hair ablaze with coppery flame. She was as clean as . . . No, he'd done snow.

'Want a cup of tea, Ness? No? Oh, well, perhaps Malen will drink a cup . . . When she's dressed.'

He sent a glance to her face, another to the parcel on the table, but she crossed her arms over her chest, afraid to touch.

'Ness,' he said. 'Take Malen and her parcel to the *tŷ bach*. Bolt the door behind you and tell her to get dressed. Then bring her back for a cup of tea. Got that?'

Nessa scratched her ear and flopped down by the fire.

Malen took the parcel.

CHAPTER NINE

Another hour passed before Owen saw his first glimpse of civilisation, although he hadn't a clue which bit of it. Save for two fairly long rests – one to cool his feet in a stream and one for his picnic – he'd been walking for five hours. He could be anywhere.

It looked more like a village than a town – it was hard to tell from here. There was a church tower flying the red dragon from its flagstaff, a few buildings and a glittering, shimmering thing reflecting red, white and blue, which was probably a car park. Everything else – if anything else existed – was obscured by the forested flanks of the hills. In spite of his wish that he need never go down, he was remarkably glad to see it. He was tired, hot and thirsty. He could see in his mind's eye a pint of chilled lager with condensation running down the glass like rain.

As he left the mountain behind him, he began to feel a little scared. At first it was barely worth noticing: a vague discomfort which bore no relation to the terrors he'd experienced in the past. Yet as soon as he noticed it, it became worse: a physical revulsion which turned his stomach, an emotional suspense which was centred at the back of his neck, making his hair stand on end. Was someone watching him again? Someone following him? He glanced warily to right and left. He whipped around suddenly to catch whoever it was creeping at his back. No one was there.

Yet some *thing* was there. He'd seen it before, this place: the precise shape of the hills, the rocks, their shadows and textures, the gorse and sedges, a cluster of stunted thorns growing from a crater-like hollow. He'd been here before – at this exact spot – and had liked it no better then than he liked it now. But that couldn't be! He hadn't walked this far with Paul last week. Had he dreamed it? Or was it a memory? He'd been born in this part of Wales, after all . . .

By the time he reached the village the panicky thud of his heart had eased to a murmur and he was thinking again of lager, a cool, quiet little pub where the sun never shone and . . . More lager.

It was called 'The Station Arms'. It had a frontage of green galvanised iron, plate glass windows and a clientele which, at a rough guess, smoked sixty a day, to a man.

The barman looked at Owen rather strangely, but all he said was, 'Hot out.'

'Hotter in,' Owen said, with feeling.

'Garden out the back.' He looked again into Owen's face, one eyebrow quizzically dipped. 'Nice and shady under the trees. Bring you a sandwich? Baked potato? Wholemeal roll? All done on the premises. Nothing plastic.'

He tipped his head from side to side, like a blackbird listening for worms, examining Owen's ears, his neck, the bulging contents of his backpack. 'We do vegetarian,' he said.

'What the hell for?' an old man demanded bitterly from the far side of the room. 'We're not bloody rabbits.'

Owen downed his pint and ordered another.

'That's the ticket,' the barman said. 'Come far, have you? On your holidays? It's not like this all the time, mind. Chucking it with rain six months out of seven and then there's the fog. We've had snow in June, before now.'

'Snow in January, too,' the old man announced spitefully. 'Regular.'

Owen escaped to the garden which, save for an overheated brace of German cyclists, was pleasantly deserted and remarkably well-tended, with climbing roses on the walls, stone urns full of herbs and a lovely old yew tree in a corner of the lawn. He sat at a rustic table in the tree's dense blue shadow and closed his eyes on bliss. When he opened them again he saw a girl crossing the lawn towards him, carrying a large oval plate on which lay a split baguette with salad and prawns spilling from the seams.

'Oh,' he said, 'I didn't order . . .'

'No, it's mine. Too smoky to eat in there.' She sat beside him, smiling up into the dark boughs of the tree. 'You don't mind?' she said. 'Nice and cool here, isn't it?'

She had on a tattered pair of denim shorts which exposed her legs almost to the groin. They were marvellous legs, with firm little muscles in all the right places, inviting hollows, a mahogany sun-tan and an exquisite glimpse of creamy pink where a seam had split just north of her thigh. Owen didn't know where to look and he had a suspicion that she knew it. Still, since she was here . . .

'Er – I wonder if you could tell me the name of this place? I've been walking on the mountain and . . .' He smiled stiffly. 'I was aiming for the Black Anvil and . . . lost it.'

'I'm not surprised,' she said bluntly. 'You're way out. It's about eight miles west of here. How long have you been walking?'

'Hours. I left home at . . . *West*? Don't you mean east?'

'No.' She was smiling, her dark eyes glinting with a cheeky, wicked light which both called him an idiot and forgave him for being one. 'I'm a local girl. I know where everything is – north, south and east as well.'

Owen stared into his glass, biting his lip on embarrassment. If she was right, if the Anvil really was west of here . . . He peered up at the forests. He was viewing them from a more northerly point than before, but they were definitely familiar.

'Where are you staying?'

He groaned and pointed upwards. 'Up there. I must have passed within a hundred yards of it on my way down.'

She laughed. 'Never mind, you won't have as far to go home as you thought, will you? If you follow the river about half a mile along, you come to a ford . . .'

It was really quite funny. He'd walked a full circle, and it was no wonder he'd recognised where he was. Dreamed it? He'd seen it from his bedroom window every morning for the past ten days!

'So where *are* you staying? Tŷ Mawr? Valley View?'

'No. I'm – er – borrowing a friend's cottage.'

'How long for?'

He shrugged. 'A few weeks.'

He was flattered by her attention, flattered that she was more interested in talking to him than in eating her lunch, which she hadn't yet touched. She was very pretty. Dark hair pulled into a pony-tail, tanned skin with a flush of heat in her cheeks, brown eyes fringed with curling black lashes. She had a soft, deep voice which matched her soft, deep breasts: breasts which would fall sideways when she lay . . .

He swallowed and looked at his hands. 'Are you a singer?' he asked.

'Oh, were you at the eisteddfod? Why didn't you say?'

'You have a lovely voice,' he said.

'Thanks.' She blushed. 'It's only for fun, though. I'm a teacher, really.'

'Music?'

She smiled. 'The three Rs. Primary school.' Wrinkling her nose, she added, 'I like it. Thousands wouldn't.' She nibbled a small shred of lettuce and with disconcerting suddenness said, 'I've got to ask. Do you know a man called Glyn Caldwell? He's a writer.'

'No. Never heard of him. Why?'

'Oh. Oh, well. You just look like him, that's all. I thought you were him, at first.'

She began eating, her eyes turned from him. Owen found her withdrawal strangely hurtful and his resemblance to Glyn Caldwell painful in the extreme. He'd thought she'd been interested in *him*, that something in *him* had excited her. But there was always another man, a better man.

'What does he write?' he asked.

'Oh. Well, funnily enough . . . You know that first song I did the other night? He wrote that. The words, I mean, not the music. Years ago, this was. He entered it in the National Eisteddfod. Didn't win anything, but it caused quite a stir locally. He had his picture in the paper . . . What's the matter?'

Without realising it, Owen had been staring at her, hoping she'd tell him what that song had been about and almost praying she wouldn't say, 'The stars'. He could cope – just about – with its being a figment of his imagination, some unsuspected poetic streak his 'nerves' had brought to the surface. But the gift of tongues? He couldn't cope with that.

With difficulty he relaxed. 'Go on,' he said.

'You sure? You look a bit green around the edges. Been out in the sun too long, I expect.'

'No, I'm fine.'

Still gazing anxiously into his face, she shook her head. 'It's an amazing resemblance, you know. I haven't seen him for years; he lives in London now, but . . .' She blushed again. 'If I see you again, I'll show you the book. It's got his picture on the cover and . . .'

'What book?'

'Oh, I didn't get to that, did I? I was telling you about the song – "Seiniau'r Sêr" – but in fact he's just written a book with the same title.'

'Is it in Welsh, then?'

She laughed. 'No. I didn't explain it very well. The *poem* was in Welsh. The book's called *Song of the Stars* – in English. You've gone green again,' she added flatly. 'Are you sure you're all right? Sunstroke can be funny, you know. My sister got it in Greece. She was sick for a week after.'

'Yes,' he murmured. 'I think I'd better go . . .'

'I'll see you on your way,' she said. 'Don't want you getting lost again, do we?'

He felt lost. He felt weak and frightened. His mind was full of shadows and thin, shrieking voices which came from far away. He wanted to run, but his legs would barely hold him.

'Down these steps, now. Hold the railing, good boy, don't want you falling.' She'd taken his backpack. Her arm was hard around his waist. 'No,' she said. 'It's no good. Sit down. Sit down now, and put your head between your knees. *Duw*, you're shaking like a leaf!'

She sat beside him on the steps and rubbed his back with a firm, coaxing hand. The shadows flickered. The shrieking voices fell silent. He heard the river tinkling over stones and the girl saying softly. 'You'll feel better in a minute. Don't worry. I won't leave you.'

He blew his nose. 'Sorry. You must think me a complete fool. I'm all right, now, I think.'

'Stop there for a minute. Don't rush it.' She laid her hand on his forehead and frowned solicitously. 'Cool as a mountain stream. It's not sunstroke, then. How about hunger? You had two pints and no lunch, mind.'

'It's that song,' he confessed weakly.

'No . . .' She scowled at him. 'Oh, well, then. It's no wonder you feel bad. All those demisemiquavers. Murder on the stomach.'

He covered his face with his hands, hiding laughter and a sudden rush of tears. 'Will you say it to me?' he asked. 'In English?'

'English? I'm not sure I can remember it in English.'

'Can't you translate it?'

'Yes, but it won't sound like poetry. The translation in the programme was good, but I only read it once. On principle, that was, mind. The great poet charged us royalties on every . . . *Now* what's the matter?'

He was staring at her again. 'There was a translation in the programme?'

'Didn't you buy one?'

'Yes!' He almost howled it, thumping his head with his fist in vain hope of knocking some sense into it. He'd read it in the *programme*!

'Christ,' he said, 'what a fool! What a bloody, stupid . . .!' He curled up on himself, hugging his knees with his elbows and his head with his hands.

'You'll let me in on all this, will you?' she murmured. 'No hurry. I've got all day.' After a brief pause, she added, 'You're looking healthier now, anyway. Your ears have gone red.'

It was difficult to explain it without explaining everything. He hated to tell anyone he was adopted, and that he'd been born Welsh – and had probably spoken Welsh as his first language – was something he preferred not to think about. He told her about his 'phenomenal memory' and hoped she'd be satisfied with that.

'It's a sort of photographic memory then, is it? You look at something and it's there for ever?'

'Something like that, but – as you've seen – it's not perfect. I remembered the poem, but not where I'd read it, or even that I *had* read it. As far as I knew I'd heard it once, in Welsh, and . . . That's what confused me. I thought . . .' A shadow of what he'd really thought flicked at his mind like a whip, making him shudder. Remembering long-forgotten poetry was one thing, remembering a long-forgotten language quite another. He didn't *want* to remember that.

'You thought you'd gone mad?'

'I suppose so.' He heard the coldness of his tone and was ashamed of himself. She'd been very kind. She'd been funny and gentle. She'd comforted him. And now she was escorting him to the ford, going out of her way, he was certain, to see him safely home. She was smaller than he'd guessed. Her head barely cleared his shoulder. At the concert, standing alone on the plat-form, she'd given the impression of being a tall, strapping lass, but she was really quite dainty. Small waist, slender hips. He'd even overestimated her bra size. But she was strong and healthy and her skin shone with a bright, open-air glow which owed nothing to cosmetics. Her nose was a little too large, burned at the tip and peeling slightly. She kept pressing her fingers to the end of it, as if hoping to cool it down, or perhaps hide it, although he hoped not that. It was by no means the prettiest part of her, but it was pretty because it was a part of her: warm and generous, unrestrained.

'I must have read your name in the programme,' he said. 'But I'm afraid I've forgotten it. *Not* a perfect memory, you see.'

'It's very Welsh. You'll never pronounce it.'

'I can try, can't I?'

She shook her head, clicked her tongue and tipped up her face to laugh at him. 'Gwen Jones,' she said. 'The Gwen's short for Gwenhwyfar, but even my mother calls me Gwen-hoover, so I've given it up as a bad job. I like it, though; it's the original of

Guinevere. I don't suppose your name's Lancelot, is it? I could do with a spot of romance.'

It was neat; it was kind; it was easy. Take it or leave it.

'No,' he said, aware that he was making one word do the work of two. 'My name's Owen.'

'Good name. Very heroic. Very Welsh.'

'Home Counties,' he said. 'And you've seen how heroic I am.'

'No,' she said softly. 'I've seen how sad you are. There's no shame in that. Did you love her?'

Owen was not greatly surprised at her question. Women usually went straight to the root of one's emotions, and although he'd hated the trait in Alison, who'd often done it to wound him, he didn't seem to mind it with Gwen.

They stood in a green tunnel of alders and willows to gaze at the river. 'I don't know,' he said. 'I thought I did. At least . . . Whether I did or I didn't, I would have been loyal. I'm the loyal type. Dull, I suppose. She said I have no soul.'

'Who was she to say so?'

'My wife.'

'No, I don't mean that.' She sat on the river bank, pulling one foot towards her groin to unbuckle her sandal. 'Let's paddle,' she grinned. 'Go on. Be a devil.'

He laughed. 'How old are you?'

'It changes from minute to minute. Six at the moment. Eighty first thing in the morning. Twenty-nine on my birth certificate. How old are you?'

He pushed off his shoes. 'Twelve,' he said.

They waded slowly down the middle, looking for tiddlers, running slimy green water-weed through their fingers.

'I've lived here all my life,' she said. 'I hate it, sometimes, but at times like these . . . Look at the sun on the water. It's like golden pennies from the fairies: touch them and they're gone.'

She scuttled about, trying to touch them, splashing and laughing, acting the goat. Owen watched, smiling down at her as if from a great height, wanting to join in, yet having no idea how to go about it. Alison had never been like this. She'd been cool and contained. Even when she'd laughed, she'd done it with dignity. There had been no joy in Alison.

'No,' he said suddenly. 'I didn't love her.'

'Good. She didn't deserve you. Everyone has a soul.'

'But I love my children.'

'Good,' she said. 'That proves it.'

'What about you?'

She glared at him comically under her eyelashes. Then, pitching her voice to a gossipy whine, 'Not *married* yet then, Gwen? Don't leave it too *late*, now, will you? They don't fall off trees when you're *thirty*, you know.'

He smiled. 'Your mother?'

'Huh. In a place like this, everyone's your mother. People you hardly know back you into a corner, say, "Hope you don't mind me asking," and then ask if you're a lesbian. Or frigid.' She grinned wickedly. 'Or worse.'

'Good God. What's worse?'

She glanced covertly around and behind, looking for eaves-droppers.

'A *feminist*,' she whispered dreadfully. 'Hush, don't say a word. Even the *stones* have ears.'

The joke was good enough, the delivery even better, but it was her accent that really tickled him. *Femmy-nist. Storns*. He wanted to hug her.

'You're a feminist, I take it?'

'Any sane woman has to be,' she said. 'But I suppose no sane man can be.' She slanted him a bright glance under questioningly raised brows. 'It goes against his best interests, doesn't it?'

Owen had always found this sort of test rather tiring, best treated with a nod, a smile and a pressing engagement elsewhere. But Gwen didn't matter. He was unlikely to see her again.

'You needn't worry about me,' he said, 'I'm not sane.'

'Thanks for warning me.'

He smiled. 'You can't have it all ways.'

While they were still at a distance from it, Owen recognised the ford and his heart thumped with panic. He stopped walking.

'What's wrong?'

'I—er. I suppose you know Gethin Morgan?'

'Oh, you've met him, have you? Yes, he terrifies all the visitors. Does it deliberately, I think, just for the hell of it. It's best just to smile and talk about the weather. He'll lose interest in you, then. If you go on being scared, he'll follow you and touch you for money.'

'How?'

'He draws money on his palm and screams his head off. You have to pay up, just to keep your brain from scrambling. Sad, really. From his point of view, I mean. It must be like living on an alien planet, all by himself.'

Snatches of the star song were creeping through Owen's mind. He said, 'Did this Glyn Caldwell chap know him?'

'Ah!' she laughed. 'Well, done. You're not just a memory, you see. You've got *reasoning* powers, too.'

They hovered for a moment, looking at their feet.

'I'd better go,' she said. 'You know your way now, do you?'

He wanted to see her again, yet had no idea how to ask without committing himself to something more. 'I'd like to read the book,' he said. 'Will I find it in town?'

'Oh, don't bother. You can borrow mine. I've read it, anyway.' She walked away, calling lightly over her shoulder, 'See you at the Station Arms. Any time.'

'Eight o'clock?'

She waved and he was left wondering, counting the hours. 'Four, five, six, seven.' And then she wouldn't be there.

CHAPTER TEN

Rhodri had noticed that whenever he stood up, Malen sat down, ramming her back into the corner of the settee like a limpet cleaving to a rock. It had puzzled him at first. The settee was stuffed with horsehair and covered with slippery leather-cloth; there was nothing to take a grip on, nothing to protect her should he decide to do his worst. It had occurred to him after a while that she wasn't as afraid of being raped as she was afraid of being stepped on. She was small and narrow and as slow to move as an invalid. He was tall. He did everything at speed. Even when he was reading, he'd shoot up like a rocket to fetch his dictionary or put the kettle on. She must feel like a snail crossing the middle of Main Street. Even if it offered no protection, who could blame her for curling into her shell when a lorry thundered by?

He made certain they were all sitting down before he discussed Malen's personal habits with Nessa.

'Days are getting shorter, Ness,' he observed mildly. 'Weather's closing in. I can't be out eight hours a day just to give Malen room to wash, now, can I? How about making some arrangement with her, Ness? Say if she sees to herself every morning while I'm out to the sheep? Think that would do? I don't want her to get dirty again, see, Ness. It's not healthy.'

Nessa was fast asleep with her feet in the air. She woke very suddenly and turned right-side-up, as Malen, shrieking, ran to the clothes rail and snatched down her wet petticoat and drawers, balling them up as if to throw them in his face. It was the quickest, most fluent series of movements he'd seen her make, but she thought better of it very suddenly, as if she'd only then realised what she was doing and remembered where she was. Had Rhodri not been so astonished, he might have laughed, for as he watched her she began, rather stiffly, to act a part.

You thought I was angry, the script went, *but you were wrong. I was just checking* . . . She held the balled garments to her cheek, as he had seen his mother do when she was ironing, testing for too much wet or too much dry. Then, *No,* she sighed. *Too wet. Dear, oh, dear. Now I must hang them up again.*

She had hung them, at first, in such a way as to hide the

51

evidence. Now, as with shaking hands she restored them to the rail, Rhodri saw it and was enlightened. Blood stains were murder to wash out.

Still, it answered one of the questions that had plagued him. Why hadn't the minister made her pregnant a long time ago? Because the bastard had chosen his moments. God, he deserved to die. He deserved to die slowly and painfully. A garotte might do it.

Malen sat down again, twisting her fists in her lap as though she could barely contain herself. And who could blame her? He'd humiliated her, and she'd already had more shame than she could bear, poor child.

'Ness,' he said softly. 'Do me a favour, will you, *cariad*? Give Malen my apologies. Tell her I'm not very bright. And tell her, when she needs them again, there's lint and safety pins in the right-hand drawer of the dresser. Help herself, tell her.'

The silence ached a bit after that. Rhodri took out his notebook and sat at the table, sucking the end of his pencil like the genius he was. He wrote, 'He's locked her in a cage,' and although he was certain it was true, he couldn't think of anything else to say about it. He felt caged, too. Her very presence in the room was like iron bars around him. He couldn't speak for fear of frightening her, couldn't move at his own pace, couldn't think. He couldn't even read. He'd taken a stab at Chekhov several times, but had never read more than a paragraph without losing the thread. He was lonelier with her than he'd ever been without her. She'd driven his best friend away and put a stranger in his place. Both were named Rhodri.

She was sitting on the mat, now, twirling her fingers in Nessa's fur, staring into the fire which, too, was enclosed by iron bars.

> *Caged*, he wrote, *confined,*
> *Her world defined by dank corners,*
> *Bars set at fingers' span apart,*
> *Clawed against the sky . . .*

He sighed and rocked the pencil end to end, aware that he was writing for the sake of writing, not because he had anything worthwhile to say. There was nothing to say about Malen until *she* said something. Until then she was a stone in a desert landscape – a prehistoric monolith about which nothing was written and very little guessed. All you could do was walk around her,

And wonder how she came there:
Dropped from the sky or hurled
Up from the earth's burning . . .

He dropped the pencil and turned again to watch her as she gazed into the fire. Her face was quiet, her hair brushed and shining. He'd bought her the cheapest jumper he could find that wasn't absolute rubbish (he never bought rubbish: waste of money) and now wished he hadn't. Brown didn't suit her. It doused the flame of her hair.

She looked up at him, met his eyes for a moment and turned hastily away, her white skin reddening with shyness.

'You're like a little wren,' he said, and her hand flew to her mouth, trapping the scream before it could fly.

'She's like a little wren,' he repeated softly. 'Isn't she, Ness? Brown and shy and secret. Not like you, you noisy tyke. You're always nattering on. It's a wonder I ever get a word in.'

Malen stroked her hair over her face, as if she'd smiled again and was afraid to show it.

What was she thinking? If she had any mind left, how the hell was it working? She'd been a bright, intelligent girl. She'd passed the scholarship, had learned Latin and French, geometry, music. She'd studied Shakespeare and Dickens, Wordsworth and Milton. Yet this room was full of books and she'd never touched one of them.

Depression, that could be. Fear . . . Yes, and confusion. He wasn't in half so bad a state as Malen was, yet he couldn't read. Or damn well write. Even his thoughts were going round in circles. How the hell am I going to get out of this? How the hell am I going to get out of this? How the hell . . .?

He knew he wouldn't take her to the asylum. Even if it was the right thing to do – and it wasn't – he wouldn't be able to live with himself after; he'd never be able to forget her, would always be wondering whether, with the charity he'd lacked, he might have healed her. But the asylum was still an option, a decision he could make if he chose. He wasn't entirely helpless. Malen was. Helpless, penniless, speechless. For her, there was no getting out of it. There was only making the best of it, whatever it turned out to be.

'Tell her,' he said. 'Tell her she isn't helpless, Ness. The fear will go, in time. Then she can read and write and walk on the mountain. She can learn to speak and make her own life as she

53

chooses. It's only fear that's stopped her, Ness, and that will go. In time.'

Malen closed her eyes and sighed. She turned her face from him. Oh, she knew what he was saying, all right, and if that sigh meant anything, she wanted to hear more of it.

'Just because she's small and not very strong, it doesn't mean she can't help herself, Ness. Remember how the wren became king? Pure intelligence, that was. Forward planning. No strength involved.'

Nessa's paws twitched as she chased rabbits through the warrens of her dreams, but Malen turned again and looked at him with a question in her eyes. *Well? Go on. How did the wren become king?*

He'd grown accustomed to Nessa's speech and the mountain's speech: they had no choice but to say what he was thinking and, in spite of his efforts to see things as they saw them, they would never have the means to put him right. But Malen . . . Even without speech, she had means. If she wasn't quite mad, her mind must be full of questions. Let her ask him, then. Let her choose.

'Right then,' he said. 'Come on, Ness. Let's go out for a while and let Malen put herself to bed.'

He'd made up a camp-bed for her behind the settee. She hadn't yet slept in it (for which, with hindsight, he was grateful) and he guessed she'd spent her nights so far wiping blood from the settee. But she would sleep now. He hoped.

The night was quiet and cold, darkening from the north, where black clouds were swallowing the mountains. While Ness wandered off to see to herself, Rhodri strolled around to the old scullery at the back of the house, where Garth and Pen kept guard over his home – or pretended to. He'd never heard them bark. Garth snarled occasionally and Pen sometimes uttered a queer little yap when she was annoyed with a sheep who'd defied her, but good working dogs are silent dogs. They command with their eyes, not their voices.

'You don't half wriggle, though,' he said as they rushed to meet him. 'What's all this? Have you missed me?'

He sat on the step and let them fuss. Garth stood between his legs and licked his face. Pen stuck her nose in his ear, in his pockets and up his coat sleeves, looking for her bedtime biscuit. 'You're not even warm,' he said. 'What's wrong with you?'

He talked to them as he talked to Nessa, never doubting that they understood and trusted him, never doubting his own under-standing of their silent communications. Yet he had no real idea what went on in their heads. They were sensitive to a fault, never forgot a cruelty or a fright and could reason things out like nobody's business. But their needs were simple. As long as he had health, wealth and sense enough to feed, shelter and appreciate them, they were happy.

Malen was different. Perhaps she was mad, but simple? No. Even at its worst, the human mind is as vast and as complex as a world.

Rhodri had often thought that if a man lived to be a hundred, committing every day of his life to learning about the world which was his home, he'd end up knowing only a thousandth part of it. Yet he could travel, take photographs and specimens, fly as the eagle and delve as the mole. He could hack everything to pieces in his explorations, reduce mountains to atoms to see what they were made of. But he couldn't do that with the human mind. He couldn't do it with Malen. Her mind wasn't as the earth; it was as a star: set firmly within a hand's reach – ten million miles away.

> 'Twinkle, twinkle, little star . . .
> How I wonder what you are.'

He sang, and was amazed again by mysteries. His voice was clear and true, yet he could not sing that song as he sang any other. Wonderment was its keynote, faint was its voice. To sing it loud was well-nigh impossible. You might do it when you were drunk, perhaps, or as bitter as death, but if those sweet, simple words meant anything to you, then soft you must sing them; the choice was not yours.

There was a right way of doing everything – singing a song or boiling an egg – and the rightness of it was usually dictated by its nature. You built a wall with your back, your legs, your arms: no use to caress the bloody thing with your fingertips. But people were different; their nature was obscured by the shadows of their lives and appearances were too often deceptive:

> A second-sight procession, such as glides
> Over still mountains, or appears in dreams . . .

So what was Malen?

He was neat and clean in his habits. He was especially careful with his notebook, and although he did not *know* he'd put it away, he was as certain as he could be that he *would* have put it away. Habits die hard. But it was there on the table – without his pencil. If he'd put the pencil away, why should he leave the book?

Malen had gone to bed. He couldn't see her, but he could see her shoes at the foot of the bed, her clothes folded neatly on the back of the settee.

Rhodri's heart was drumming to a strange, ominous rhythm. She'd moved his notebook? Opened it? Read it? The secrets of his heart, the soiled linen of his mind, the many-holed sock of his genius? Oh, he didn't like that. He didn't like it at all. It reminded him that he was not the man he wished he could be. It reminded him that he was still very nasty, deep down.

He didn't see the farthing until it was almost too late. She'd set it tail-side up in the centre of the book, with its device clearly lit by the oil lamp.

The device was a wren.

'It began many thousands of years ago,' Rhodri said, 'when the birds of Wales decided to choose a king to rule them. They wanted a wise king to settle their disputes, a strong king to conquer their enemies, a noble king to command the respect of both men and beasts and speak out bravely at their councils.

'Many of the birds thought the eagle should be king. He was bigger and stronger than most of them and more knowledgeable in the ways of the world. Sadly, however, he was also very proud. He thought himself better than anyone else, and no bird is better than any other. Each has its good side and its bad; each has its strengths and its weaknesses. Because the eagle cannot sing, he must be a lesser bird than the nightingale. Because the eagle has few colours, the bullfinch must be a better bird than he. Nevertheless, the eagle is a great and noble bird. Of all the birds that fly in the air, none is better suited to be king.

'Yet the other birds at that council were reluctant to give him sovereignty over them. They were afraid that if they awarded him the crown uncontested, he'd become prouder than ever: an aloof and cruel tyrant who would make their lives a misery.

'Eventually, after many discussions, they decided that the bird who could fly highest should be king. They knew the eagle would win, but at least he wouldn't win easily. The hawk, swift and skylark would give him a run for his money. He'd need to put his back into it, make an effort, prove that he was worthy of the crown.

'The wren, who hadn't said much during all the discussions, was sitting beside the eagle when the contest was announced. He saw how he preened himself in advance of the race. He saw the smug grin on the eagle's beak and the arrogant gleam in his cold, golden eyes. Then, "Hmph," the wren thought, "I'll show you, boyo," and, without saying a word to anyone, he hopped unnoticed on to the eagle's back and rode with him as he launched himself effortlessly into the sky.

'Higher they flew and yet higher. Far below, the robin and the chaffinch tumbled wearily to earth. The swift and the skylark gave up and went home. The hawk stayed longer, but not long enough, and at last only the eagle was left, flying high above the mountains, as high in the sky as he could go. "I am king!" he cried.

'But as he turned, regally, to make his descent, he saw a tiny brown bird flying a little way above his head. The wren had just that moment taken off from the eagle's back and was as fresh and strong as he could be. But the eagle was exhausted. Try as he might – and try he did – he could fly no higher than the wren.

'The eagle was ashamed to have been outdone by a bird so small and the other birds were angry because their new king was not the one they had chosen. But the wren knew his limitations. He didn't want to be king and was glad to give his crown to the eagle. For now the eagle knew that pride and strength could take him only so far. Intelligence and humour fly higher.'

Rhodri bolted the door and banked down the fire. He swept the grate and set the guard, doused all the lamps but one.

As he passed Malen's bed on the way to his own he held the lamp high to smile a goodnight. But her eyes were closed and her mouth softly open. Her breathing was deep and regular.

She hadn't heard a word of it.

CHAPTER ELEVEN

Before his marriage Owen had possessed three suits, a tweed jacket, a blazer, a few pairs of slacks and a dozen or so shirts in various shades of white. It hadn't – as Alison had accused – been lack of taste on his part so much as lack of motivation. He'd been wearing hospital white for most of his adult life. As long as he was clean and relatively neat underneath, he'd thought the rest hadn't mattered.

Alison had taught him otherwise. He'd been willing enough to learn and had enjoyed the security of knowing his clothes were the most appropriate for given situations. But he still didn't know what to wear tonight. Meeting strange girls in seedy pubs had not been one of the subjects on Alison's curriculum.

He gazed into his wardrobe, half-heartedly searching for the right shirt. Blue would accentuate his eyes, red the black of his hair, white the tan of his skin, yellow the streak through his spine . . .

He wouldn't go. His legs were aching. He was tired. An early night would do him no harm. Far less harm than if she didn't turn up. But if she did turn up . . . A pretty girl, a summer night, the sweet relief of another person's flesh touching his? How could he risk missing that?

He chose the blue and sat at the end of the bed for the best part of ten minutes, staring glumly at the wall. He hadn't deserved this: this cruel return to callow youth, this aching loneliness, this need. He'd married to be rid of it. He had the same sexual hungers as any other man, but a doctor can't afford to be hungry – or even mildly peckish – when every hour of the day he's telling women to take their clothes off and lie down. A doctor needs to be married. He needs to be happily married. In that lies his virtue, his professional purity, his self-respect, his peace of mind.

Alison had taken all that. She'd taken every bloody thing and left him back where he'd started: homeless, childless, loveless and . . .

He wouldn't go. Didn't he have enough trouble, without courting more? He wasn't ready – not nearly ready – to be playing around with his feelings like this. One thing at a time. His life was in ruins. He had to build it again, not start throwing explosives into what was left of the foundations.

Yet this day had been the happiest he'd spent in a year. The mountain, Gwen-hoover Jones. They'd each, in their way, put him in touch with solid ground.

He'd told Gwen he hadn't loved Alison and known for the first time that it was true. He'd *thought* he'd loved her. At least, he'd thought that what he'd felt for her was as near to love as he was ever likely to get. God knew he'd seen enough evidence of lousy marriages to know that his marriage had been, if not perfect, far from lousy. He still knew it. Even counting the long, lonely passages of leaden boredom when he'd asked himself, 'Is this all?' it had never crossed his mind that it could be different with anyone else. Passion fades. Interests diverge. The balance between two people changes more or less as the weather changes. So what? You make adjustments, carry a brolly, switch off the heating, turn on the fan.

The trouble was, he supposed, that they hadn't made a habit of complaining when they were too hot or too cold. When Alison had frozen him he'd had his work to keep him warm and he'd always assumed it was the same for her. She'd had her job at the university, the children and their doings, her social life . . .

She'd mocked him, in the end, for not noticing how many lunch dates she'd had with 'Caroline' and 'Julie', her lover. He *had* noticed. It simply hadn't occurred to him that she could be lying. Why should she lie? He'd never lied to her.

Yes, he had. He'd told her he'd loved her.

He was still not convinced, though, that this had been so far from the truth. His marriage had been everything to him. He had loved *it* and since Alison had been an indivisible part of it, he must have loved her. You can't love the woods without loving the trees, even if the things you love most about woods are their sunlit clearings, the shelter they afford from the wind or the flowers which grow among their roots.

And yet, if he'd loved her, he'd hated her, too. Hated her values, her politics, the white roots of her mind which, like the roots of bindweed, roamed over everything, enhancing nothing but themselves. He'd never heard her ask, 'What will people think?' but this had been her guiding principle, the reason she'd taught him how to dress, told him what to eat, even what books he should read in bed. She'd turned him into a designer husband, a fashion

59

accessory, a thing she could wear, drive or sit upon to announce her status to her friends. He'd never put up much resistance; it had amused him on at least as many occasions as it had annoyed him, although in fact he'd scarcely thought about it until, like a coat or a skirt, he'd gone out of fashion – or beyond Alison's power to change him – and been given away, with a shudder, to the charity shop on the corner.

He'd told himself he wouldn't go to meet Gwen – that he was too vulnerable, too impressionable, too desperate – and he was half-way to the ford before he realised he'd been functioning on automatic ever since: being controlled, like a space rocket, by the little men back at Mission Control. They'd even remembered to put his wallet and house keys in his pockets.

He stopped walking. This was how men came to grief: how they murdered, raped, took their first shot of heroin. They abandoned all reason and let instinct take over. Owen had never been that sort of man. He'd always thought things through – to a fault, he supposed. Dull, safe, pedestrian . . .

In the entire eight years of their marriage, Alison had never failed to laugh at him when he'd taken the lawnmower for its annual service. She'd called him an old woman, fussing over trivia. Why couldn't he be like everyone else – wait until the damn thing broke down and then get it fixed?

He'd never been able to explain – even to himself – how important such things were to him. The lawnmower was a good one; he'd been told when he'd bought it that if it was serviced regularly it would last him his lifetime and he supposed that was what he most needed: things that would last, things he could feel attached to, things he could hold and never let go. His home, his lawnmower. His marriage, his children. He'd been like a kidney bean, putting its roots into a jar of wet cotton.

Planted in the garden, a bean is like a cat with nine lives. Its roots are long and deep, its force for life almost unstoppable. But put it in a jar and let the cotton dry out . . . Put it on the kitchen windowsill just as Alison decided to spring-clean . . .

She'd cleaned him out. She'd reduced him to nothing. There was nothing left except . . .

He shrugged. This morning there'd been nothing. Tonight there was Gwen-hoover Jones. Which of them was better?

He walked on.

CHAPTER TWELVE

Two *could* live as cheaply as one, but only if one of them went hungry and, as the 'one' in question, Rhodri didn't much care for that. He didn't mind a little abstinence now and then. A *little* abstinence was strengthening. But that didn't last. Abstinence made the heart grow fonder of stew and suet dumplings.

He put in his usual order at the Co-op – 'Heard about the minister, Rhodri?' – and then wandered the town, buying the extras piecemeal so that no one should suspect he was eating enough for two.

'You'll never guess . . .'

'The grief, it must've been. Turned his mind, poor man.'

'Never a word to no one. Just upped and gone . . .'

'And taken Malen with him!'

It had snowed in the night – low down as well as high – and the clouds which had brought it now squatted, grey and chill, over everything, sucking the light from people's eyes and the evil from their tongues, making Rhodri shiver.

'Oh, *I* knew he wouldn't put her away. *I* knew he'd find some way around it, respectable or not. Stands to reason, doesn't it?'

'But he hasn't done himself credit, Rhodri. Going off like that without so much as a by-your-leave. Chapel packed to the rafters and no minister? There was bound to be talk, wasn't there?'

'You're quiet today,' Enid Griffiths, Library, observed thoughtfully. 'Chekhov too much for you, was he? I noticed you didn't bring him back.'

'He's slow,' Rhodri murmured. 'Like poetry. Every word counts.'

(He'd counted some of them forty times over.)

'You heard about the minister, did you?'

'Do you think I'm deaf?' He was picking over the library's selection of Jane Austen, wondering if *Pride and Prejudice* would suit Malen in her present state.

'It's a bit worrying, though, isn't it? Where would he have taken her? She's got no family living now, has she? You don't think . . .?'

'I don't think anything.' He'd been a bit severe with everyone who'd mentioned it and although he liked Enid he was certain she wouldn't care much for him when the truth came out.

'Jane Austen?' she enquired coolly when he gave her his books to stamp. 'Why are you taking her? Trivial, you said she was.'

'I've decided to give her another chance,' he said. 'In the name of justice.'

'Now, look,' she spread her hands and glared at him through thick pebble glasses that made her eyes bulge and spin like two globes of the world, with a bloodshot British Empire. 'I didn't say he'd done wrong, did I? I was fond of the girl. I feel sorry for her, that's all. What's wrong with that?'

He laughed. 'How can you ask? When I know the truth about the minister and Malen Price, I'll talk about it. But I'll *never* know and neither will anyone else until someone invents a machine that can read minds!' His hands shaking, he pushed the books into his satchel and swung it to his shoulder. 'George Orwell,' he concluded with venom. '*1984!*'

About half-way down through the town he stopped walking and heaved a sigh. The thought came to his mind, *Methinks he doth protest too much*, and knew that the outburst had done him no good. Why did he feel so guilty, so dirty, so wrong?

Because you want her, his conscience murmured. But for the act, you've done everything they'll say you've done. You're as dirty in your own mind as they are in theirs.

Yet the act was everything. If blame could be apportioned just for one's thoughts, everyone in the world would be a murderer, a thief. Rhodri would have killed his mother, his father, Mr Roberts and a fair few others. He'd have robbed Barclays' Bank ten times over.

'Hello, stranger.'

Young Sue Philips, done up in rubber boots, hair curlers, lipstick and a pink chiffon scarf, moved in her own cloud of Woodbines and operated her own fog-horn: a deep, mournful voice that seemed to emanate from a mile further off than her mouth was. 'What's wrong with you, then? I haven't seen you for weeks.'

The right side of her face had been badly scalded when she was a child: the skin there was silvery pink, slippery and tight, with tiny pleats on the side of her neck where half her ear had melted away. That apart, he'd always thought her a tidy looking woman and now was appalled to see how ugly she was. How old.

'I'm writing,' he lied, knowing that she, too, would plaster his name with filth as soon as she knew about Malen.

'Oh, there's nice.' She pursed bright, glistening lips to a fresh cigarette, jetting the smoke expertly from the corner of her mouth. 'Drop in for a spot of inspiration some time then, will you?'

'Right. Thanks, Sue.'

Never again, he added silently. Her flesh had tasted of burnt toffee. He'd lapped it up quite happily until, noticing how her bedroom walls ran with condensation and nicotine, he'd realised he'd been chewing her tobacco at one remove. Forty a day she smoked and wondered why she never had a penny to call her own.

Yet even cigarettes were cheaper than Malen was turning out to be. Oranges and apples, green cabbage, *fresh* bread! Fresh bread was against Rhodri's religion. It sliced thick. It tasted wonderful. It didn't last five minutes. But Malen had turned up her nose at the stale bread by Wednesday, just for a spot of mildew on the crust.

'That's good for you,' he'd said. 'Penicillin. Lovely stuff. Cures all the diseases known to man, they say. TB, pneumonia, scarlet fever, the lot.'

But she wouldn't eat it. The look in her eyes said she'd rather have TB and pneumonia, scarlet fever, the lot.

Her eyes were beginning to speak now she'd had a few nights' sleep to rest them. She was still shy and afraid, but she was alive: thinking and reacting, perhaps even caring a little. He'd cleaned the cottage this morning as he usually did on Saturdays: a quick sweep through, a slosh over with the mop. Nothing too drastic. 'There,' he'd said when he'd finished, 'How's that for housework?' and she'd bitten her lip on a tiny smile and pointed to a grey frieze of cobwebs over the dresser.

He'd loved her then. Loved her so much it had paralysed him. He'd been sick with the shock of it ever since. He didn't know what was going on, couldn't identify his feelings, his motives. He was almost certain he didn't love Malen. How could he? He didn't know her. She was not so much a person as an idea, a romance, a poem he was writing; and when she'd pointed out those cobwebs . . . It was as if he'd completed the first line.

There is love in the first line of a poem. You write and rewrite it, change it, delete it, rescue a word from the scribble and write it all again. And suddenly it's there: not merely saying precisely what you wanted it to say but, in its meanings and rhythms, engendering the next line and the next. It was like the first flower of spring which tells all there is to know about summers gone and still to come – and more than that, much more than that, ten thousand years more than that.

> *I am the seed of the seed, it says,*
> *Of the flower that bloomed here before the Saxons came.*
> *And that was the seed of the seed, it says,*
> *Of the flower that bloomed beneath the seven hills of Rome.*

A poem exists in its author's history, his experience and lineage, things he knows or only guesses, things he loves or hates or only wishes for. But there are things unknown inside his mind, too, inside the secret hoard he calls his soul, which will creep unbidden into the heart of a poem. Hybrids, mutants, alien strangers which, when they reveal themselves for the first time in a word or a phrase, make him ask in awe, 'Who am I?'

If Rhodri lived to be a hundred, spending every day of his life in exploration of the world that was his mind, he would never learn the answer. So how could he hope to know Malen? How could he 'write' her, whose experience and lineage were so different from his own? No, he didn't love her. He loved the mystery of her, the beauty of her, the tender bloom on her skin and the blazing fire of her hair.

He wanted to touch her, to blow warm breath into her ears and heal all her wounds. Change her, delete her and write her again, until she said . . . precisely what he wanted her to say.

That wasn't love. It was arrogance.

CHAPTER THIRTEEN

'I think,' Gwen said, 'Owain Glyndŵr would have looked like you.'

Owen frowned. 'I've heard of him. Shakespeare, was it?'

'Welsh chieftain. Early fifteenth century. Claimant to the Welsh crown. Prince Hal beat him to it.' She quirked her eyebrows as if to add, And I haven't yet forgiven Prince Hal.

'The Welsh still dislike the English, then?'

'Mmm,' she wrinkled her nose. 'Resent would be a better word. For most of us it's gone underground, but it's still there, the same as it always was. You conquered us, you ground our faces into the dust . . .'

Her voice was soft: more wistful than bitter. She was like an ageing mother reminding her quiet, respectable, sixty-year old son what a demon he'd been when he was twelve. All forgiven now. Nothing to get excited about. Yet the son could still blush for his crimes and recall as if it were yesterday the indignities of his punishment. Owen's heart was beating so hard and so loud he could scarcely bear it.

'Don't blame me,' he said suddenly. 'I'm Welsh, too.'

For a while after that everything went a little hazy. He could hear Gwen's voice – a faint humming sound beyond the periphery of his panic – but hadn't a clue what she was saying. What had *he* said? And why had he said it? He felt like a traitor, yet had no idea whom he'd betrayed. Himself? His Welshness? Or the 'Englishness' he had so determinedly claimed since the first stranger had enquired of his name, 'Owen? That's Welsh, isn't it?'

They were sitting in the garden again, in the last pool of sunlight. He found himself staring up at the church tower, at the red dragon which limply hung there, folded up on itself, defeated, its flames burning its own feet. Gwen was asking questions he wouldn't answer. He said, affecting dreamy reverie, 'I've never known what that means. Presumably there's a legend behind it?'

'What?'

'The red dragon.'

She laughed. 'Don't change the subject. What are you ashamed of? Being English, or being Welsh?'

He didn't know what she meant. He didn't want to know. He wanted to go home, but no longer knew what that meant, either.

'I was born . . .' he said haltingly, 'in Bangor. I lived in Wales until I was three. I don't know if that makes me Welsh. I've always thought it did.'

Her eyes were warm and humorous, brightly challenging. He thought she was going to attack him again, but suddenly she looked at her hands and pressed them gently together as if to say, Look, no weapons. I will not harm you.

'I suppose,' she said, 'the red dragon symbolises the same thing as the Cross: death and the promise of resurrection. You've heard of Merlin?'

He smiled. 'Who hasn't?'

'When he was a boy, at the time of the Saxon invasions, he let loose two dragons from under Snowdon: a white dragon and a red dragon. As soon as they were set free, they began to fight and the white dragon won. We weren't Welsh then, of course – just Britons, the ancient, pre-Roman race, like Boadicea – Boudicca, if you're fancy. We call her Buddug, from *buddugoliaeth*, victory. Ironic, really – she was defeated, wasn't she? But all our heroes are the same: they make mincemeat of the opposition,' she clenched her fist and shook it, 'and then run out of steam at the last minute. Buddug took poison. Caradoc was captured and taken to Rome. And Glyndŵr dropped dead, with the Welsh crown actually in his grasp. *Actually*, mind, not just inches away!'

Her clenched fist met the table with soft restraint, but her eyes burned with indignation at the unfairness of it all. It was no wonder the Celts were unquenchable: their history was still alive for them, their heroes still manning the barricades even two thousand years since they'd died in the attempt.

'So anyway,' (Gwen pronounced it 'swennyway'), 'Merlin said the white dragon represented the Saxon conquerers, the red dragon the defeated Britons. But, he said, the tide would turn and the red dragon live to win another day.' She smiled. 'We're still waiting.'

'So the original defeat had nothing to do with the English?'

'Well, not *exactly* . . .'

'Not at all, surely, because the people living in England – the Roman-Britons – had been defeated by the Saxons, too. And at Hastings – what, six or seven hundred years later? – they were defeated again. What's the difference?'

66

'The difference,' she said, 'is mountains.'

'Mountains?'

'We're a difficult country to invade. The Romans didn't make much of a go of it – Caradoc kept them out of Wales for years before they caught him – the Saxons did better, the Normans better again; but where England was overrun until there was no alternative but to assimilate, we could keep aloof, keep our identity to a certain extent. Invasions of England have always resulted in "us and them" becoming "we". No prolonged resistance was possible. The Welsh, the Scots and – of course – the Irish, resisted and were beaten, resisted and were beaten again. That's where the bitterness comes from. If you don't resist, you can't get beaten. We defy nature, I suppose. We don't adapt.'

'Do you think that's wrong?'

'No. It's not sensible, but being sensible and being right aren't necessarily the same thing. While you have a hope of defending what's yours, it's wrong to surrender, isn't it? Are your parents Welsh, then?'

This question took him by surprise, but not as much as had the one which had preceded it.

He'd never fought for anything. Suddenly he saw a clear image of himself as Alison must have seen him and knew why she'd cried when he'd said goodbye. He'd kept quiet, he'd 'surrendered', not because their marriage had not been worth fighting for, but because there had seemed no hope of winning. When your wife doesn't want you, when her lover is waiting and all the practicalities of her removal neatly arranged, what can you do, what can you say to defend what's yours?

Yet he'd felt the same about everything, all his life. He'd had no mountains to defend him, no birthright to protect. He hadn't quite seen himself as a leaf on the wind, doomed to fall wherever he was set down, but he knew now that it had been so and realised that the only thing he'd really cared about was to fly with grace, to fall with dignity and hope that something – even if it was only the damp – would fix him to the spot so that he need never fly again. He'd swallowed more rage in his lifetime than he'd swallowed bread and butter. And it was all still there: battened down so hard it could find no expression except . . .

He hadn't seen the monkeys just lately. They'd left him alone for more than a week. But he knew now what they were, what they represented. Disgust, revulsion, an utter contempt by himself for himself which would never be forgiven.

'The gnats are biting,' Gwen said. 'Let's go inside.'

The stench of cigarette smoke and cooking oil seemed far worse after the freshness of the garden. The change of place and pace and noise level was distressing and disorienting. Everyone looked up and stared at him. Most called out greetings to Gwen. One stocky, middle aged man in crumpled jeans and a sweat-soaked shirt demanded, 'Come on, then! Introduce us!'

'Bossy devil.' Gwen laughed off-handedly. 'This is Owen. This is John. John's a farmer, Owen, but you'd never know it. He thinks he owns this place and everyone in it. You included.'

Owen smiled nervously. John scowled and set his hands on his hips. 'Well?' he said. 'Go on. I'm a farmer . . .?'

Gwen scratched her ear. 'And Owen's a . . .'

'Cabinet maker,' Owen said. He didn't know why. He had never before wanted to deny his profession. He'd been proud of it. Now he wasn't. It didn't seem quite real any more. It didn't seem appropriate. A doctor needs to be married.

John pulled up a stool and sat astride it, setting his elbow on the table and his rank, damp armpit a little too close to the end of Owen's nose. 'Oh, there's interesting. Good stuff, is it? I like good furniture. You should see my granny's dresser. Two hundred years old, twelve foot long, black as pitch and carved with . . .'

Owen laughed. 'Oak leaves and acorns, right?'

He blinked, hearing the echo of his voice with a sense of amused bewilderment. *Ork* leaves? He'd never been much of a mimic, but the Welsh accent was beginning to seem as natural to him as was the idea of being a cabinet maker.

John rattled on about his granny's dresser and a ten foot long refectory table which had never been moved because it was set into the floor. 'Mind, you'd never move it even if it was free. The boards are three inches thick. The legs – oh . . .' He drew his hands nine inches apart and then laughed at the expression on Owen's face. 'Look at him!' he said. 'His bloody mouth's watering! What you drinking, Owen? Gwen?'

There was no such thing as a private date at the Station Arms. A young girl who looked like a young boy wearing lipstick came to consult Gwen about a newspaper quiz. John introduced Owen to a chap named Rhys, who invited him to play darts.

'I—I—er—I—'

'Go on,' Gwen laughed. 'Enjoy yourself.'

Owen hadn't played darts since his student days, but he'd been good at it then and, after hitting the wall with his first few throws, he found his aim well enough to lose the first game with merit.

The room wasn't a big one and there were fewer than a dozen people in it, all of whom shouted encouragement and advice to the players and cheered when Owen won the next game. He felt very comfortable and easy of mind. Recognising his ease and wanting to test it, he let his thoughts turn to his children who lived now with another man on the far side of the world. They seemed happy enough.

As he took aim for his next shot, Gwen called out, 'Wait, Owen,' and as he turned to look at her a chilling shriek tore past his ears, making him stagger, just as he'd done when he'd first heard it. Rhys took his elbow. 'It's all right. Nothing to worry about. He's deaf and dumb, poor bugger. Can't do nothing else but scream.'

Gethin Morgan was ordering a drink. He screamed again, slapped the counter and made urgent jabbing motions at the brew of his choice. He was much taller than Owen had guessed when he'd seen him sitting like a gnome among the verdure of the river bank. Tall and strong and as brown as a nut.

'How old is he?' Owen murmured.

'No one knows. He was a young kid when he first come here. My dad was about nineteen – he'd be ninety-two now if he was alive – so I reckon Gethin must be up over eighty. Looks younger, though, doesn't he? *Duw*, I'd love to know what goes on in his head. I worry about it sometimes. Keeps me awake for hours, it does. How can you think about anything if you don't know what it's called?'

'Can he lip-read?'

'I don't think so. Hard to tell what he knows and what he doesn't. You can't cheat him of money, though. He went crazy when we went decimal – couldn't understand it – but he worked it out a hell of a lot quicker than the rest of us. Play on now, Owen. He's coming over. If he screams at you, don't jump. He likes scaring strangers. Bit of fun for him, isn't it? He plays it for all it's worth.'

Owen's darts went everywhere except where he'd aimed them. He scored one, three, and a large splinter of plywood from the edge of the backing board, horribly aware that Gethin was standing just behind him and might hit ninety decibels at any moment. As Rhys took his place at the oche, he sent Gethin an approving smile. 'Thanks, Gethin *bach*. You've put him off his stroke just nice.'

Gethin sat down. Owen reached past him as if he wasn't there, took a few sips of his own beer and played again. His hand was shaking: not with fright but with triumph. He couldn't have done this a week ago. He couldn't have entered this pub a week ago, let alone enjoyed being in it – and in such company! A deaf mute, a dozen sweaty rustics, Gwen-hoover Jones.

She came and sat at the table opposite Gethin. 'Come on, Owen. Triple twenty, now, is it?'

'Not with Gethin watching,' he said. 'He's putting the evil eye on me.'

'I'll fix him.' She touched Gethin's arm. She looked into his eyes, and recited calmly:

> '*I know a bank whereon the wild thyme blows,*
> *Where oxlips and the nodding violet grows*
> *Quite over-canopied with luscious woodbine . . .*'

'He loves this,' she went on in the same cool, conversational tone. 'Look at his eyes, now, Owen. He's hungry just to be noticed, just to have someone try to get through.'

It sounded pathetic, heartbreaking; yet there was nothing pathetic about Gethin Morgan. He sat at the table just as he'd sat on the river bank, looking as much as if he belonged there as a king in his castle. There was a relaxed pride in his posture, an expression of watchful authority on his face which made Owen think more of his old anatomy professor than of a man in sore affliction. His intelligence was undeniable. His mind was working like an engine; you could almost hear it running.

'Why has no one taught him anything?' he asked. 'He could be . . .'

'He could be festering in a mental home,' Gwen said quickly. 'That's what happened to most of them when he was young. But he's free. His own man. And I think he's happy, in his way.' Her face fell, her eyes filled with longing. 'Oh, Gethin,' she sighed. 'What would you tell us if you could speak?'

His eyes were like glittering pools of blue water, watching Gwen's mouth to catch the merest inkling of sense, yet the thought crossed Owen's mind, as it had evidently crossed Gwen's long ago, that Gethin Morgan had far more to tell them than they to tell him. He'd been watching the world for eighty years, interpreting it for himself without any influences or explanations beyond those his own – quite unimaginable – reasoning powers could deduce. What must it be like in his mind? How did he fit things together, or explain things to himself?

Owen pulled up a chair and sat at the end of the table, fixing Gethin with a professional, 'tell me everything' smile.

'Do you live alone?' he asked.

'Yes,' Gwen said in a ghostly voice. 'In my own little house by the river. I keep it clean and tidy, just as my aunty showed me . . .'

'Showed him with the hard end of a broom-handle, too,' Rhys said. '*Duw*, she was cruel.'

'She was a saint,' Gwen said firmly. 'She was an angel.'

Rhys laughed and folded his hands in prayer. 'God save us from saints and angels,' he said. 'Gethin's still got bruises she put on him forty years back, I reckon.'

'But why?' Gwen demanded fiercely. 'So he could see to himself when she was gone! There's nothing kinder than that, is there? He's worked hard all his life – he was a farm labourer, Owen – started when he was thirteen. Fifty-odd years he worked for his independence, and he damn well deserves to keep it. What would the social workers have done to him by now? Put him in a home, locked him up . . . He'd have died, Rhys.'

She was right. Owen had seen too many independent old people die of being properly looked after. In the cold and squalor of their own decaying homes, confused and hungry, lonely and often afraid, they still had something to keep them going. He had never paused to wonder what that something was. It wasn't wise to wonder about things which go against the conventional line of duty.

'Not everyone round here is as tolerant as Gwen,' John called from the far end of the bar. 'If it wasn't for her, people would have shifted him out of here, years ago. He's a bloody nuisance. I was in the Black Bull up in town last Saturday. Heaving, it was. They'd just had a coach party in. Could have taken five hundred quid just in sandwiches, let alone drink. In walks Gethin, shrieks for his pint and the next thing you know everyone's making hell-for-leather out of it: terrified. It's the same in the shops. It's the same in the streets. We depend on tourists, but one shriek out of him and they're gone. *And* he begs for money,' he added darkly. 'Which is a crime, I'll have you know, Miss Know-it-all!'

Gwen smiled wryly. 'One crime Gethin's never committed is tell lies about you, John Philips.'

'Lies?' He was laughing. 'What d'you mean, lies? Ooh, you're a hard bitch, you are. I wouldn't marry you if you paid me.'

'You're safe, then. I've got horse manure for the roses. I don't need bullshit, as well.'

'Oh, there's poetic,' Rhys murmured.

'But tell the truth now, John: how many left and how many stayed to stare at Gethin and thank God they weren't born the same?'

'Puh!' John pushed himself off the bar and marched cheerfully towards the dartboard. 'Bloody women. I don't know why I bother arguing with 'em. Come on, then, Owen, give us a game. Best out of three, is it?'

CHAPTER FOURTEEN

Rhodri's cottage stood only a few dozen feet above the road, yet in weather like this it was invisible. A few years back he'd walked straight past it in the mist and not known his error until he'd begun to walk downhill, on the other side of the mountain. Since then, he'd built a *carn* at the foot of his path to show him the way, but even so was never confident of getting home safe until his hand was on the door latch. He'd heard of shepherds – older and wiser ones than he – who'd gone out in a fog to check their lambs and walked the best part of twenty miles before finding their way home again.

He was accustomed to coming home to an unlit house and always, before, had set a candle and matches just inside the door to light his way to the oil lamps. He hadn't done that today. Malen was here to light him. Yet everything was dark and the only thing he saw was a glimmer of white as Nessa came creeping across the floor, the tip of her tail twitching trouble.

'Ness?' He fondled her ears and she sat at his feet, very upright and good. 'What's wrong, girl? Where's Malen?' He crouched to feel Nessa's shoulders. She was trembling.

He groped for the mantel and the tub of spills he kept there. Nessa followed him, stepping and sitting her way by stages across the flags. *I am good*, she said. *It wasn't my fault, Rhodri, I swear.*

'It's all right, Ness. Calm down, now.'

He was scared. If Malen had gone out in the fog, she was as good as dead. He thrust the spill into the fire, lit a candle and carried it swiftly to the end of Malen's bed, holding it high.

She was huddled in the corner, as tight to the wall as she could get without pushing the house down. Her hands were flat over her ears, her elbows and knees curling her as small as the unborn. 'Oh, Ness,' he sighed. 'What's gone wrong here, then? What's wrong with Malen?'

He lit the lamps, tended the fire, put the kettle on to boil and then sat with Nessa's head on his knee, stroking her until she stopped trembling. He wished he could do the same for Malen, but knew that it would only scare her. All he could do was wait.

He unpacked his satchel. 'Look, Ness, what I've brought for

Malen. Oranges and apples, a nice fresh loaf . . .' He made the tea and poured it: weak and black for Malen, strong, with a syrupy spoonful of condensed milk, for himself. 'Tell Malen her tea's ready, Ness. And tell her I've brought her a present.' He rummaged in his coat pocket for the gift: a chocolate Wagon-wheel – tuppence, and barely a whisper of nourishment to make it worthwhile – which he'd hoped might bring a smile to Malen's face.

But she was crying: sniffing and gulping behind the settee, breaking her heart for a mystery which, knowing women, could be something as silly as a spider he'd swept loose from the cobwebs.

'Malen,' he called softly. 'Come out here now, will you? Your tea's going cold.'

She screamed. He heard her fists pummelling the wall and began to suspect temper rather than terror. Could she be crying just because he'd gone out and left her?

Irritated, he gazed around the room, noticing for the first time how the lamplight reflected from his mother's china on the dresser, from the brass knobs on the drawers, even from the wood itself. Strange to be noticing such things for the first time. He'd lived here five years, going on six, and never seen . . .

Frowning, he stood up and crossed to the dresser, taking a lamp with him. She'd washed all the china. It was shining like new. She'd polished the wood and the brass.

'I don't know, Ness,' he said glumly. 'You spend an entire afternoon polishing the place up to make a nice home for her, and I walk ten miles to bring her fresh bread and oranges, and all she can do is cry. Makes you spit, doesn't it? Beats me how you took down all this china without breaking it, though. You're a won-derful dog, Ness. The fairies did me a good turn when they sent you here, didn't they?'

Malen blew her nose. He heard the metal legs of the camp-bed scraping on the stone floor. He saw her feet, like bear's paws, furry and grey in a pair of his socks, padding slowly towards the table. She sat and buried her face in her hands.

'She can write,' he said. 'Why doesn't she write it, Ness? Why doesn't she tell me what's wrong?'

But he'd tried that before. She wouldn't write. She bit her hands instead of speaking. Instead of writing, she hid them behind her back.

Suddenly she snatched open the drawer, took out a pencil and a sheet of scrap and drew a cross on it. Rhodri stepped closer. She put a circle at the top of the cross with three dots in it: eyes and nose. No mouth. She drew a hat on top of the circle: a trilby, plain as plain. She picked the paper up, slapped it down. She pointed to the door and burst into tears again.

Rhodri turned cold all over. Many men wore trilbies; the minister wasn't the only one. But it would be just his style to come after her on a Saturday, when he knew Rhodri would be from home.

He had come close enough to touch her, and his hand moved to her shoulder without his realising it until she failed to scream and run away. He held his breath. He didn't dare move.

'Did Roberts come here?' he asked quietly. 'Did you let him in?'

She screamed, bit her hands, shook her head. She pointed to the settee. *I hid.*

'Was the door locked?'

She shook her head.

'He didn't try the door?'

She pointed to Nessa.

'Ah, Ness did her stuff, did she? She's a good dog. I told you she'd look after you, didn't I?'

Malen sighed and drank her tea. She looked rather puzzled, disappointed almost, and while Rhodri was still trying to think what else could have happened, she screwed up the drawing and threw it on the fire.

He didn't know how much her fright had changed her until, as he put on his coat for his bedtime visit to Garth and Pen, Malen decided to go with him. A scream, a mad scuttle to put on her shoes and coat, a wild, 'Don't leave me,' look in her eyes.

He'd been trying to get her to go out for a walk all week. Now he tried to persuade her not to: partly because of the snow, which was deepish along the side of the cottage and partly because this was her chance to get ready for bed in privacy. Not for money would he give her the use of his bedroom – not, at least, until she *asked* if she might share it.

'No,' he said softly. 'Stay here. Go to bed. I won't be long.'

Her shoes were still unlaced, her coat unbuttoned. He slipped out very quickly and shut the door behind him. He heard her wailing and, even without words, knew that she had said, *Wait for me!* He saw from the corner of his eye a flash of yellow light as the door flew open and slammed shut. Her hand caught the belt of his coat. Her teeth were chattering and she was making urgent little noises in the back of her throat: *Take me with you!*

'No, no. It's too cold for you. Go back, Malen.'

She screamed.

He stood for a moment, holding the lamp to see her face. She looked very fierce, very determined. 'Button your coat,' he said. 'Fasten your shoes.'

For a moment her hands flew to her mouth. Then, shaking with cold, she obeyed.

'Now, hold my hand.'

He was sure she wouldn't do it. If she didn't, he'd manhandle her back indoors and lock her in. The last thing he needed was to lose her in the fog on a night like this.

But she held his hand. She held it tight, trusting him. *Look, Rhodri, how good I am.*

He laughed. He felt wonderful: excited and scared, as if he'd kidnapped her all over again and the adventure was just beginning. A faint, chill breeze touched his face and, illuminated by the lamplight, the mist swirled and thinned and he caught the glimmer of a star in the black vault of the sky. He laughed again. 'Look, Malen,' he whispered. 'We're coming out through the clouds. See the stars?'

He avoided the drift on the north side of the cottage and led her higher, telling her where to put her feet. The mists turned to smoky wisps which the breeze blew away. The sky was clear and bright, full of stars.

He let go her hand to point above the mountain ridge. 'Look – there is Orion, the hunter. See, Malen? The red star, Betelgeuse, is the point of his right shoulder. See? Over there?'

She shivered. *See if I care. I'm freezing!*

He smiled and took her hand to lead her down again. 'You will come out with me in the summer,' he said. 'And I'll teach you all their names: Cassiopeia, Andromeda, Perseus . . . The whole catalogue of mythology's up there, Malen: the finest stories in the world set forever in diamonds.' He paused, taking a last look before the mists again veiled his sight, and the last star, like the first, was seen through a torn curtain of cloud.

He had been aware, without being aware of its consequence, that Malen had drawn closer to him while he stood there, using his body to shelter her from the wind. On a cold night, his dogs would do the same, although they generally sat on his feet, using his legs as a windbreak – huddling together for warmth. All animals will do it, but only with animals they trust. The lamb will not lie down with the lion.

Slowly, with infinite care, he curved his arm around Malen's shoulders. Gently, he cupped her head with his hand and held her warm against his chest. 'There,' he murmured. 'There's nothing to be afraid of, Malen. I will not hurt you.'

He held the lamp higher to see her face. 'You know that now, don't you?'

Her mouth twisting down with sulky denial, she turned away and stood with her back to him, putting him firmly in his place. Rhodri smiled. She was lying.

The clouds stayed with them for another two days. The third brought a vicious north-easterly wind and more snow. The fourth was as bright as summer. Malen strayed outside and looked back over her shoulder, asking Rhodri to walk with her.

They didn't go far. She was as strong as a woman in her eightieth year: free enough in her joints, but with no puff to keep them going. Even with Rhodri's help she had to rest every few yards to get her breath back.

'Are you ill, Malen? Does your chest hurt?'

She shrugged, shook her head and pointed down into the valley. *How could I get strong? When did I go out?*

'It will come,' he said. 'Soon you'll be running ahead, leaving Nessa behind. You must walk every day when it's fine. We'll put roses in your cheeks in no time.'

She shook her head and turned away.

'Malen?' He walked around her to see her face. She looked grim and cold, her mouth set tight, her eyes burning with bitterness. Rhodri took a sharp breath and averted his eyes, as if he had seen her undressed – which, upon reflection, he supposed he had. Until now, he had thought of her as a wounded child, a little thing not quite formed who, with patience, he might heal and strengthen and make new again. He knew now that she was not a child. She'd learned more about life in her sixteen years than most women learn in a lifetime. The pain of it had gone too deep for him to touch. She was like Young Sue Philips, forever burned, forever marked.

They say skin deep, yet skin alone
Contains the heart, the tender soul.
Mar it and an inner beauty spills,
Like milk corrupted on the dairy floor
That no amount of weeping can restore.

'Come, Malen,' he said softly. 'We'll go home now.'

She called out to him as he began to walk down: a thin, desolate cry, like the mewing of a buzzard. He turned, astonished, and immediately she began to speak, drawing sharp, clear pictures with her hands and the expressions on her face. *I am a prisoner*, she said. *How can I break free? He's put iron bars around me.*

'You are not a prisoner here, Malen. I will . . .'

She screamed and bit her hands. Baring her teeth, she crossed her arms, palms outwards, several times, erasing what she'd said before. She began the mime again. *No! The minister will come again. He will lock me up, he will put me away. And you* . . . She stabbed her index finger at him, *can do nothing to stop him!*

He suspected that she was right, but could not bring himself to say so. 'I will kill him first, Malen,' he said. 'I will do everything I can to keep him from you.'

Her face fell. She began quietly to weep, and he knew that he had not understood her. She was saying something else, and without words, how could he discover it?

He walked back to her. He held her hands and stooped to look into her face. 'Will you write it for me, Malen? You can write, *cariad*, can't you?'

No! She snatched her hands clear of his and hid them behind her back.

Wearily he straightened, wearily looked up at the mountain and silently asked of it, 'Help me.'

But the mountain was in one of its vicious moods: showing him its sweetest face while spreading filthy rumours behind his back. Two men were walking the road below the cottage, armed with stout canes to help them in their climb. They were watching their feet when he first saw them, breathing hard and talking politics, but as if with one voice their legs had demanded rest, they stopped, raised their heads and looked straight up at Malen.

Although they were too far off for Rhodri to see their faces, he recognised them. Mr Jenkins, town council, and Thomas Parks, his son-in-law: old women the pair of them and chapel to the marrow.

'Let's go home,' he said urgently, 'Come, Malen, good girl.'

But as he took her hand to guide her out of sight, the mountain, laughed, *Oh, no you don't,* and sent a cruel wind to lift Malen's hair against the snow, making it fly and blaze like a beacon.

Here is Malen! the mountain cried.

And the men on the road heard its voice and stared at her, amazed.

CHAPTER FIFTEEN

It was one in the morning before they left the Station Arms. Gwen had a reconditioned Morris 1000 convertible, almost exactly like the one Owen's father had bought him for his eighteenth birthday. Cream paintwork, red leather-cloth seats. It smelled the same inside and had a similar litter of books and loose-leaf binders on the back seat.

'My God,' he laughed. 'What's happening to me? I feel . . .'

'Eighteen again,' she said. 'So? What do we do next?'

'Make love,' he said wistfully. 'Everyone made love in those days. No reason not to. The Pill had been invented and AIDS hadn't. Morals were out of fashion. I wore myself out my first year at medical ssss . . . *Damn.*'

'Ah,' she said. 'I thought you were lying. My dad was a doctor. I think I must have recognised you. The corset-like restraint, you know.'

'Rubbish. I've never worn a corset in my life. Does the roof open?'

He lay back as she drove, tipping his face to the stars. When they'd left the pub, everyone had called out, 'No star! No star!' but they couldn't have looked properly; there were *millions* of them!

He sighed deeply. 'You know,' he said. 'I'm happy. I know it won't last, but I'm happy *now*. That's something, isn't it? Think I'll remember it tomorrow? I'm not drunk, you know. I only had three pints. I counted.'

'So did I. I counted the five whiskies, too.'

'Spoilsport.' He sighed again. 'Oh, Gwenhwyfar, Gwenhwyfar, I never want this night to end. Did I say it right?'

'Almost. The "r" shouldn't sound so much like a pneumatic drill, though. Have you got any food in? I'm starving.'

He giggled like a child. 'It's one o'clock in the morning!'

'I bet you didn't say that when you were eighteen.'

He began, very quietly, to weep. He knew he was drunk. He knew that the grief he felt now was at least three parts booze and another three the 'over-excitement' his father had trained him out of thirty years ago. He'd never had a night like this since then: the innocence of it, the laughter. The hill farmers were lonely men who came into town not for drink but for company: stories and jokes, songs and games, old-fashioned fun of the sort Owen – and most of the rest of the world – had forgotten. They'd played darts and quoits and forfeits, a crazy game of hunt-the-thimble: 'You're getting warmer! Warmer! *Cold!*' He'd laughed until his ribs ached and he hadn't done that, hadn't done that since . . .

He couldn't remember.

Gwen parked the car in the drive, and they sat there for a while, listening to the tick of the engine as it cooled.

'Come on,' Gwen said at last. 'Let's sober you up, shall we?'

'The stars look so close when your eyes are full of tears.'

'Got any spaghetti? I fancy spaghetti.'

'Why are you so cruel? John said you were cruel. He said he wouldn't marry you if you paid him and I don't blame him. You got no symphony. Sym-path-y.' He grinned. 'You got no spaghetti, either.'

'That's true. Come on. Where's your key?'

'Oh, I know where that is,' he said. 'The little men at Mission Control,' he fumbled in his pocket, 'saw to all that.'

'Oh, did they? You *are* in a bad way, aren't you?'

'No, really. They do it all by telescope, you know. Press a button here, press a button there – it's all organised. If it hadn't been for them, I wouldn't have come tonight. I'd have missed it.'

He leaned against the wall. He pressed his hot face to the cold stone and was sad and almost sober, wanting nothing more than he wanted to go to sleep and forget everything. It seemed rather empty now: the games, the talk, the silly laughter. He felt like Gethin Morgan, for whom such things had no meaning.

Gethin hadn't stayed with them long. Once he'd made certain that no one would buy him a drink (Owen had been warned not to), he'd banged his empty glass on the table and hurried out, shrieking, into the lingering dusk. They'd been quiet for a while afterwards, tumbling into his loneliness as if into a black hole from which there was no escape – except to forget him. *Forget* him. Think of Gwen instead.

'I don't suppose you'll stay?' he asked, but was careful to speak too softly for her to hear him and refuse.

He couldn't find the spaghetti, but while he was looking for it he found something else: an appreciation of the cottage as his own domestic base, a nest, rather than just a twig he'd landed on before flying (or falling) off again.

'Now this is nice,' Gwen said, her voice travelling downwards, not up, so that 'nice' struck his ear with a thud, startling him into looking around, as if he'd never seen it before. There wasn't much to see. Jill's tastes were simple almost to a fault. The walls were white, the floor pale grey, the curtains a bright sunny yellow.

'She's blonde, isn't she? Your friend, I mean.'

'Well, yes . . . Sort of.' He looked again and saw Jill personified in the bleached kitchen dresser and its plain white china, the clutter-free benches, the unadorned table. Peace and comfort were all she'd asked of the place. Peace and comfort were all it gave. No gloss, no frills, no smug declarations of status.

'And no bloody stupid bunches of dried herbs hanging everywhere,' Gwen added, making him laugh, making him love her. The only things he'd regularly criticised about Alison's brand of home-making had been her bloody stupid bunches of dried herbs hanging everywhere.

They ate bread and cheese and drank tea at the kitchen table. Gwen talked about her job, the pleasures of teaching, of watching children grow. 'My dad wanted me to do medicine,' she said, 'but I knew it wasn't right for me. I hate illness. I hate misery. I hate death.'

'So do most doctors. That's the whole point, isn't it?'

'No, I don't mean it like that. If someone tells me he has a headache, I don't want to cure his headache, I want to thump him for being pathetic enough to mention it. As you said, I have no sympathy. I'm an optimist, I suppose. I believe in positive thought as a power for health. And happiness.'

Owen was glad of that. A hypochondriac was the last thing he needed. He didn't even want to talk about medicine; it made him feel sick. But she'd think him weird if he changed the subject now, and he was even sicker of being weird.

'That's all right when you're well,' he said. 'It's hard to be positive when you're in pain.'

'Everything's hard. Everyone suffers. I saw you looking into Gethin's mouth when he screamed. How many teeth's he got left? Six, eight? He's never been to a dentist, so how did he lose the others? No one to turn to, no one to tell. Toothache's agony; and how many other agonies has he suffered, I wonder, with no one to turn to, no one to tell? He's a bloody hero, that man.'

'He's probably mad,' Owen said.

'I know.' Suddenly she was crying, her throat a moving staircase of broken sobs. Owen circled the table to hold her head against his chest, to stroke the dark silk of her hair.

A phrase came into his mind out of nowhere and escaped his tongue before he could stop it. *'Be' sy'n bod, cariad?'*

He was standing in an ancient privy. The rim of the toilet bowl was about level with his waist. Beside it was a pail full of ashes. There was a hole in a corner of the roof with pale trails of sun-starved ivy growing across the underside of cobwebbed slates. The whitewashed walls were dancing with the sunlight that filtered through the leaves of an elder tree outside the open door. He was crying and someone behind him was saying, *'Be' sy'n bod, cariad?'* What's the matter, love?

Gwen scraped her chair backwards to gaze up at him, amazed. 'Good God,' she whispered. 'Where the hell did that come from?'

Owen felt rather faint. 'My parents,' he whispered.

'Ohh.' Sweet and low, softly humming . . . 'So they *were* Welsh.'

'But they left me.'

'Left you? What d'you mean, left you?'

'I . . .'

He couldn't tell her. The feelings and the words seemed to fight one another, like tentacled sea creatures whose object was to smother, strangle and suck dry. All his life his feelings had been the stronger. All his life the words had died inside. But it was better that way. Even if the words could win, who the hell would understand them? Who the hell would care?

'Nothing,' he said. 'I'm drunk, that's all. Why were you so sad about Gethin?'

Gwen said nothing. Her eyes were narrowed, the tip of her tongue curled thoughtfully over her teeth. 'I'll tell you,' she said at last. 'I love him, Owen. I've known him all my life. Everything I know about language and music, everything I know about myself and other people, everything I know about the world, I've learned through him. I owe him a debt of gratitude I can never repay, or even tell him about.'

She smiled wistfully. 'Once you start thinking about him, you see, Owen, you find yourself thinking about everything, and the more you think, the more awe-inspiring it all becomes. Why, for instance, are there so many different words to say much the same thing? Because our inner worlds are so complex, our thoughts and feelings so precise, that even to say, "I am sad," we could use up half the dictionary. And it's so necessary to say that, sometimes, isn't it? Not just to let off steam but to have someone else share your load. Gethin can never share his load with anyone.' She flicked Owen a glance from under her eyelashes. 'That's why he's mad, isn't it?'

Owen turned his face to the ceiling and closed his eyes. Yes, that was why Gethin was mad and it was the reason *he* had come so close to madness. He'd made a mute of himself, condemned himself to isolation not for Gethin's want of words but for his own want of courage. His own want of trust. Well, he'd said it now – *They left me* – and nothing terrible had happened. The world hadn't caved in. And Gwen was still here, still listening.

'I was adopted when I was three,' he said. 'My parents – they're dead now – were both doctors, too old to adopt a baby in the ordinary way. I think until then I was in some kind of orphanage; I'm not sure. It seemed to me a terrible place, but it might have been terrible only because I missed my real parents so much. I remember crying for them, watching the door for them. No. No, I don't remember that; I remember *waiting* for them, being . . . Being incapable of doing anything else because I was waiting so *hard*. I couldn't understand why they'd left me there, just gone off and . . .'

'Why do you say they left you? They probably died, Owen.'

'No.' He shook his head. 'No, I'm sure they didn't. I *know* they didn't.'

'How do you know? Did you ask?'

Owen was silent for a long time. Then: 'Didn't I tell you?' he asked softly. 'I have a remarkable memory.'

CHAPTER SIXTEEN

Although he ran down the mountain very early, not to leave
Malen alone at the usual time, Rhodri walked back the following
Saturday with lead in his legs and iron his soul, reciting the names
of the shops in Main Street to keep his mind from his rage.

There were Evans Departmental, Evans Hardware, Evans
Greengrocer and Evans Baker. There were Jones Carpets, Jones
Books and Jones Fish and Chips. These names, with as many of
Williams, Jenkins, Thomas, Morgan and Price – oh, yes, and
Roberts – peopled the entire country and could be identified, one
from another, only with help from a few other names and occu-
pations. Thus, when one spoke of a Jones, one said, Jones Carpets
to mark him out from Jones Books. And if there were two Jones
Books they became, 'Robert Jones Books and Idris Jones Books.'
The complications were endless, often resulting in four or five
appellations, as in 'David *George* Lloyd-Evans Glove Factory',
the general manager, to distinguish him from his cousin, 'David
John Lloyd-Evans Glove Factory', who did the accounts.

As far as Rhodri knew, there was no other Rhodri Thomas in
the locality, but they always called him Rhodri Thomas Mountain,
not so much to identify him, as to comment on his madness in
choosing to live so far from his fellow men. Now, he supposed,
they'd call him Rhodri Thomas Dirty Bugger, with – unless the
minister showed himself very soon – Rhodri Thomas Murderer
following soon after.

Mrs Cadog Evans Co-op had looked at him with knives in her
eyes and a lemon in her mouth. She had served him in silence and
not once, until she'd totted up the bill, had she met the eyes she
would die for. 'Twenty-two and three,' she'd remarked with acid.
'Eating well all of a sudden, aren't you? Come into money?'

'I'm sure you would know of it,' he'd said, 'if I had.'

'Oh, I know nothing.'

'I am glad to hear it, for what you do not know you cannot
judge.'

The pursed-up smile of her was like poison, the triumphant
squirm of her shoulders a sickness to his heart. 'Always the same
tune then, Rhodri? Speak no evil?'

'That's right, Mrs Evans.'

But as he'd reached out for Malen's oranges, Mrs Evans caught his wrist, squeezing hard. 'Oh, Rhodri, what are you doing, *bach*? Where is the minister? What have you *done*? Will you ruin yourself?'

'I might well come to ruin,' he'd said through his teeth, 'But if I do, Mrs Evans, the wrong of it will not be mine.'

He hadn't gone to the library. He couldn't face Enid Griffiths. He couldn't face her glasses. Chekhov, already beloved but still half finished, had ridden to town on his shoulder only to ride back again, unstamped, with a tuppeny fine to add robbery to insult.

But all along Main Street women turned from him, smirking, or sucking their cheeks, or calling out sweetly, 'You're early today, Rhodri! Anything *wrong*?' and whispering behind him as he passed.

He hated them. Only give him a stick and he'd whip them all home, burn out their tongues, make them as mute and as helpless as Malen was.

In one of the ancient tales of the *Mabinogion* – in fact in a postscript, barely linked with the rest and hardly understood – it told how the Welsh settlers of Brittany had cut out the tongues of their women, 'lest they corrupt the language'. Rhodri had always been shocked by that passage; it had spoiled an otherwise beautiful story. But that was what the tongues of women did: they corrupted and besmirched, they spoiled the beautiful stories.

And in his dream the emperor saw a maiden sitting before him in a chair of red gold. No more than it would be easy to look on the sun at its brightest, no easier than that would it be to look at her in her excelling beauty . . .

The wind had ice in it and a strength which threatened to push Rhodri back down the mountain as fast as he could climb it. But his rage was its equal; the wind stood no chance either of cooling or slowing him down. He knew in his heart that they would take Malen from him.

It was strange how soon she'd possessed him, how completely she'd filled his mind. Two weeks! Yet it was as though it had been for ever: as if he had never lived – and could never live again – without her. She was inside him even now, in every pulse of his blood, in every thought, every thrust of every muscle.

*And when he awoke, neither life nor existence nor being was left in him
for the maiden he had seen in his sleep. Not one bone-joint of his, not a
single nail, to say nothing of a part that might be greater than that, but
was filled with love for the maiden . . .*

The last bend in the road was a good way down from the *carn* he
had built to guide him, but he'd scarcely set his steps straight
when he saw Roberts rounding the higher bend, clutching his hat
to his head as he nipped out of sight on the mountain, just below
the cottage.

Rhodri opened his throat and roared, 'Roberts! Touch that girl
and I'll kill you!'

But the wind thrust his words into his throat, making him
dumb. Without pausing to mark the spot, he slung his satchel into
the heather and ran.

CHAPTER SEVENTEEN

Owen threw off the covers and awoke, his overheated limbs rejoicing in the runnels of cool air which spilled over the window-sill. His eyes were sticky and swollen. He opened his eyes and closed them again, having registered the grey haze over the mountain which promised yet another scorcher. Somewhere nearby an early-rising wood pigeon remarked upon the weather: 'Too, *too* cruel.'

He remembered, from a time very distant in his childhood, rescuing from the cats a fallen nest of unfledged house martins and being appalled at the lice which sucked at their naked little bodies. He felt lucky and comfortable and too sleepy to remark on the strangeness of it.

An unconscious while later, the pigeon spoke again: 'Too, *too* cool,' and again was right, twice in a day, like a stopped clock. Shivering, Owen reached behind him to snatch at the duvet and caught instead a handful of someone else's hair. His eyes widened painfully. Memory poured over his mind like water over stones, too insubstantial to be caught by the fingers alone. He turned over, establishing beyond reasonable doubt that he'd spent the night with Gwen-hoover Jones.

She opened one eye, shut it again and blushed, curling her hands to her cheeks to cool them. 'What's the time?'

'Er . . . twenty to seven.'

His eyes closed again of their own volition and he remembered resting his head on her soft, unsympathetic breast, telling her everything he knew and thought he had forgotten, wishing she could mend it. She hadn't. Yet the pain he felt now was mostly embarrassment. He almost said, 'It was the whisky talking,' but realised at once that she would think the whisky had made love to her, too, and he didn't want her to think that. It was probably true.

Yet he remembered enough about it to know that he hadn't, by that time, been half as drunk as he'd been desperate. He'd felt so lonely, as if, even holding her, even speaking to her, he was floating silently in space, caught in an orbit of darkness he would never escape. Unfastening her blouse had been more an attempt to catch and be caught by the earth's gravity than an invitation to sex, although now he came to think of it they were probably the same thing.

'How are you this morning?' she asked, and he smiled at the no-nonsense briskness of her tone. No sympathy. That was her trademark. She carried it like a banner. Yet there was something in her eyes which added a defensive rider: 'I don't want your pain. I have my own.'

He traced her lips with his finger. 'Ashamed of myself,' he murmured. 'As you said, everyone suffers. You, too, I'm sure. Tell me about it. Trust me. I'm a cabinet maker.'

She laughed. 'Oh, well in that case, I've got woodworm.'

'No! Where?' He began carefully to examine her: her throat, her chest, the damp, silky channel between her breasts, the smooth plane of her belly.

Her stomach rumbled. 'Ah, there it is,' he said, and she drew up her knees and chuckled, put up her hands to pull him into the shadowy cradle of her thighs.

By eight o'clock the sun was hot, its light as bright as torture. It had been Owen's idea to have breakfast in the garden, but his temples ached and his eyes were so sore he wished they'd stayed indoors. 'Ve haf vays,' he murmured through his muesli.

'What?'

'I went to a shrink after Alison left. I thought if I could talk about it . . . But I couldn't. I've never been so embarrassed in my life. I don't know what's worse – saying too much when you should keep your mouth shut or saying too little when you're meant to tell all.'

Gwen didn't reply and her silence sickened him, making him admit to himself that he'd said all that just to have her tell him, 'There's nothing to be embarrassed about.' It was the sort of thing *he* would say. Reassurance was part of his job.

'Don't you ever lie, Gwen?'

She widened her eyes at him and burst out laughing.

'What's funny?'

'What isn't? You take everything so bloody seriously.' She closed her eyes and tipped her face to the sun. 'It's a new day. A beautiful day. Why let yesterday spoil it?'

Owen smiled, frowned and scratched his neck, wondering if she was right, wishing she was, knowing she wasn't. The things that ate at one's mind could not so easily be dismissed. If they could, he'd have dismissed them years ago. He'd tried to dismiss them, tried to live his life regardless; but it was like Hamelin trying to live regardless of rats. *They bit the babies in their cradles.*

Yet it was clear that Gwen had had more than enough of his plague of rodents. His burdens, for her, were like feathers at the end of her nose: an irritation she could easily be rid of.

'Feel like a walk?' he asked.

'Can't. I'm meeting my sister at eleven and I'll have to go home first, to change.'

Will you come back? he asked silently and the silence deepened and expanded, covering the world. He felt as if he were the only creature left alive in it and realised, quite suddenly, that he'd felt something similar all his life. Like the last of the dinosaurs, the last of the dodos, there was nothing to do but kill time.

'What's the best thing you can do with an electricity bill?' Gwen asked suddenly.

'What?'

'You heard.'

'Pay it, I suppose. Why?' He frowned. 'Have you had one you can't pay?'

'No. You have. At least, I think you have. Debt begins with a single unpaid bill, doesn't it? And then grows, mushrooming out of control until you can't pay the rent and you're homeless, destitute, a vagrant without a future, and a past you'd rather not think about. But if you do think about it, you can always trace it back to a single bill and the decision you made not to pay it.'

'Does one decide such things?'

'Yes. It probably doesn't seem so, because in that kind of situation you have very little choice. Either you pay the bill or let the kids go hungry. Yet there must be a moment when you decide to feed the kids, mustn't there? You fork out the money for food and think, there, that's it, now I can't pay the electricity bill, but it's still a decision and once you've made it you can't change it. The mushroom of debt is already growing. See what I mean?'

He stared bleakly down the garden. 'Yes,' he murmured. 'You mean it's too late.'

She laughed again, mocking him. 'Too late is when someone puts flowers on your grave.' She stood up, smoothed her skirt and stretched her arms, like a Druid, to the morning sun.

'I'm not sure I quite understand you. What bill?'

'Your parents.' She leaned over him to ruffle his hair, to smile into his eyes. 'I'll ring you, okay?'

90

He didn't believe her and, long after she'd gone, the touch of her fingers in his hair irritated him, angered him, made him ache to have her touch him again. He could scarcely believe he'd met her only yesterday. Last night had seemed like a lifetime; he'd given her – told her – his whole life and she'd calmly walked off with it, saying she'd *ring* him.

He wandered back to his room, intending to make the bed which had never been so wrecked when he'd slept in it alone. She'd made love as she wore her hair: loose and generous, holding nothing back. Yet she'd held everything back. He knew almost nothing about her that meant anything.

He sighed and lay down, stroking her pillow as if the dent her head had made in it was not now an empty space, his whole life not an empty space, a waste of time, of work, of love and judgement. Sex was everything only while it lasted. While it lasted, it wiped out all that had gone before. When it was over you were back where you started, only worse, lonelier, wishing you could do it again.

They left me.

Gwen still doubted him, but he was certain they hadn't died. He was sure he would have remembered the aching incredulity of death, its whispers falling like goose-feather snow until one was covered, one knew. No, they had left him, believing, perhaps, that a child of two is too young to notice the difference between one pair of arms and another, one voice, one face and another.

In fact, he had no recollection of faces, before or afterwards. His memories were all of hands and voices, places – like the earth-closet in the garden – and moods of peace or black terror. He remembered his mother's hands (he was sure they were hers) and a table and a loaf of bread, diagonal stripes cast by sunlight through a small window.

But the thing he recalled most clearly was his own point of view, his closeness to the ground, the vastness of the world which loomed above him like a sky full of magic carpets from which those large, godlike hands had reached down to comb his hair or wipe his nose, to lift him up, perhaps, although he could not remember being lifted. He only remembered being held, being so much a part of another person's body and she – or he – being so much a part of his, it was as if they'd been the same.

It was a version of heaven as impossible to define as it was impossible to forget. He'd felt it with his own children and learned something about it through them. When Jonty was three, Em a little older, they'd broken free. There came a time when you held them and felt a space between, which *they* chose not to fill. It was almost as if they'd been born twice: the first simply to enter the world, the second to become independent beings with minds of their own.

He had never reached that point of voluntary separation. He'd been torn from his parents by a violence so great it was as if he'd lost a part of himself: a leg or an arm, a slice of his brain, nothing that could be returned to him by someone else. Even his own children hadn't managed to give him back that missing part, but they'd given him a future . . .

His stomach lurched with the onset of panic. A familiar seething blackness filled his mind. He bared his teeth, uttered a groan of despair and in the next instant said, very reasonably, 'That's enough of that,' and jumped off the bed to stare at himself, narrow-eyed, in the mirror. 'Know what's wrong with you?' he demanded caustically. 'You've got a hangover.'

He continued to mutter to himself as he went downstairs in search of Alka Seltzer: something about a brisk walk, something about water under the bridge, something about suicide. He knew the time for suicide had come and gone, that it wasn't an option any more and would never be so again. He felt sorry about that. The easy way out was closed to him. It was like missing the last train, resigning himself to the long walk home.

He washed the breakfast dishes, moving the mixer tap in dreamy arcs, a child playing with water. He realised, as he reached for the towel, that his headache had gone.

He thought, 'Only another forty years to go,' and remembered all the comforting platitudes he'd doled out to grieving patients and realised how poor a comfort he'd been. 'Just take it one day at a time, Mrs Brown.' People didn't naturally live one day at a time and, when they were forced to do so, their 'one day' felt exactly the same as forty years.

Yet during the decade he'd spent in general practice, Owen had lost only one of his patients to suicide – and for bankruptcy, not bereavement or divorce. The others had lived their one day at a time for as long as it took and then come to him with a cold they wanted to clear up before they went climbing in the Himalayas, or got married again, or took their Grade 3 test in flamenco dancing.

It would happen to him. He'd learn the flamenco and start living again. It was hard to believe, yet he did believe it now. Yesterday, as the armchair philosophers had it, had been the first day of the rest of his life. Today was up to him. He'd walk into town, buy some bread and a newspaper, write to the children. He could tell them about his walk on the mountain. He wouldn't think of Gwen. He was certain she wouldn't come back.

CHAPTER EIGHTEEN

The man standing at the door was not the minister. He was taller and thinner and it seemed he'd bought his lovat gaberdine second-hand, for it fitted only where it touched, hanging in folds over his chest, fighting his legs in the wind.

Rhodri stood gasping for breath, battening down murder with relief enough to make his knees sag. Inside the cottage, Nessa was doing her stuff, mingling blood-curdling howls with a deep-throated bark which meant, Rhodri knew, that she was terrified.

'All right, Ness!' he yelled. 'Pack it in, now, good girl!'

She was quiet. In his mind's eye Rhodri saw her, too, sagging at the knees. She would fight to the death if the fight was asked of her, but that didn't mean she fancied it.

The stranger took off his hat, not for courtesy, but to keep the wind from knocking it from his head. His thick white hair, released from confinement, leapt upright, like the crest on a white cockatoo.

'Oh,' he said. 'Mr Thomas, is it? Rhodri Thomas?'

Rhodri frowned and said nothing.

'I am John Evans,' the man said. 'One among thousands.'

Rhodri smiled and said nothing. He turned his face from the wind and looked at the visitor sideways, admiring the patrician cut of his nose and his sharp, poetic cheekbones. He was carrying an old, pigskin briefcase, but in other respects looked nothing like an insurance salesman.

'Nice place,' John Evans said, nodding towards the cottage.

'It keeps the weather out,' Rhodri said, recognising flattery. Even with a dozen coats of limewash to cover its flaws, his home still looked as if he'd knitted it and dropped half the stitches.

They stared at each other, half-smiling. The man nodded again. 'I've come about Malen Price,' he said. 'Can we talk?'

Rhodri's face slammed shut.

The man gazed with watering eyes beyond curtains of shifting mists which covered, revealed and covered again, as though the mountain exhaled smoke with every breath. 'I have not come here to hurt you.'

Again they stared at each other. 'Round the back,' Rhodri decided at last. 'Out of the wind.'

94

Garth and Pen came to meet them, Garth grumbling, Pen's shoulders braced to dash at the visitor and shut her teeth where they'd hurt. Evans sank slowly into a crouch and held out both his hands for them to sniff at. 'Good dogs.'

To the dogs he said, 'John Roberts has passed on, God forgive him. It'll be all over the papers on Monday. I wanted you and Malen to be the first to know.'

They sat in Rhodri's bit of a barn, the dogs quiet at their feet. Evans, too, was a minister of the chapel. He'd known Roberts for years without knowing him, except to suspect there was something amiss with his soul. They'd preached the same circuit, stayed in each other's houses, been polite to each other without saying much beyond the limits of chapel business.

'When Malen went dumb,' Evans said, 'I guessed what he'd done to her. His rage was suspect, you see: an act, over-acted. But it could have been someone else, someone she'd met in the street, like he said. What could I do? It's a terrible thing to suspect a man of, a worse thing to accuse him of when you've nothing to prove it. Now I feel almost as guilty as if . . . But I still don't know what I could have done. If I'd been wrong . . .'

He shook his head. When Rhodri made no reply he went on pensively, 'He came to me last week to tell me you'd taken her. He lied about your motives – very plausibly, too. Last night, he came again. I don't know where he'd been in the meantime; he looked like a beggar. He put a letter in my hand and then went out and threw himself in the river. My house is by the river, you see. I watched him go, never thinking for a minute what he had in his mind. By the time I reached the bridge, he'd disappeared. We found him three miles down, stuck in the roots of a tree, bless him.'

'You are too generous,' Rhodri whispered.

'Oh, no. He could have left it, Rhodri, left all the blame heaped on your head, not his. You might not know it, but the talk about you is already . . . Well. He only did it for you and Malen. He wanted to put it right for you and Malen.'

'It will never be right for Malen.'

'No.' From his briefcase he took a folded wad of paper which he carefully unfolded and, after separating a few sheets from the top, handed them to Rhodri. 'The rest is just business,' he said.

John, I have lied to you. I am Malen's ruin, her mother's and my own. I couldn't help myself. I know this makes me no better than an animal, but the truth of it is no less true. I couldn't help myself. I was driven by the devil's scourge to violate her. Pity me, for I am lost to heaven, but pity Malen more.

I married the mother that I might wed the child and when she refused me I forced her, and dared her with threats to speak of it. I told her I would throw her mother out in the street and keep Malen for myself. I didn't mean it. I meant for her to keep silent on that subject only, not cease to speak at all. I drove her to madness.

Her mother suspected me and hated me for it, but she was as helpless as Malen was. She had no money of her own, no family, nowhere else to go. She died of grief and had no comfort.

All I can do now is pray for courage to die the same.

I knew after Anne died that I could not keep Malen with me, that I'd have to put her away, but when I told her what would happen, she flew at me and clawed my face. I felt no pain. The scourge was on me and I wanted her again.

What I told you about Rhodri Thomas was a lie like all the others. I am as certain now in my heart that just as I was driven by Satan to hurt Malen, he came on the Lord's work to save her.

No, Rhodri thought, it was the devil in my case, too.

He scanned the next page – which was about himself and as true as made no difference – and handed it back. He felt like crying.

'Nicely written,' he said. 'Pity to blame it on the devil, though. I'd have liked him better if he'd blamed himself.'

Mr Evans's cheeks, seared crimson by the cold, were beginning to turn blue. His teeth chattered when he asked, 'Are you in love with her?'

'No.'

'Then why? Were you called, like he said?'

Rhodri laughed. He could believe in that sort of thing sometimes, when he was private in his thoughts, but when anybody else talked about it, it sickened him, made him angry. Why couldn't men do good without being driven? And why couldn't they do evil, likewise? The responsibility was theirs, not God's or the devil's. He didn't doubt the 'scourge' part of it: lust *was* a scourge, fear a scourge, hunger, cold, pain and loneliness; but if you gave in to any of them it was your own bloody fault. Men are not animals.

He looked at his dogs, who looked patiently up at him, flickering their eyebrows like feelers as if to divine his thoughts. Animals are better, he added silently.

'No,' he said. 'I wasn't called. I felt sorry for her, that's all. For a mad five minutes I was Sir Galahad: sword and buckler, white charger, the lot.'

John Evans nodded. 'And what now, Rhodri? I can't leave her here. Not like this.'

'Like what?'

Evans tucked his hands under his armpits and beat a warming tattoo on the floor with his feet, watching them as they tapped up and down. 'She's old enough to marry,' he said. 'What's this floor? Concrete?'

'Solid rock.'

Rhodri covered his face with his hands. He was aware that his doom had fallen on him and that he had, on a whim, chosen it. Chosen Malen. He wished to God he hadn't.

'The trouble is,' John Evans went on quietly, 'that I am responsible for her now. I have to do my best for her, as I would for my own daughter. I can't leave her living in sin with you, now can I? You'll be lepers, the pair of you.'

'*I* haven't touched her.'

'I believe you, *bach*. Who else will?'

'What if I won't marry her?'

John Evans shrugged. 'There's nothing else. I am a widower, living alone. You know the alternatives as well as I do. That was why you took her, wasn't it? To save her from that?'

'No. To save her from him. Don't you see, Mr Evans? Married or not, I can't *ever* touch her, because if I do . . .'

'You think he's defiled her?'

'No, I think he's defiled *me*. I was as clean as a whistle two weeks ago. Now I'm up to my eyes in other people's dirt. *Duw*, what a mess. But I brought it on myself. I can't complain. How long can you give her, before you decide?'

'*I* decide?' John Evans queried gently. 'No, Rhodri. This is your decision and Malen's, not mine.' He leaned across to grasp Rhodri's wrist. 'Romance and reality are different things, and the right thing is wrong if you do it for the wrong reasons. You were right to take Malen from him. I am not so sure that you would be right to marry her. Asylums are not what they were. They might heal her, *bach*.'

They would cut her hair with a basin and dress her in grey, take her shuffling around the garden, three times a day . . .

'Give me another week,' Rhodri said.

97

CHAPTER NINETEEN

As Owen was leaving the house, he found Glyn Caldwell's book on the hall table. It was a small, tastefully produced hardback, the cover design a soft watercolour of mountains against a dark sky. He flipped it open. It had been signed by the author, with a short message written in Welsh, the only word of which Owen could decipher was Gwen's name, written in full. He smiled as he pronounced it: 'Gwen-hooey-va-rrr.' She'd have to come back now.

He turned the book over and saw Glyn Caldwell smiling at him from the back cover. In spite of his being forewarned, he was shocked to find it such a powerful likeness. Caldwell's bone structure was remarkably like his own: same long nose, same squared-off jaw, same forehead. The eyes – perhaps – were longer, and perhaps lighter, although with a black and white portrait it was hard to tell. The mouth was different. No, just the smile was different. It was the smile of a happy man.

Owen stood at the hall mirror and smiled. He smiled broadly, coyly, smugly, lecherously, sadly and sarcastically, but however he smiled he couldn't reproduce Glyn Caldwell's smile. He shrugged, set the book down again, stared at the photograph for a moment and then tried the half-face test, laying his hand first over the left side of Caldwell's face and then over the right. It didn't always work, but it was the best way Owen knew of revealing a complex personality in a photograph. Covering the left made no difference except, marginally, to make Caldwell's expression more cheerful. The right . . . It was like looking at his own face in a mirror. The smile was blotted out, the brightness in the eye quenched. That side of his face was cold and sad, the face of a ghost, robbed of life.

Taking the book with him, Owen ran upstairs to find his passport and the most recent photograph he had of himself. It was too small to obscure with his hand. He laid the edge of a bookmark over the right side and produced almost exactly the same effect: a haunted, empty expression which wasn't apparent when the full face was exposed. The 'alive' side of his own face was childishly innocent and he realised that his right eye was slightly larger than his left, the right side of his mouth softer, the unsmiling corner of it optimistically uptilted. Optimistic? Him? Yes, in a way, he supposed he had been, until this past year.

And now? His heart was racing with something he clearly recognised as hope, although he recognised too that it was a ridiculous, childish hope, scarcely worth thinking about. Many people had doubles and when their physiognomies were structured according to recognised ethnic types – Celtic in his case – they probably had numerous doubles, related by blood, perhaps, but so far back in history it no longer signified. Glyn Caldwell was not Owen's brother. He was not Owen's brother. Owen had never had a brother. He was certain of that. Almost.

He opened the book at the first page and read the opening lines.

It had rained all week. Now, suddenly, the wind turned and strengthened, blowing dry and cold from the north-east, clearing the sky. Tonight there'd be a star-white frost and ice crystals in the peat, crunching underfoot like spilled sugar.

Winter. He was glad it was winter in Glyn Caldwell's book. He'd forgotten what winter was like.

He was crossing the bridge at the foot of the mountain before he entertained his next reasonable thought. It was, How the hell did I get here? He hadn't been conscious of the walk. His mind had been in free flight, enjoying the beauty of the day, the heat of the sun on his skin, the green of the trees against a sky so densely blue it seemed almost solid, a block of pigment from God's own paintbox.

Owen didn't believe in God and, until this moment, would have said that he lacked spirituality of any kind. Now, standing in the middle of the bridge, he began to think there might be something more than he'd imagined. Why was he here? What – leaving Paul's BMW out of the equation – had brought him to Wales, to this particular corner of it? There'd certainly been no choice involved, no active decision. Paul had said, 'Come to the cottage with us, will you?' and Owen hadn't even stirred himself to reply. He hadn't, at the time, quite understood the question. Words had ceased to mean anything very much. He'd been like Gethin Morgan, watching people's mouths opening and closing and wondering why they did it, what it signified.

He leaned on the parapet of the bridge and stared into the river, listening to its quiet burblings as if to an alien language: Turkish,

Armenian, Farsi. Perhaps it meant something. Perhaps everything meant something if you listened hard enough, paid attention.

Why was he here? Paul could just as easily have bought a cottage in Tenby or Montgomery. It needn't have been here, where Gethin Morgan was, where Gwen was, where all the pieces had begun to come together. It was almost as if his life had been a maze and this the centre of it, the monster's lair. Unpaid bills . . .

Gwen was right. He'd spent his life believing he owed his parents nothing except to forget them as they had forgotten him. But that wasn't the point. When you paid an electricity bill, you weren't giving anything away; you were lighting your own darkness. The benefit to the electricity board was immaterial; it didn't matter. All that mattered was to keep the lights burning, to stay alive, stay solvent.

He became aware that he was grinning to himself. He realised also that, in spite of his own fully acknowledged stupidity in the matter, he believed that Glyn Caldwell was his brother. He couldn't help it. He wanted it to be so, and no matter how many times he called himself a fool, an idiot, a man barely sane, he still wanted it.

He bought bread, pasta, the *Times* and, in defiant mood, a bottle of Australian wine, with kangaroos on the label. Alison had sent him a snap of the kids beside a browsing kangaroo and its joey (although now he came to think of it, it was probably a wallaby; kangaroos were bigger). Alison had written on the back of the photograph, 'Guess where we live now?' as if he didn't know, hadn't noticed, had let it slip his mind somehow. A victory was never complete for her until she'd rubbed his nose in it.

He still couldn't think of her without rage. He knew that he was at least partly to blame, that he hadn't understood her, but he'd never understood anyone, had given up trying to understand many years ago and – in his way – been happier for it. Trying to understand people was like trying to understand cats. They sit and stare at you with cool, assessing eyes, they curl up in your lap and purr, they swipe at you with their claws or wind themselves around your legs, crying for attention. No point asking the bloody things why they do it. They do it, that's all, and if you're a decent, fairly kindly person, you respond as best you can *without* understanding.

One of his patients, once, had said to him, 'The trouble with most of us is that we don't realise we're alone in the world until we're in pain.' He'd meant, It doesn't matter that you understand the source of my pain; it makes no difference how sympathetic you are; you can't *feel* it.

Owen had understood this for as long as he could remember and had assumed that most people felt the same. It had never occurred to him to think that it was a fairly rare condition. Most people, he realised now, thought they were *not* alone. They thought that when they were in pain, someone else could feel it, that when they were sad, someone else would weep. Alison had been like that. She'd fling around the house with her mouth set in a grim line and when he asked what was wrong, snap, 'If you don't know, I certainly shan't tell you!'

'Then how can I find out?'

'Use your imagination!'

Imagination. What the hell was the use of that to anyone? If he used his imagination (construct a fantasy, in other words) he might imagine she'd contracted rabies and treat her accordingly. A married woman with two young children, a job, a house, two cats and a car, could choose from a few dozen reasons for storming around in a temper. How was he to guess which one of them had set her off? If the boot happened to be on the other foot, he'd damn well tell her what had upset him, not ask her to *imagine* it.

But no . . . He wouldn't tell her. He'd never told her anything. He'd never given her a chance to know him, and how can you love someone you don't know? How can you care?

The streets were crowded and the town much brighter than he remembered, with baskets of flowers hanging from every lampost, sunlight glinting from windows, quartz crystals in the granite slabs shining like stars. He wondered what had happened to it – or to him – that its shadows had fled. I'm better, he told himself and at the same time was aware that if better and worse were divided by a line, he was still balancing on the line, teetering between light and dark and by no means certain which side he would fall.

He was passing the entrance to a deserted side street when he heard Gethin Morgan's scream. As Jill had said, it was terrifying even when you understood its source; you couldn't help wondering what it meant, why it sounded so desolate, so passionate. If he was only saying hello, couldn't he tone it down a bit, scream in a friendlier fashion?

But Gethin wasn't just saying hello. He was begging. He'd cornered two young girls in the doorway of a boarded-up shop and was stretching out his palm, hooking his fingers, shrieking, 'Gimmee, gimmee, gimmee!' or its equivalent, as the girls shrank from him, their eyes bulging with terror.

Owen called out, 'It's all right; he won't hurt you,' and as the girls looked at him, desperate to be rescued, Gethin looked too, and grinned. He *was* mad. He had that sly, triumphant look in his eyes that sane people adopt only when they're winning at Scrabble.

'God, what's *wrong* with him?' The girls were edging crabwise out of the doorway, clutching each other's arms.

'He's deaf, that's all. Nothing to worry about.'

The girls sobbed and ran for it. Gethin screamed again and stretched out his palm to Owen.

'You old sod,' Owen said. 'I know you, remember? You can't fool me.'

Gethin narrowed his eyes.

Owen mimed holding a dart and rocked up on his toes to mime throwing it. 'Remember?'

Gethin's eyes widened with recognition. He reached out thin, brown fingers and made hooking motions at Owen's mouth. *Talk to me.*

His loneliness was almost worse than his voice. It made Owen's hair stand on end, brought him out in gooseflesh. He couldn't think of a single thing to say and, when he cast about for a few lines of poetry to quote, he could remember none; not even a nursery rhyme. It was weird. The very fact that it didn't matter, that Gethin couldn't hear what he said, made it all the more difficult, somehow.

'Oh, well,' he said at last. 'Looks like we're a matched pair of dummies, Gethin.' Gethin tipped his head to one side, watching Owen's mouth for the next burst of mysterious activity.

'You aren't entirely alone, anyway,' Owen went on. 'None of us can say what we mean. Few of us can hear what we're told. We don't even listen to ourselves, you know.' He smiled. Gethin jutted his chin, waiting for more. 'You know something, Gethin? I should have been a cabinet maker.'

He turned and walked back to the high street, half expecting Gethin to stop him, or to scream again, but nothing happened. As he turned the corner he glanced back, almost hopefully, to see if the old man was watching him, but he'd turned to the wall and was quietly peeing against it.

Owen shrugged, smiled and walked on and, now that he no longer needed it, remembered a line from Wordsworth that he'd liked all his life for its joyous, spring-heeled rhythm:

> . . . *as the morning comes*
> *Out of the bosom of the night, come ye.*

Had he done that? He thought he probably had. A week ago he'd been counting his way through the days, counting out agonies he could scarcely bear to confront. He tried it again.

'One, two, three, four . . .'

But it seemed a waste of time. He wanted to get home, read Glyn Caldwell's book, find out where he'd come from.

Out of the bosom of the night, come ye.

Yes.

CHAPTER TWENTY

When Mr Evans had gone, Rhodri walked back down the mountain to find his satchel, letting his thoughts run in circles through the fog. He saw Mr Roberts hurling his sins into the river and felt a pang of sorrow for a soul forever lost. No man was born evil. He was born only with weaknesses which his experience either protected or laid bare. Rhodri thought it likely that Roberts had known this and turned to God for protection, but God's business is not to protect. Like the mountain, his business is to test, to challenge, to open two paths where only one will do and say, 'You choose.'

But how could you choose when even your own feelings lied to you? Rhodri had loved Malen this morning and now he didn't. Little more than an hour ago he had come up this mountain raging because they would take her from him and now he wished they would, wished they would take her by force or by stealth so that *he* needn't say, 'My fault.'

Garth was the one with the nose for finding things, but he was asked to seek so rarely, he went *twp* with the responsibility of it, zig-zagging all over the mountain with his nose sucking the ground like a hoover. They searched for more than an hour before at last Rhodri saw the satchel: just the gleam of a buckle, several yards lower down. It was only then, with the gleam, that he realised the mists had gone, the sun come out. The wind had turned, whistling in from the east, as keen and clean as a blade.

'*Diolch yn fawr*, Garth,' he said nastily. 'Bloody hopeless, you are. There it is, down there.'

It was useless to tell a dog to seek unless you also let him find. Useless to tell him anything unless, through success, he came to comprehend the nature of the task. Dogs have no real knowledge of human language; they associate sounds with actions, moods, routines. Even had Garth found the satchel straight off and been given no praise for it, he wouldn't know he'd done right; he'd think he'd failed; he'd go on hoovering the mountain until hell froze.

Rhodri couldn't wait that long. His ears were freezing and hell was next. 'Come by,' he hinted tactfully and, as Garth moved

104

closer to the satchel, wondered if he too was a dog, God's dog, needing words of guidance and praise simply to tell him what he was doing, let alone whether it was right or wrong.

He couldn't marry Malen. Had he wanted to be a monk (and he never had) he'd have chosen a nice, safe monastery, free of temptation, not a two-roomed hovel with the only woman . . .

'But wanting her is not loving her,' he told himself.

And want unsatisfied could turn to hatred a good deal faster than Garth . . . But Garth had found it.

'*O, da iawn!* Good dog!' He opened his arms and Garth leapt into them to lick his face and bound away, laughing with the triumph of the moment.

And even if it was love, how could he live with it, with her, without touching her? He'd go mad – and what might a man do when he was mad? He saw Mr Roberts hurling his sins into the river and suddenly was raging. Why should he pay the price for another man's evil? Why should he be sullied by his filth? He wasn't the same! He wasn't the same!

Prove it, the mountain said.

'I don't have to prove it. I know.'

Much good that'll be to Malen when you put her away. What'll you tell her? That you're doing it for her own good, her own safety? Safety from what? You?

The sun had dissolved behind a high blanket of aluminium cloud below which clots and wisps of darker stuff were racing the wind. In such a light, the mountain was the colour of armies: rank upon rank of them, silent and vengeful, waiting only the word of command. It was possible, still, to give the peaks their names: Old Tom, the Devil's Horn, the White Seeker, but they were like the names of enemy battalions, of little consequence when ranged against one man whose name they could obliterate in moments.

Rhodri Thomas Mountain, ho-ho. You believed it, didn't you? You thought yourself so big, so high. Well, pride ever goeth before a fall, boyo. What are you now? An ant on the toe of my boot. Nothing.

'And what is Malen?' Rhodri demanded bitterly. 'An ant on the toe of mine.'

As he walked back to the cottage, rehearsing the precise way he would speak to her (explain first about Roberts and Mr Evans, tell her that asylums were not as they were), he remembered something else Evans had said and turned up his face to heaven, thanking God. 'This is your decision and *Malen's*, not mine.'

105

'Well, there's obvious,' he said. 'It's not my choice at all!'

But he'd damn well make *her* choice clear. He'd tell her precisely what marriage meant and make no bones about it. And why the hell not? Maybe he had thought himself a touch better than he was, but he'd never set out to be saint and never would. Not for Malen. Not for any woman. Not for Roberts, either.

You burn in hell, he thought. *I* don't have to.

Malen was standing in the middle of the room, staring at the door. She had a way of keeping her eyes wide open and frowning at the same time: a frightened, anxious expression which somehow had hope in it too. Rhodri smiled briefly and set the satchel on the table.

'It's all right,' he said. 'Safe and sound.'

But she hadn't been worrying about the groceries. She screamed and waved her arm, jabbing her finger in the direction of the barn.

Mr Evans! What did he want? What was he doing here? What the hell's going on?

'You knew it was him who came before, didn't you? Why were you afraid of him? He seems a decent enough man.' He narrowed his eyes suddenly. 'Or do you know different?'

Malen was quiet, her mouth pressed tight, her grey eyes glittering with the frustrated rage of her silence. Rhodri turned away to stow the groceries. For some reason he was afraid to speak, reluctant to tell her anything at all. In many ways . . . In some ways, at least, he had been happy with things as they were. He had liked the uncertainty of it, the feeling that although things could not go on the same, they might change for the better. Now, whichever way they went, they must change for the worse. For Malen at the mental. For himself, alone. God knew she hadn't been a great conversationalist, but she had been company: someone who filled the empty space, someone who softened the air with her presence.

He gazed into the sink. 'Mr Roberts is dead,' he said. 'He drowned himself last night.' Raising his head, he looked out over the mountain, hating it. 'He told Mr Evans what he had done to you and asked him to see you all right. That's why he came here, to let us know. He did not come to hurt you.'

He turned to look at her and she hid her face in her hands.

'Malen?'

She stared at him, shaking her head in disbelief. He knew she was remembering, for her mouth was curled with sickness and her face as pale as the wall.

'Sit down,' he said. 'You'll be all right when you've had a cup of tea.' He took the end of a loaf from the crock and smiled at her sideways. 'Fancy a bit of toast? We'll have to use the bread up before it goes mouldy. Terrible stuff, mould. They'll never find a use for it. Not in a million years.'

CHAPTER TWENTY-ONE

A steamer chair in the shade of a tree, a glass of iced wine and a book. Owen was aware that, by most men's standards (including his own) he had entered a state of bliss only a churl could fail to appreciate. There weren't even any midges.

'So *now* what's wrong with you?' he muttered.

The chair and the tree were fine. The wine was okay, considering. Thus . . . it was the wrong book. Perfect bliss demanded a tome by Tolstoy or Trollope, something large and largely irrelevant, from which one could extract little nuggets of wisdom or brilliance and say, 'Well, well, fancy that.' Glyn Caldwell's book was no such tome. If Owen could only bring himself to read the bloody thing it would be over in a few hours. But it sat on his lap like a time-bomb, steadily ticking. The oddest thing was, he didn't fear an explosion. What really scared him was the thought that it might turn out to be a damp squib. He wanted it . . . He wanted it to . . .

'What d'you think of it, so far?'

He hadn't heard Gwen's car, or her footsteps on the path. He jumped, uttered a loud, braying gasp which made his eyes water with embarrassment, and fell back into his chair, feebly laughing.

'Sorry. Did I scare you?'

'No. No.'

'If you'd rather read . . .?' She half-turned, smiling, to go back the way she had come.

'No! I'm . . . er . . . Please. Have a drink. Sit down. There's another chair—' He jumped up and sped around in welcoming fashion, finding her a chair, fetching her a glass, shouting from the kitchen, 'How was your sister?' as if he cared.

'Fine.'

He put the glass into her hand, poured the wine. He felt as he'd felt at Alison's drinks parties (his too, but it had always been easier to disown them), trying to seem cheerful and interested when he was neither, trying to think of the right thing to say. All he wanted to say was, *Oh, thank you, thank you! You came back!* and sod her bloody sister, but he didn't think it quite suitable. A touch over-eager, perhaps.

'Do you get on well with her?'

'Mmmm,' Gwen pulled a face. 'No, not really. We don't *not* get on. We don't squabble or anything. We're different, that's all. We look alike, but otherwise you'd never know we shared the same blood. Asking us to communicate is like asking a guinea pig to communicate with a rabbit. There's a certain amount of nose-wiggling—' She demonstrated the process, '—and that's it.'

Owen pretended to think about it. 'You just wiggle?'

She grinned. 'Oh, we're very discreet. Even my mother doesn't notice; she thinks we're the best of friends.'

'Is there much difference in your ages?'

'Three years. She's thirty-two. Married. Two kiddies. Very conventional, very nice.'

'You don't like nice?'

'Oh, nice is . . . nice enough if it's all you've got. I couldn't bear it if it was me, though. I'd go mad. It means telling lies all the time. You can't say what you mean or do what you want. You can't be yourself if you're nice all the time.' She threw back her head to glower at the sky. 'I don't mean *good*,' she wailed. 'Good is something *different*, Owen!'

He laughed. 'Was I arguing?'

'I'm right though, aren't I? That chap in Glyn's book: Rhodri; if he was just nice, you wouldn't like him; you wouldn't care; he wouldn't mean anything. That's what upsets me about Eluned. She doesn't mean anything. She's like something dead.'

Niceness apart, Owen had the feeling that he and Eluned were very similar and that Gwen would soon discover this and hastily remove herself. 'I haven't actually started reading it,' he said. 'How did you pronounce his name? *Hodree*?'

'You make the *R* with your tongue and push the *h* through it.'

'And he's a good man, is he? Is it—?' He snatched a breath to fill lungs that had suddenly emptied. 'Is it autobiographical?'

Gwen quirked her eyebrows. 'You mean is Glyn Caldwell a good man? I don't know; I haven't seen him for years.'

'But he signed the book for you,' Owen frowned. 'And you said he charged royalties on the star song.'

'Yes, but that was all done by *magic*, Owen.' She folded her arms and produced a teasing little smile. 'You're in Wales now, you know; we do everything by magic: telephone, e-mail, fax, postage . . . Brilliant, it is. I don't know how you manage without it in England. Still go by stage-coach, do you?'

109

Owen tried not to laugh – and failed. Even when she was mocking him her sense of humour was lovely – partly, he guessed, because she was also mocking herself.

'I bought the book as soon as it came out,' she said. 'Don't ask me why: curiosity, I suppose. And I *posted* it to him to sign. Cost me a fortune, too. Postage, return postage, padded envelope. And then he charged us bloody *royalties* on the poem! Tight little sod. Who does he think he is? You'd think he'd be honoured, wouldn't you?'

Owen felt a little hurt, as if his loyalties were being torn, as if Glyn Caldwell really was his brother. He wasn't. Couldn't possibly be. Yet still he felt compelled to speak up for him. 'Maybe he's broke,' he suggested warily.

'Maybe.' She shrugged. 'Not being very fair, am I?'

Relief made him smile. 'Not answering the question, anyway.'

'What was the question?'

'Autobiography.'

'Oh, yes.' She widened her eyes, thinking it over. 'Yes, it's mostly that, I think, but all muddled up to fit the story. The main thing I noticed was about his mother.'

Owen felt like a trout dying on the river bank. He couldn't breathe. His blood pumped so loudly in his ears he barely heard himself saying, 'His mother? What about her?'

'She hasn't seen him for twenty years. No one knows what it's all about, but you can see it's breaking her heart. He was her only child, and she's getting old. Her time's running out. You haven't read any of the book?'

'I'd just opened it,' he lied, 'when you came.'

'There's a bit – it won't spoil it for you if I tell you? – where Rhodri says about his mother, "He would never have come back except to her funeral," and I couldn't bear to think of Glyn's mam reading that. It's so final, isn't it?'

He tried again to find something to say, not this time because he couldn't think what to say, but because he didn't dare say it. Was Glyn adopted? Could he be my brother? He wanted to ask, but the same terror which had stopped him before – when he was seven, twelve, seventeen and thirty – stopped him now. What if the truth was better left alone? What if the 'history' he had longed to possess was worse than the torment of having none?

He had a nightmare, sometimes; had had it all his life, off and on, which he was certain was a memory of something that had

110

really happened. He was alone in a place having a great deal in common with the most barren parts of these mountains. Running around in circles, searching for something so important he knew he'd die if he didn't find it. On one level it was a perfectly typical anxiety dream, but on another . . . He knew it had happened, that they'd left him – a child of two – alone on the mountain. What kind of people could do that to their own child? He wanted to know. He didn't want to know. He wanted to change the subject.

'You're not drinking your wine,' he said. 'Too dry?'

'Too alcoholic. The police can be funny round here. I think they get bored – breathalyse you for wearing too much hair spray – and I was wondering if you'd fancy a drive. Doesn't matter if not. I just thought, with the top down . . .?'

He didn't need to be asked twice.

CHAPTER TWENTY-TWO

Rhodri spent the rest of that day repairing his lambing fold which, even in good repair, amounted to nothing very much: a small enclosure of dry-stone walls whose functions, although slight, were essential. First, to keep the lambing ewes within easy reach of his aid, second, to afford the vulnerable newborn some shelter from the wind and third, to keep the shepherd from freezing while he ministered to their needs.

Dry walling was not one of Rhodri's talents. He understood its basic principles but lacked the necessary skills. As with most arts, an intellectual grasp of the task was less than a third of it, hard work and enthusiasm less than a third. The rest was all rainbows and lightning-bolts. You couldn't make them, only hope that if you hung around long enough they might happen.

He supposed the same would be true if he married Malen. If he hung around long enough lightning might strike. He tried to imagine it: Malen looking at him one day with love in her eyes, but it gave him no hope. All it gave him was an itch he couldn't scratch, for the day he touched Malen without her consent he would be little better than John Roberts.

He thought himself incapable, deliberately, of frightening or hurting her. His every impulse was to heal her, make her happy, make her whole. But what of himself? He couldn't sacrifice himself to her needs, condemn himself to a lifetime of chastity, childlessness and worse: the hope that somehow she would be healed before he was too old and dispirited to care. No, he couldn't do it. He'd rather die.

Cold and bruised both outside and in, he returned to the cottage, looked Malen straight in the eye and told her flat: 'Asylums are not what they were. They are hospitals, you see, not for the sick, but for the sick at heart. They have the means to heal you, Malen. I don't. You cannot stay with me.'

Then he opened the door, went inside – and said nothing at all.

They spent the evening in an electric silence which, properly harnessed, could have lit up Barmouth front. Rhodri kept rehearsing his speech in his mind, saying it over and over until every word was honed to perfection. *Not for the sick, but for the sick at heart. They have the means to heal you.* It had a certain beauty, a certain symmetry. He saw it, for some reason, as being egg-shaped and when, by Malen's bedtime, he still hadn't managed to say it, he understood why. Eggs are easily broken. It was a lie. It was worse than a lie. Asylums are for the insane. Sick at heart they might be, but they're crazy all the same. He was certain Malen wasn't. Malen was only sick at heart.

'So,' he told Pen a few minutes later, 'If you'd rather stay here, I will marry you, Malen. It will, of course, be a proper marriage; you will be my wife in every sense: lie in my bed, mother my children . . .'

Pen chose that moment to rootle among her private parts, exhibiting a lack of concern for his feelings that made him laugh, if only to keep himself from crying. '*O, dammo*, Pen,' he said bleakly. 'What am I to do?'

She answered as she always answered: briefly and to the point.

'Oh, shut up,' he said when she'd finished. 'What the hell do you know? You're only a bloody dog.'

Malen was waiting for him. He had never before seen her in her nightgown, had avoided the sight out of tact. But he needn't have bothered. It had all the charm of a cardboard box. Same corners. Same colour. The Co-op could deliver groceries in it and no one would know the difference.

He bit his lip, painfully, on a smile. 'Unbleached flannelette,' he said. 'Marvellous stuff. Last for years. Why aren't you in bed? Won't it bend?'

Malen jerked her head the other way. *It's not funny, damn you.*

But the joke died when she turned to look at him again. He thought at first she was having some kind of fit. Her eyes were wild, her mouth opening and closing with a strange, tortured energy, as if she was gagging on a poison she could not quite throw up. 'Aaah,' she moaned feebly. 'Aaaa, ahh . . .'

Frightened, he took a step towards her, holding out his arms to catch her should she fall. 'Malen?' he whispered. '*Be' sy'n bod, cariad?* Are you ill?'

He did not comprehend that she was trying to speak until she formed her lips into an 'O' and moaned again, her eyes narrowing with the effort. 'Ooooh . . .'

'It's all right,' he said. 'Try to relax, Malen. It will come.'

She shut her eyes, took a deep breath and tried again. 'Oo-ooh?'

'Who? Is that what you're saying?'

She screamed. She waved her arms, pointed at the door. Her hands fell to her sides for a moment. Then she pointed south-east, towards the barn.

'Mr Evans?'

Yes!

He sighed. 'Sit down, Malen. I'll tell you everything he said, exactly as he said it. Will that do?'

She sat. She looked at her feet and then intently at him, watching his mouth, watching with narrowed eyes for the lies he might tell her. She reminded him of the women he'd seen in Germany just after the war: hungry, bewildered, defeated, wanting still to stay alive, but not knowing how to go about it, whom to trust. He had pitied them, even knowing that many were as culpable as their menfolk for the crimes of the war. But Malen was not culpable and neither – yet – was he. He couldn't bear for her to look at him like that.

He stared into the fire, scratching Nessa's ears, telling the tale in the softest voice, the gentlest voice, easing Malen's way through the minister's letter. He couldn't remember all of it – just the essence – but he didn't look at Malen again until it was over. She wasn't watching him now. Her eyes were closed, her face so quiet she looked like someone dying.

'Then,' he said, 'Mr Evans asked me if I was in love with you. I told him no; I had brought you here for your safety only, to get you away from your stepfather. He told me that you are old enough to marry, suggested—'

She stared at him, appalled.

'No, no . . .' he murmured. 'Stay calm now, good girl. No one will hurt you. No one. But we can't go on as we are. The talk . . .'

He looked again into the fire, his voice hardening. 'Talk is all some people live for, Malen. Talk without truth, without pity. Sometimes I think it's just . . .' He blinked and swallowed, forcing himself to be generous. 'Just a cultural deficiency,' he said. 'If they could talk about Tosca, maybe, or Carmen, if they could talk about people they can't hurt . . . But no, Malen, they will talk about *us*.' He smiled stiffly. 'It's a weakness of mine,' he explained. 'I cannot bear it, Malen. It's dangerous. If anything happened to me, if you were left alone, no one would raise a hand to help you. They would say you were no better than you should be. They would make an outcast of you. So we have only two alternatives.

Marriage . . .' He glanced at her to see how she felt about it now: frightened, wary, but not – quite – terrified. '. . . or the asylum.'

Afterwards he wondered why he had said it so bluntly, without a word of comfort to ease it for her. He wondered what had happened to the egg-shaped 'sick at heart', which might have soothed her, if only for a moment, before it shattered.

She had almost reached the road when he caught her. He caught her from behind, more tenderly than he should have, and she twisted in his arms and jabbed her elbow in his eye. It knocked him silly. He thought for a moment she'd blinded him. By the time he recovered his senses (but not yet his temper), she was a few hundred yards downhill and still running. 'Go, then,' he hissed. 'See if I care.' But he still went after her. She had nowhere else to go.

It was dark, without moon or stars, and she no more than a pale glimmer on the road. Ghostly, almost gliding, like an owl. It scared him, the way she moved. It was as if she had no substance, as if she was a wraith, floating a few inches above the ground. He stopped, his heart hammering with sudden fright.

Not gone mad up there yet, then, Rhodri?

Had he? Had he slipped at last into the dark regions, where women could walk on water or dance on air? He had dreamed of such things and in his dreams known the bliss of deep enchantment. But he wasn't so sure he liked it now. It was . . . frightening.

He dragged his hand over his face and stared into the darkness for the best part of a minute before he realised what was happening. Malen wasn't gliding; she was standing still. And what he'd thought were her feet, floating on air, was the white tip of Nessa's tail, gently swaying back and forth. He could have cried, more with shame than relief. He'd forgotten Nessa. Now that he remembered her, he knew precisely what she'd done. When a dog intends to turn a sheep, she does not run behind; she runs in a wide circle and then comes at her object from in front. She'd probably run a mile, bless her, rheumatics and all. Now she had a mouthful of Malen's cardboard box clamped between her teeth, and although she was being polite about it, she wouldn't let it go.

'She wants you to come home, Malen,' he said gently. 'So do I.'

She was shuddering with the cold, but otherwise seemed quite calm again. 'Come on, *cariad*, back into the warm. You will not go to the asylum. I swear it.'

She looked up and stared at him. He could scarcely see her face, yet in a curious way saw it clearly, the sadness in her eyes, the submission. What was it to her, after all? Marriage, the asylum. Whichever way she chose, she'd be on the road to hell.

'Hold my hand,' he said. 'When we get home, I will tell you about the farmer and the fairy. Hold my hand now, good girl. There was this farmer, you see. Tall he was, and very handsome, but so poor . . . He was so poor, he could only eat on Wednesdays.'

Malen took his hand. He'd noticed from the first that she'd trusted him most – or, rather, distrusted him least – when he'd said something daft to make her smile and it was this more than anything else which had made him certain she wasn't mad. In a way, he supposed, humour *was* sanity; probably the last thing you lost before you went religious, or fascist. Or celibate.

Yet he knew he was going to do it. He'd known it all day and been fighting it off ever since, a pathetic, rear-guard action against the massed armies of conscience and compassion: the minister's guilt, Malen's sorrow.

Her life was as dark as the night, and maybe she saw it all as he'd seen it a moment ago: a world of floating spectres among which doubt of one's own reason was surely the worst. What had brought him back from that? Nessa. Her courage, her fidelity to the prime purpose of her life: to bring the stray lamb home.

Funny how a dog, with no great intellect to speak of, could pose the biggest question a man could ask of himself. What is the prime purpose of my life?

He didn't know the answer any more.

He hoped to God it wasn't sex.

CHAPTER TWENTY-THREE

Driving over the mountains was an experience very different from that of walking over them. The land seemed to unfold as they climbed. Deep valleys opened like buds and snapped shut again; strange formations of rock sprang up like mushrooms and as quickly shrank away as the land closed around them to reveal something new.

A few miles of the roadside were fenced, and on virtually every other fencepost a buzzard sat, poised for flight. As the car approached them, one by one, they tipped forward, spread their great wings, flapped once and floated away, soaring effortlessly, as though drawn through the air by invisible strings.

'Ohhh,' Gwen thumped a fist against her chest. 'They're wonderful, aren't they? *I* want to be a buzzard!'

'Think of the winter,' Owen said.

Gwen took her eyes off the road just long enough to glare at him. 'Bloody spoilsport,' she said. 'Miserable old buzzard.'

'There,' he grinned. 'You wouldn't want to be like me, would you?'

She changed into second for a precipitous bend. 'Oh, you're not so bad,' she said, her voice deepening, her chin lifting as if with pride in her own judgement. 'At least you can laugh. And if you can laugh at yourself you're halfway there, aren't you?'

'So they say. Halfway where, though?'

'Halfway up a bloody mountain, for a start. And then there's life.'

An English voice would have concluded with an ellipsis, a wistful trailing away to imply, *Think about it*. Gwen had concluded with a thudding stop, which implied something else: *But you know all that; I needn't go on.*

Yes, he knew all that. But halfway up was exactly the same as halfway down when your legs had given out, and laughing took you no higher; it just made being stuck in the middle more ridiculous, as if you'd set out without your compass and survival gear and thus barely deserved to be rescued. Bloody idiot.

At the highest place they could achieve without climbing on foot, Gwen pulled into a gravelled lay-by and turned off the engine. Neither of them spoke. As the car's voice died it was as

117

if the mountain held up a silencing hand: *Now you will listen to me.*

Even the crunch of their feet on the gravel seemed a sacrilege.

Heat pulsed out of the ground, beat from the sky. The road ahead dissolved into lambent ripples and beside it the mountain basked like a sleeping dragon, its hungers sated. Far below – and about three miles distant as the buzzard flew – lay a blue lake, with neatly hedged fields of gold and green and a tiny farmstead, its blue slate rooftops shimmering like water in the bright summer haze. It was all so tightly enclosed by the cupped hands of the mountains that there seemed no way out, no way in. A secret land, a land of peace, a Shangrila whose existence only the buzzards knew.

For the first time in years, Owen's mind slipped into a high, cruising gear in which consciousness of himself barely figured. He became a rock, a part of the landscape merely, a thing so old and deep-rooted that he and all his torments of soul were things of the moment, arriving and departing on the same breath.

They had passed the crag of Einion Ddu a few miles back and now stood between two others: one a vast, wart-like excrescence of many-layered rock, the other a near-vertical face of pinkish stone, veined with red iron. By contrast, the grassy flanks of the mountain seemed as soft as curtains, purple velvet in the shadows, green damask in the depths, a jade-tinted silk where they framed the clear window of the sky.

'What are you thinking about?' Gwen asked softly.

'Hmm? Oh, I don't know, really. Endurance . . .'

'What about it?'

'Oh . . . There are insects, you know – mayflies, that sort of thing – that live only for an hour or two. If they live three hours, they get a telegram from the Queen.'

Gwen laughed. 'Oh, yes?'

'It's hard to imagine – packing an entire life into an hour. You wonder why they bother, what it can possibly mean to them. And I was thinking . . . These mountains – if they were aware – would feel much the same about us.'

'That we aren't important, you mean?'

'Hmmm. If I could believe that . . . It's the answer to everything, isn't it?'

Gwen looked at him with sternly narrowed eyes, as if *she* knew the answer to everything and was about to share it with him. 'What you need is a nice cup of tea,' she said.

Owen knew they were approaching civilisation when the sheep-cropped grass turned to bracken and swathes of foxglove, scabious and bright yellow poppies sprang up along the roadside. They stuttered over a cattle grid between hedges of thorn wreathed with briony. There was a farm, a white-painted cottage, the deep shade of trees, a little stone bridge and the river.

'Little sod,' Gwen jumped on the brakes for a gilded bantam rooster which, with his dowdy hen and a panicky retinue of juveniles, chose that moment to run squawking across the road. 'That's Caradog,' she said.

'Who is?'

'The cockerel. Brave as a lion, he is. Every time a car comes he plays chicken with it.' She turned into an earthen track on the far side of the bridge, drove slowly across another bridge and into a cobbled yard where a white-painted sign announced, 'Teas,' and 'David Samlet, Woodcarver.'

'What do you want first? Tea or sawdust?'

'What sort of woodcarver? Souvenirs?'

'Welsh dressers.'

Owen closed his eyes on a smile. He groped for her hand and patted it. 'Thanks.'

David Samlet stood at a work bench in the corner of a barn. Small, thin, his white hair cropped close to his head, he turned, smiled shyly into Owen's face as Gwen made introductions and bent again to his work: a large oval frame with a design of vine leaves and grapes. The wood was English oak. He carved it like wax, the gouge in his hands making scarcely a sound, the wood whispering at its touch like a contented lover.

'A mirror?' Owen asked.

David Samlet blushed and nodded. With a stroke of his hand he indicated a table by the door where several volumes of colour photographs catalogued his work. Dressers, tables, chests, chairs, doors, coats of arms, lecterns, picture frames, mirrors and boxes. Hundreds of pieces, each of them finer than the last.

'What period of time does this cover?' Owen asked.

'I retired ten years ago.' Samlet's voice was a soft rustle, like dry leaves rubbing together. 'Inland Revenue. Purgatory.'

Owen flicked him a glance and found that he was smiling, his dark eyes wide and bright, as coy as a little girl's.

'I am in heaven now,' he added sweetly. 'Do I look dead?'

'No, you look – er – fine. The wings suit you.'

Samlet chuckled and got on with his work, easing a third dimension from his carefully sketched design as if for him, as for the angel he claimed to be, miracles were second nature and not to be remarked upon.

'Ten years? You must have done some work before that?'

'Ohh, bits and pieces just.'

'Are you self-taught?'

'No, indeed. I have learned everything from the wood. If I'd realised how much she had to teach me, I would have begun sooner. Ten years or twenty do not reveal the half of it.' He shrugged and sighed. 'I needed fifty.'

His Welshness rendered his use of English as precise and as lovely as poetry, every syllable pronounced as though it were a separate word – purg-a-tory, re-al-ised – but he spoke in soft, dreamy phrases, separated by long silences while he worked, bowing to the wood as one who kisses the feet of a queen. Owen had never seen anything like it; never seen so much love so humbly given. He ached to say that he felt the same, but couldn't allow himself to speak. It would be like telling a survivor of Belsen, 'I, too, have suffered.'

Only dimly noticing that Gwen had disappeared, Owen browsed through the photographs a second time. 'Were all these pieces commissioned?'

'No, indeed. My object was to furnish the tea-rooms, you see. I began with a dresser. It had been in its place only two weeks when my wife sold it to an American lady. I made another and she sold that, too. So it has continued . . .'

Owen laughed. 'Any furniture in the tea-rooms, yet?'

'I have bolted it to the floor. If they want it now, they must take the house with it, and I do not think my wife will sell that.' There was another long pause. 'But you never know. Women's minds are deep and subtle; they know so many things.'

Owen suspected a joke. He approached it with caution. Women's minds, women's feelings and women's politics had always seemed to him a minefield of paradox and complexity about which he preferred to keep his mouth shut, especially in conversation with men who seemed so much more certain.

'Do they?'

'Yes, indeed . . .' Minutes passed. 'I can think of only one thing at a time. My wife thinks of everything all at once: children and cookery, politics and poultry. I listen to her sometimes and think, Dear, dear, I have married a genius.'

'Ah, but your understanding of just the one thing?'

Samlet nodded. 'Oh, yes . . . *totally* inadequate. You have heard the Shaker maxim: "Do all your work as if you would live a thousand years and as if you would die tomorrow"? I try; but I know I will *not* live a thousand years and that tomorrow, or any other day, will come too soon.'

Owen turned away, his stomach griping with envy. Samlet's work was nothing like the Shakers' except – he guessed – in one respect: that he perceived work and worship to be indivisible parts of the same thing: the love of all things. Owen knew no such love. He knew only that he desired it, as all men did, as the Shakers had. Oh, God, could he do this? Would he dare? He hadn't a tenth of Samlet's ability, but he was young and strong. There was still time.

He swallowed. He opened his mouth to speak and shut it again. Then, in a voice he barely recognised as his own – higher than usual and louder – he said, 'Would you say you make a living? Do you sell enough to—er—?'

'Oh,' Samlet scratched his chin. 'I don't know. Mari sees to all that. Anything to do with money reminds me of Purgatory, you see. Show me a tax return and I tremble.'

He laughed. Owen didn't. He'd been feeling much the same about medicine without daring to go the whole hog and think it through. Even now, he couldn't think. When he envisioned himself going back – even to London, let alone to work – it was as if a door slammed, slammed so hard it made his heart leap with fright.

He heard Gwen's voice in the yard and another whispering, 'Ohhh, yes, *isn't* he?'

She was tall and gaunt with straight grey hair cut in an unfortunate bob which lengthened her face to horse-like proportions. Huge blue eyes, a wide mouth, pale skin with two bright spots in her cheeks which looked like patches of pink tissue paper, stuck on.

'They could be twins,' she said. 'He's taller, though, isn't he?' Suddenly she strode towards him, smiling, stretching out her hand. 'I am Mari – pleased to meet you.' Still shaking his hand, she twisted around to look at Gwen. '*Duw*, it's incredible.' She turned again: 'And you've never even *met* him?'

'Er . . .'

'Now what is she talking about?' David Samlet widened his

121

eyes and gazed at his wife in apparent wonderment. 'Of course he's met me. We've been talking an hour, woman.'

'Not *you*, you fool! Joyce *Caldwell*'s boy! Isn't he the living *image*?'

'Who?'

The women laughed. Samlet smiled into Owen's eyes. 'There,' he said, 'That proves it. She's so clever, I don't even know what she's talking about. Marvellous, isn't it?'

'Perhaps you've never met Glyn Caldwell,' Owen suggested faintly.

'Oh, yes, I've met him.' He turned away, took up his gouge and went on with his work in a manner which seemed – for him – curiously decisive. Bewildered, Owen looked at Mari, who shrugged and stretched her mouth as if to say, Whoops, that's torn it. Gwen was looking at her feet.

'What happened there?' he asked when, more than an hour later, they drove away. 'Doesn't he like Glyn?'

'No, not much.'

'Why?'

She shrugged. 'He likes his mother, I suppose.'

'Mrs Caldwell? What kind of a woman is she?'

'A rip. She can talk the hind legs off a donkey, make you laugh until you wet yourself, sing, dance . . . She plays bingo, takes herself off on coach trips, hangs her own wallpaper, grows her own vegetables. She's the same age as David: seventy-one, coming up.'

Owen did some swift mental arithmetic. According to the author-biography on his book's jacket, Glyn was thirty-eight. 'She was thirty-three when she had Glyn, then? Quite old for those days. I don't suppose . . .?'

He couldn't say it. He looked, with pretended bewilderment, at a landscape he was beginning to recognise quite well. 'Where the hell are we? Have you taken another road?'

'I don't suppose what?'

'What?'

Gwen laughed shortly. 'Doing a Gethin, again?'

He turned his face to the road, letting the wind cool his skin, brace his nerve.

She stopped the car. 'It was you who chose to confide in me, remember. I didn't torture you for it. But now you've begun, I see no point in not finishing. You want to ask if he's your brother, don't you?'

He felt sick. 'Is—? Was he—adopted?'

'No.' She played with her keys, swinging them back and forth in the ignition. 'I was beginning to think he might be; that's why I wanted to see Mari – she's known Joyce Caldwell for years, since Glyn was a toddler. He was a right little devil, Mari says, and his mam used to say the only thing she'd ever managed to force him to do was come into the world. She had a hard labour with him, apparently. They were both nearly dead by the end of it.'

'Ah . . . I see.'

Disappointment settled in his stomach. His heart-rate slowed. After a while he realised that he felt perfectly all right. Better than before. The answers, it seemed, didn't have to be the ones he wanted, just as long as they were answers, just as long as they resolved a doubt. He smiled and shrugged. 'Ah, well, at least I can read the book now.'

CHAPTER TWENTY-FOUR

In ancient tales of chivalry, when men were princes and women were wallpaper, the rules were clear and true. If you wanted a wife you rode forth and took one, whether she fancied being taken or no. It made little difference, for she loved you in the instant she saw you (or so the bards had it) and slept with you the same night.

There was no word of how she fought and screamed, punched you in the eye, ran off down the mountain barefoot and came back frozen to the bone. There was nothing about her nose going red or her lips going blue, nothing about her howls of pain as the circulation came back to her finger ends. Women had suffered in silence in those days and quite right, too. The 'fair damosel' wasn't half so romantic with her nose in a mug of Oxo.

'Better now?' Rhodri asked grimly.

Malen flicked a glance to his face and looked away again, blushing – or so he hoped – for the black eye she'd given him.

'Now look,' he said. 'Before we go any further, I think you should understand that we're both on the same side, Malen. Neither of us wants you in the asylum and neither of us wants you to be hurt. That's right, isn't it? No arguments so far?'

Malen hitched a grey army blanket over her shoulders and stared sullenly into the fire.

Irritated beyond patience, Rhodri gave Nessa a prod with his foot. 'Tell her, Ness, will you? I can't do this on my own. She's got to cooperate. She's got to help me.'

Nessa opened one eye and closed it again. *Tell her yourself,* she said. *I'm a dog, not a bloody telephone.*

Snow tapped the window and rattled the door-latch. A wolf-wind in the chimney howled for admittance. Rhodri put his feet on the fender to keep them from the draught. This was the coldest night they'd had yet, and there were three months of worse to come. Then, if his luck held, another month of worse still, just in time for lambing.

'It was a beautiful day in May,' he said suddenly. 'The sky was a crown of sapphire, the sun a radiant diadem set at its heart. There was gold-dust in the grass, emeralds in the trees and lustrous clusters of pearls dripping from every hedgerow.'

Malen looked at him, amazed.

'The farmer and the fairy,' Rhodri said. 'Remember? So poor he ate only on Wednesdays? Half-day-closing, see, Malen. The bread's half-price, come dinnertime.'

She pressed her fingers to her mouth and tipped her head to one side. She was pleased. Either that, or she was planning to take him to the mental.

'So although he was poor and hungry, although he knew that the jewels of the day were fairy treasure and not his for the taking, the farmer felt very rich. He was not entirely happy, however. He was lonely and felt that he must be lonely all his life. He could scarcely feed himself, let alone a wife and children; and what woman would have him when he had so little to offer? Oh, he was tall and fair of face, he was kind and softly spoken; but such things are not enough for most women. They like eating, too.'

A light came into Malen's eyes, so near to laughter as made little difference. But she was still hiding her mouth and Rhodri turned in his chair, averting his gaze from her so that, should she smile, he might catch her unawares.

'Still,' he said, 'it was a lovely day and no time to be sorrowful. It was Wednesday. The farmer bought his bread (the cheapest stuff was left over from Tuesday, so it was rather hard) and, as he ate, he wandered through the fields at his leisure, admiring the pretty flowers.

'Dear, dear, that loaf was hard. He wanted to eat it quick – he hadn't eaten for a week, see – but the crust was too tough; he couldn't get his teeth into it. He tore off little bits and swallowed them whole until, eventually, he swallowed a piece too big which stuck in his throat, half-way down. He hadn't thought to bring any water with him and for a nasty moment he thought he would choke to death. But then, through the trees, he saw a large, glittering lake beside a pebbled shore and there he ran, lest he die before he could drink.

'The water was cool and sweet. It soothed his throat like balm and when he felt better he sat back on his heels and gazed about him, his eyes wide with wonderment. It was lovely, that lake, sparkling in the sun like a polished silver platter. The farmer laughed out loud. "Oh, I am rich," he said. "For on a day like today the whole world is mine!"

'But he was still hungry, and although he still had some bread left, he was afraid to eat it in case he choked again. He put the loaf

125

in the water, soaked it until it was soft and swallowed it down at a gulp.

'In the instant that he swallowed it, he heard a woman singing. Her voice was silvery and sweet, but so sad it brought tears to the farmer's eyes and he called out in pity, "Where are you?"

> *"I ache for the sound of a loving voice,"* she sang.
> *"And for gentle arms around me,*
> *But the lake is deep*
> *And the lake is dark*
> *And no love has ever found me."*

The farmer looked behind him and to left and right along the shore, but the sad lady wasn't there. She was out on the lake, standing on the water as if it were solid ground. Her hair was red as blood, her skin as white as milk and she wore a gown of silver thread, a veil of finest silk.

'"Ohh," the farmer whispered, "Oh, there's beautiful."

'But he knew she was a fairy: one of the *Gwragedd Annwn* who, like the sapphires in the sky and the gold among the grass, was not his to take, but only love in his heart.

'He called out to her across the water: "I love you, lady!" and the lady reached out her arms to him as if she would love him too.

'"Oh, come to me, come to me!" he cried. "Marry me, lady, for I shall love you till I die!"

> *"No, mortal man,"* the lady sang, *"I cannot wed,*
> *Til you give me to eat of mortal bread."*

The farmer was horrified. Bread! She wanted bread, and he'd eaten it, every crumb! He scrabbled around among the pebbles to see if he'd dropped a piece he could offer her, but he'd been too hungry to miss any and he felt as bad about that as if he'd eaten a roasted ox. He called himself a glutton, and when he looked again at the lady he knew that she agreed with him.

'"No," he wailed. "No, don't look at me like that! I'll bring more bread next Wednesday! I'll give you all of it, I swear!"

'He waited in agony all that week, longing for Wednesday that he might see the lady again. He suffered even greater agonies on his walk to the lake, for he was ravenous and scarcely trusted himself not to eat the loaf on the way. Still, he managed it – some men will suffer anything for love and the farmer was one of them – but by the time he reached the lake, he could bear it no longer. He had to eat something. If he didn't, he'd die. But he couldn't eat the lady's bread, so he took up one of the pebbles from the shore and chewed on that, instead.

'The lady came to him soon after, closer to the shore this time, holding her hand out for the bread. Love her as he did, it still pained him to give her the bread he was starving for, and he gazed at it longingly one last time before he bowed and handed it to her. But she frowned as she took it to her mouth and instead of eating she said, "Oh dear, it's mouldy," and threw it, like a stone, into the middle of the lake.

> "Oh, mortal man," the lady sang, "I cannot wed,
> Til you give me to eat of wholesome bread."

The poor, hungry farmer was heartbroken. Mouldy! He hadn't thought of that! He was hungry enough not to care about a bit of mould, but the noble *Gwragedd Annwn* are accustomed to better things. He called himself a knave, an insensitive fool, and when he looked again at the lady, he knew that she agreed with him.

'"No!" he wailed. "Don't look at me like that! I'll bring you fresh bread next Wednesday! I promise!"

'The trouble was, as the trouble had always been, that he was too poor to buy fresh bread. And the trouble was, as it had never been before, that he would starve to death before another week was out. But it was worth it. There is no honour greater, after all, than to die for the love of a lady.

'As he walked home, still chewing the pebble he'd found on the shore, he noticed that it tasted bitter and spat it out. But as it fell into the road it sparkled in the sun, and he knelt and took it up again, laughing with delight. It wasn't a pebble after all! It was gold. It was solid gold!

'So the farmer was rich. He could buy anything he wanted. A new house, a new cow, some chickens. He could buy fine clothes and a horse to ride . . . But he didn't want any of those things. All he wanted was a loaf of fresh, wholesome bread for his lady.

'"Now will you marry me?" he asked when she'd eaten it, and the lady smiled and accepted him.

'"But," she said, "If you ever touch me without my consent, I will return to the dark regions forever and you will never see me again."

'The farmer was appalled. "What?" he said. "Not touch you? Oh, I don't know about that, *cariad*. That will be very difficult, won't it?"

'"No," she said. "Not very. You gave me your bread when you were starving. What is more difficult than that?"

'So they were married and lived in great happiness for many years. Even though it *was* very difficult, the farmer never touched his fairy bride without her consent and she was gentle, kind and merry and very loving, in her way. She helped him on the farm, kept the house like a shining pin . . . And she had a wonderful touch with pastry. Apple tart, bacon turnover, cheese and onion pie . . . The farmer almost forgot what it was like to eat only on Wednesdays.

'Then, one cold winter's day, the lady went out visiting and did not return at the usual time. Darkness fell. Suppertime came and went. The farmer was worried sick. What could have happened to her? Had she had an accident on the way home? He kept walking to the gate to watch the road, tearing his hair out with worry.

'At last he saw her, hurrying home through the moonlight. The moon had turned the road to silver, and he saw her as he'd seen her the very first time. Her hair was red as blood, her skin as white as milk, and she wore a gown of silver thread and a veil of finest silk.

'"Oh!" he cried. "I love you, lady!" and he threw open the gate and ran to meet her, folding her in his arms as if he would never let her go.

'But when at last he did let her go, he saw that she was weeping and knew what he had done.

'"No!" he cried. "No, no, I didn't mean it!" But even as he looked, a soft white mist blew across his sight and, when it had passed, his fairy bride had gone.

'Moaning and stumbling in his sorrow, the farmer returned to the beautiful house he had built with his gold, but that, too, had gone, as had his cows and his chickens and horses. All that was left was the hovel he'd lived in before, with its empty grate and its empty larder and a heap of cold straw for a bed.

'He walked every day to the lake after that, but he never saw the lady again. He never heard her singing. And he lived in misery for the rest of his life, thinking himself lucky if he ate on Wednesdays.'

His heart thudding, Rhodri stared into the fire. He hadn't meant the story to go like that. It was a traditional Welsh tale: *The Bride of Llyn y Fan Fach*. He'd added the half-day-closing only to make Malen smile, meaning to lose it on the way, yet out of that alteration had sprung a dozen others, over which – it seemed now – he'd had no control.

The most ancient tales were generally short on morals and if *The Bride*, in its original version, had had one, it was only that a man should keep his marriage vows. *His* story had said more than that, more than he'd wanted it to say, more than he'd meant.

A man could take celibacy upon himself and, as long as he did his best to keep faith with it, could fail and be no less for failing. But if he took vows: pledged himself openly to a course he couldn't hold, he was diminished. He wouldn't do that to himself. He wouldn't do it to Malen.

She was gazing at him as if hypnotised, her grey eyes wide and dreamy-soft, her thoughts beyond his guessing.

He laughed shortly. 'Don't get carried away, now, Malen. It's only a story.'

She blinked and turned away, her mouth tightening.

'And the farmer was a fool,' he said softly. 'Not because he touched her, but because he promised not to. A man should not make promises he cannot keep. He was a young man, Malen, with a young man's needs . . . As I am. Do you understand that?'

She didn't move. She stared into the fire, taking comfort from that, its rose-red caves and golden forests, its amethyst flames.

'So,' he said. 'I will make you no promises, Malen. All I can say is that if you marry me I will do my best for you. I will do my very best for you.' He closed his eyes. 'And that's the best any man can do.'

With his eyes closed he began to pray: 'Let her say yes, let her say no,' and hated himself for meaning both in equal measure.

Malen screamed: the thin wail of a buzzard calling bleakly to its mate. *Open your eyes! Look at me!*

'All right,' he said. 'I'm still here.'

She bit her lip. She laid her hands in her lap, looked at them for a moment and stretched out her left hand, palm down, like a child saying, 'Look, I cut my finger.'

Her hands, although small, were long and tapering, with the opaque, fine-grained skin typical of redheads. Apart from that and a trace of coal-dust under her fingernails, there was nothing to be seen, save that she was trembling.

'Come on, *cariad*, tell me.'

She pointed to her third finger and drew a line where the ring would be. There was no query in her eyes. No fear. Just a bleak determination that reckoned fear and futility the same.

'You *will* marry me?'

Still biting her lip, she jerked her head around to look at the wall, glaring at it as if she saw in the bumps and whorls of Rhodri's inexpert plaster-work the face of John Roberts, who had brought her to this. She nodded.

Rhodri looked up at the ceiling to hide a sudden rush of tears. He didn't know what to say.

He wished she'd said no.

CHAPTER TWENTY-FIVE

There were swifts nesting under the eaves of the cottage, hunting low, as swift as their name, flittering like bats in the last of the twilight. Owen sighed, recognising a moment of rare contentment, holding it in softly folded hands, like a prayer. He'd walked a few hundred feet up the mountain, wanting to breathe. He'd breathed, watched, let himself float and sink like a homecoming crow, black against the sky. Things were falling into place. He could see them falling, could identify them as they fell; but – like Gwen's fairy pennies – they wouldn't be caught.

At its zenith the sky was the intense blue of Bristol glass, at its edges palest jade, against which the cottage chimneys and the spiky tops of the trees were painted in Indian ink. It seemed as permanent as a drawing; as old as a medieval scroll. Hard to think that it had only just happened, this warm, summer dusk; even stranger to think that although it was unique and would exist like this for only minutes (*exactly* like this for scarcely a second) it had happened before and would happen again, just like this, for as long as the world lasted.

He had read only a few chapters of *Song of the Stars* and been surprised to find Rhodri's mountain so different from this one – so cold – and Rhodri very different from himself – so warm. Save for his height (the same as Owen's) and his forget-me-not eyes (Owen's were forgettable), Caldwell hadn't described Rhodri in any detail, yet the picture in Owen's mind was already fixed. His hair was long, his clothes patched and darned, his skin burned gypsy-brown by the wind. He was vital and alive. He talked all the time and his voice was clear and strong, rattling on in two languages, singing, laughing, raging, cursing. Working it out.

It was almost as if the book was about Owen, or at least following a parallel track: one he might have taken if only he'd had the courage, the sense. A parallel track . . .

A second-sight procession, such as glides
Over still mountains, or appears in dreams.

Strange that Rhodri had quoted those particular lines. They

seemed to sum Owen up. His entire life had been a second-sight procession, a dream he'd observed powerlessly, as if from the sidelines of sleep, wishing he could wake up and find everything different.

Shrinks aside, no one took much notice of dreams any more. Something to do with modern life, he supposed; modern language, a declining ability to recognise symbols. The ancients had been drawing symbols on cave walls long before speech could have progressed beyond a few painfully articulated grunts, and it seemed reasonable to suppose that the next stage after that had been poetry: symbols expressed in a few words (because a few was all they'd had) rather than prose. Now it was all prose: long, wordy explanations of things that were best understood through intuition and imagination, things men no longer trusted, no longer believed in, no longer knew. God and ghosts, dreams and portents.

Owen stood up suddenly. He turned his back against the deepening dusk and spoke to the night, to the black bulk of the mountain. 'So,' he said. 'Tell me, if you're so clever—?'

He turned away again, embarrassed, afraid someone might hear him. One didn't – except in dreams – converse with mountains. The sky was easier, gentler, more forgiving. If it spoke at all it was only to say, 'I don't know,' which, in a way, was the answer he really wanted. If you don't know, it doesn't matter; you can't be blamed; you're a child, absolved by your ignorance of the sins you commit day by day.

Not that he'd committed any worth mentioning. A spot of youthful screwing, drinking. A few amphetamines to serve the long nights of book-bashing. That aside, he'd been decent, loyal and law-abiding. He'd been patient; he'd kept his temper . . .

Only because you were shit-scared of losing it, the mountain said.

Shit-scared of losing everything. His hold had always seemed so tenuous, he'd had so little to call his own. No roots, no relatives, no identity except as a camouflage can be called an identity. He could recall various occasions when he'd put on a new camouflage – 'happy family man' had been one of them – consciously trying to merge with his background, wanting more than anything else to belong, to seem right, to dig himself in so deep they'd need a bloody bulldozer to shift him.

It was quite dark now. He could still see the cottage chimneys and the topmost spires of the forest, but now they were outlined

132

against the lights of the town, the ubiquitous muddy orange that dimmed the stars. It wasn't a thing one noticed in the heart of London – except, perhaps, to be glad it wasn't pitch-dark – but out here it seemed all wrong, tragic, almost nightmarish, as if beyond the furthest horizon a great fire was raging.

Gwen was down there somewhere, among the glowing embers, perming her mother's hair. He'd asked what was wrong with hairdressers and she'd laughed and looked at him sideways, her dark eyes driving little daggers into the quivering membrane of his soul. He hadn't known what she was saying to him. Mind your own business? No, I won't sleep with you again? Or . . . Don't be so pathetic.

'You're pathetic,' he said aloud.

And it isn't necessary, you see, Owen. The answers are here, there, everywhere, standing before your eyes even as I stand at your back. You know. But you don't want to know, because you're scared, yellow, a coward to the bone. You always were.

'I can't help it!'

Ha, ha. Where've I heard that before?

'Oh, fuck off,' Owen said.

He was almost asleep when the monkeys came. It began with just one – a gnarled, near-black face very close to his own, with solemn brown eyes which gazed at him in silence. Then – it was as if a switch had been pressed – the face suddenly leapt backwards and became two identical faces. Then there were four faces, eight, sixteen. As they multiplied (each time so suddenly it made him gasp with shock) they became smaller and further away, yet the intensity of their gaze never lessened and he lay in its thrall, rigid with horror. He didn't know how it would end. Every time it happened, he tried to recall how it had ended last time and never could. His terror was not of them, but of what they knew and wouldn't tell him. They were examining his mind, turning it over like dank stones, watching dispassionately as the vermin they uncovered scuttled away to hide again.

He couldn't bear it. He had never been able to bear it, yet this time – for reasons beyond his grasp – he felt not only that he *could* not, but that he *would* not bear it. His first thought was to switch on the light, but he knew – even if he dared reach out his hand among the dark throng of watchers – that this wasn't the answer. He had to face them out. He had to *know* what they were.

What were they? Not monkeys, certainly. They were a symbol, created by his mind to represent something else, something vital, something in *him*. Except in films, he'd never seen monkeys or any of their kin in a wild state. He'd seen them caged, scratching their armpits, hanging languidly from dead tree boughs or simply sitting, as these monkeys sat, gazing solemnly into remote distances, wishing they were free.

We were not made for this.

Owen closed his eyes. When he opened them again the monkeys had gone. He knew he'd never see them again. He knew what they were, now: the last, wizened survivors of a famished land who, too hungry to speak, could only look at him and hope that he might feed them.

He lifted his head from the pillow and let it fall again, amazed to find it so simple and himself therefore so incredibly stupid. He'd known it all along. In dozens of ways he'd known it, recognised it, even described it to himself as a kind of starvation. In fact, he'd come so close to understanding it, it now seemed tantamount to idiocy that he hadn't made the connections. Yet it was obvious now. They weren't monkeys, after all. They were children.

He'd met a nutritionist a year or so back who'd done a stint in Ethiopia during the worst of the famine: thousands upon thousands of diseased and starving children patiently waiting to be fed. The worst, most eerie thing about it, apparently, had been the silence. Hungry children cry; starving children don't. They can't; it demands more energy than they possess. So they sit very still . . . And watch . . . And wait . . .

Owen switched on the light.

Like most people, he supposed, he'd seen those countless little faces on the news bulletins, reflected guiltily on the three properly balanced meals he'd eaten that day and perhaps, by virtue of his guilt, felt that those kids were judging him. So he'd written a cheque and put it from his mind. Put it from his *conscious* mind as something he'd dealt with and could no longer afford to contemplate.

Meanwhile, somewhere deeper and darker, the symbol-makers had been at work, muttering, 'Starving children, silent children, disinherited children . . . When he's ready, we'll play that back to him. He's a bright enough chap. He'll understand. Eventually.'

He'd known from a very early age that his mother had rued the

134

day she'd fulfilled her desire to have a child. It wasn't easy to adopt a disturbed three-year-old who went rigid when you touched him, wet the bed until he was six and could exist the best part of a week without eating. It would break any mother's heart, but when the kid isn't yours to begin with . . .

He remembered the exact moment when he'd looked at her and known she'd loathed him. A moment, of course, is a finite thing and for all he knew she'd been awash with tenderness a moment later. He couldn't remember; it wasn't important. When a child has seen loathing in his mother's eyes, everything else, however sincere, is like dew on a rose leaf, running off before you can catch it. Only the moment of truth sticks. It had stuck in his mind all his life, dictated his every action, informed his every decision, corroded his faith in himself until all that was left of his soul was a tiny, shrivelled, gnat-like thing, unable to tell him what was wrong because the starving can't speak.

How old had he been? Five, coming up six? Too young, anyway, to be making cold-blooded decisions about his own survival. Yet he had made it. Adapt or die. Be what she wants you to be.

It had been the last thing he'd done. He'd been someone else since then, someone he didn't know, didn't like, someone he held in contempt for abandoning . . .

His eyes widened even as his mind opened to the one idea that could heal him. His parents hadn't abandoned him. *He* had.

CHAPTER TWENTY-SIX

Rhodri and Malen were married in January, two days after her seventeenth birthday. John Evans made all the arrangements, which, to Rhodri's dismay, included the hire of a motor car to take them to and from the chapel. Afterwards, nervously fingering his wallet (he'd already forked out for the wedding ring, the marriage lines and a pair of nylons for Malen), Rhodri asked bravely, 'How much do I owe you for the car, Mr Evans?'

'It's not true what they say about you, then?' the minister asked coyly.

'As true as anything else they say,' Rhodri said. 'One half lies and the other half fiction. How much do I owe you?'

'No, no. Put your money away. The car is paid for – and not out of my pocket. I didn't tell you before, because . . . Well, it seemed wiser not to until all was fair and square. John Roberts left a bit of money, to see Malen all right.' He put a small white envelope into Rhodri's hand. 'Use it for her, Rhodri, and God bless you both.' He shook Rhodri's hand and backed off down the mountain, calling, 'See you in chapel one day, isn't it?'

Rhodri smiled and waved, thinking of the scrap of white paper in his hand and the money it contained. A five pound note? A ten pound note? Not much to pay for a young girl's ruin. Yet Rhodri itched to see exactly how much and, while he watched Mr Evans to the first bend in the road, found himself working out the compound interest on ten pounds for a year.

Use it for her, Rhodri. He already had, at least three times over. Three months, bed and board? Mr Roberts owed him that much.

Rhodri opened the envelope. It was not a banknote; it was a cheque. And it was not made out for ten pounds, but for five hundred and seventy. There it was, written in full: 'Five hundred and seventy pounds . . . *only.*'

He pressed a hand to his heart to make sure it was still beating, that the shock of getting married hadn't killed him and sent him, all unsuspecting, to heaven. Five hundred and seventy pounds!

Use it for her, Rhodri.

But Malen knew nothing about it, and what would she do with it if she did? Only spend it. Women were like that. Money burned holes in their pockets. It made them covetous and dissatisfied, greedy to spend more. And then, when it was gone . . .

He walked back to the cottage in a daze. Malen was clearing up the remains of their poor little wedding breakfast – a slab of Co-op fruit-cake (half-price, left over from Christmas) and a bottle of sweet sherry. He saw her as if in a dream, her face and hands lit by slanting sunbeams, the outline of her hair ringed with flame. She was trying to say something, but he couldn't concentrate, could barely care. Her frown, her fluttering hands and tortured murmurs only served to irritate him, distracting him from something of greater importance: five hundred and seventy pounds.

'Wait,' he said. 'I'll just go and change.'

She slapped her palm on the table. *No! Listen to me*!

She tried again to tell him and he narrowed his eyes and watched her with pretended concentration, half-fearing she knew about the money and was trying to ask about that. She kept jabbing her breast-bone with her fingers, *It's mine*, making gathering motions with her hands: *Give it to me!*

But she could be saying something else. She could be saying anything. And it wasn't *his* fault he couldn't understand her. *He* hadn't made her dumb.

'No,' he said when she'd finished. 'I don't understand. I don't *understand*, Malen. *Wait*, will you?'

He fled to his bedroom and leaned for a while against the door with his eyes shut. He took the cheque out again to make sure he hadn't imagined it. The blood that had rushed to his head when he'd first opened the envelope was now draining out through his boots. He felt weak and sick. Dear God, he'd almost doubled his money, and the interest on twelve hundred pounds would grow so fast, he'd be rich before he knew it. A farm in the valley, a decent house, a wife and children . . .

But he'd just this morning married Malen! And where were the children to come from? The bloody fairies?

'Oh, come on,' he whispered. 'You wouldn't have the money if you hadn't married her. Pull yourself together, will you?'

But he couldn't find the ends of himself. He couldn't find the reality. Malen had been one kind of fantasy, the farm in the valley quite another. He'd had a different wife there: a tall, solid, laughing woman who could put her back into things (his bed included), and work with him and for him towards . . . What?

He relaxed suddenly. He fell upon his bed like a stone into

water and his thoughts roamed idly through a green river valley, where the only sounds were of birdsong, running water and the soft breath of cows in the grass. But he had dreamed once of a farm in the mountains, of solitude and self-knowledge, of poetry, wisdom and integrity. What had become of it? Where had it gone?

He'd been married in his demob suit. A woman at the chapel door had whispered, 'Oh, there's smart,' and another had hissed, 'But wouldn't you think he'd have his hair cut? Who d's he think he is? Bloody Samson?'

She'd made no mention of Delilah, although now he came to think of it, the devil himself couldn't have conjured such a thought. Malen, reunited with her clothes from the manse, had worn a blue serge costume with a tam to match. Red hair notwithstanding, she'd looked about as sinful as a Girl Guide. He could wish – now that he was rich – that he'd bought her a bride's frock and veil. She'd deserved at least the outward symbols of virginity, poor child.

Her hair was red as blood, her skin as white as milk . . .

He jumped off the bed, stripped off his suit and climbed into his everyday corduroys. The cheque he put with his bank book in a tin chest under the bed. He'd tell her about it. He *would* tell her about it. He'd tell her about it later.

But he walked through the kitchen without meeting her eyes. 'I'll see to the sheep,' he said.

CHAPTER TWENTY-SEVEN

Gwen was sunbathing, face down, on the lawn, her chin propped on the heel of her hand, her lycra-clad bum arching up from her spine and tucking sweetly into muscular brown thighs that glistened with sun oil. She had a beautiful behind. Wide in proportion to the rest of her body, but wonderfully firm and neat. Owen liked the bikini, too. He liked it enough to want to take it off.

He coughed and snapped his book shut, trying to distract himself.

'You all right?' Gwen spoke through her teeth and a stem of grass, turning a page, not caring.

'Fine. What are you reading?'

'Giraldus Cambrensis. Twelfth century cleric. He did a journey through Wales in 1188 and saw beavers on the River Teifi, the last ones before they were hunted out of existence. I suppose it was like us seeing otters now: they've become wonderful just because humanity's so bloody horrible.' She sat up and reached for her sunblock, leaning forward to show the rounded swell of her breasts. Owen caught his breath, half rejoicing, half despairing at his sexual reawakening. He hadn't felt this rampant, this meltingly sentimental, since his student days.

'Do you happen to know what the seven deadly sins are?' she asked.

'Funny you should ask. I've just been thinking about three of them: lust, lust and lust. Oh, and lust. How many's that?'

Gwen somehow missed the hint. 'I used to think greed was the worst,' she said, 'But it's not, is it? It's only a symptom, really, of the human need to dominate.'

'Lust's the same,' he said.

She laughed. 'Shut up, will you? I'm trying to tell you something.'

'So am I.'

'No, hang on. Greed, Pride, Envy . . . what else?'

'Lust?'

'*Wrath!*' She counted them up on her fingers. 'Oh, well, never mind. What I'm trying to say is, they're all the same and what they add up to is, "Me, me, me." It's our most primitive urge, isn't it? To be better – in inverted commas – than anyone else.'

'Not better, necessarily. Just stronger. The most primitive urge is to survive, and that usually means being dominant.'

'But you're not, are you?'

He slid off his chair and knelt with her on the lawn, cupping her face in his hands. 'I've never wanted to survive – until now.'

'Ah . . .' Her face, under its tan, turned a dusky pink and she turned to brush her lips against his palm. 'What's changed, then?'

'Everything. Almost everything. I still panic when I think of the children. I'm afraid they'll forget me, or . . . think I've rejected them. I couldn't bear that, Gwen. It's the last thing I'd ever do and I can't rely on Alison to tell them otherwise because, although I didn't know it, I *did* reject her. I told you more about myself in a few hours than I'd told her in eight years of marriage.'

'Why, though? Why did you tell me?'

'I don't know. Perhaps it was because you didn't seem to care, because I thought it wouldn't affect you, because I hardly knew you and didn't really expect to see you again.' He flopped down on one elbow, tracing a finger through the grass. 'I suppose I just thought you couldn't use it against me.' He laughed shortly. 'Also . . . It was because you're Welsh and proud of it. I've always been ashamed of it.'

'Why?'

'Oh, that's complicated. I've always suspected, I suppose, that there was something wrong with my parents, that they were immoral, perhaps even criminal. That's why I never wanted to know, never wanted to ask about them. My father – my adoptive father, that is – asked me when I left school if I wanted to make the relevant enquiries. It was as if he'd . . . Oh, I don't know. It seemed gross, indecent, a violation. I walked out. He never mentioned it again.'

'Do you still feel like that?'

Owen shook his head and found himself stroking the cover of Glyn Caldwell's book. 'I want to find them,' he said. 'I want to know. Is there a—?'

'What?'

He laughed and rolled over on his back, narrowing his eyes against the sun. 'This book – Glyn's book. You know when you—? You've never been to Russia, say, but when you read Chekhov you almost think you have. That feeling . . .'

He clenched his fist to suppress a growing surge of excitement. 'It's so *strong*, Gwen. I know I've been there. Rhodri's cottage, even the view from the windows . . . I've *been* there. I've been reading as slowly as I can, searching for specific descriptions. There aren't any, yet I know every detail of it. I know where everything is and what it looks like.'

He leafed through the book to find his place. 'Here – where they've just got married and Malen's clearing away the cake – "her face and hands lit by slanting sunbeams." I remember that, Gwen, only it was bread, not cake. And there's a little mirror in a green painted frame hanging on the wall over the sink. It's Rhodri's shaving mirror. But it's never been mentioned. How can I see that? How can I know?'

'You're remembering something else, I expect. Some other cottage.'

He relaxed. 'I know. I know it's wishful thinking. But I can't help wondering if Glyn . . . Was he really an only child? Could she have had another – me, for instance – and for some reason—?'

Gwen hugged her knees and rested her chin on them. 'I've been thinking along the same lines,' she said. 'I don't think Joyce would have abandoned a child, but she might have a sister. Or a sister-in-law. Cousins can be alike, can't they? All it needs is for the genes . . . Well, you know all that.' She took off her sunglasses. 'Let's go and see her, shall we?'

The air left Owen's lungs as if he'd been punched. He tried to laugh, but only managed to gasp, 'See her? No, I couldn't.'

''Course you could.' She rocked up on the balls of her feet in one easy, athletic movement which propelled her neatly towards the cottage and her clothes.

'I'd much rather go to bed with you.'

''Course you would.' She smirked at him over her shoulder.

'Gwen!'

'Come *on*, will you? I haven't got all day.'

'Why?' He raced after her. 'What else are you doing?'

She'd gained the bathroom before he reached the foot of the stairs. She stood with the door poised to slam, smiling down on him with lecherously narrowed eyes. 'Depends,' she said. 'What else are you doing?'

'I won't go,' he said. 'I won't *go*, Gwen.'

'All right; I'll go home, then.' She was still smiling. 'See you around, isn't it?'

The door closed. Owen sat on the stairs, torn between laughter and rage. No sympathy? She'd lied about that. She had more sympathy than he knew what to do with: a profound under-standing of his needs which bewildered him, demoralised him, made him feel weak and helpless, like a child. He wasn't at all sure he liked it. Having someone else care for him so purpose-fully, so positively, was a bit like being tickled: as delightful as it was outrageous, as lovely as it was terrible. He wanted her to go on doing it. He wanted her to stop.

He knew he'd safely walked the line between madness and sanity, but now he was walking another line and had not yet identified what lay on either side. He saw it in his imagination as two deep pools of water: one of them quiet almost to the point of stagnation, the other an icy, tumbling whirlpool. He dreaded each of them in equal measure, yet seemed to be inclining towards the whirlpool. It was the sort of thing any normal man would *want* to explore. Done up in crash-helmet, orange waterproofs and a wide, manly grin, he'd hurl himself into the spray just for the hell of it, his uncertainty of coming through alive the very goad that drove him.

Gwen was right. Domination was the name of the game; but what did a man dominate who threw himself into a whirlpool?

Not the whirlpool.

Mrs Caldwell lived in a part of the town Owen had never seen. It was part way up another mountain, on a leafy plateau which had the feel of a public park, with massive clumps of rhodo-dendrons growing from a rocky cliff-face behind the houses.

'This is a bit grand,' Owen said. 'I think I was expecting Rhodri's cottage.'

Gwen laughed. 'Mr Caldwell was a bank manager, not a hill farmer.'

'When did he die?'

'Oh, donkey's years ago. I don't really remember him. Glyn would have been about sixteen, seventeen.'

She parked the car outside a pretty Regency house, painted pink. It had a long front garden with a central path on each side of which stood a healthy hedge of Queen Elizabeth roses, the blooms almost exactly matching the pink of the house. Owen was impressed.

'Does she have a gardener?'

'Who?'

He clicked his tongue. 'The Duchess of Bedford.'

142

'What? *Oh!* No, this is my house. My mother's, I mean. Joyce lives over the road, there. It's just occurred to me – with you looking so much like Glyn, she might be a bit shocked if you just turn up on the . . . Are you listening to me?'

The roses were underplanted with catmint: great swathes of silvery blue creating a misty perspective which ended at the front door. It was so pretty, so perfect . . . And Gwen lived here. He hadn't tried to imagine where she might live, but had, vaguely, pictured something pebbledashed and suburban, built in the 1930s perhaps, with a stained-glass fanlight over the door and three empty milk bottles on the step. He couldn't quite place her here. It didn't seem to fit.

She jumped out of the car. 'Hang on,' she said. 'I'll just warn Joyce she's about to see a ghost.'

She disappeared behind a tall laurel hedge on the far side of the road and almost immediately Owen heard a high-pitched shriek of welcome, a gabble of Welsh which he tried to understand (and couldn't) and then silence. He supposed they'd gone into the house and was shocked rigid when Gwen reappeared at the gate a moment later to call him in.

He couldn't move. The whirlpool seethed at his feet, making him dizzy. It thundered in his ears, making him deaf to everything but the promptings of his own terror: Run, run! Jump the other way!

Yet the other way was stagnation, a return to a life he didn't want any more. Had never wanted.

Gwen stood beside him on the pavement. 'Come on, brave boy,' she said. 'Be a soldier for me, will you?'

He laughed feebly. 'You've got me taped, haven't you?'

'Come on.'

When he'd imagined what Joyce Caldwell would look like, he'd pictured a typical septuaganarian: small, stooped, grey and – taking Gwen's description of her into account – determinedly jolly. Instead she was a tall, buxom woman with thick brown hair (dyed, he supposed) which made her look about fifty and rather coarse. But she was as shy as a bird newly caged, fluttering and twittering, bumping helplessly into the bars.

'Oh-oh-oh, well, now, you do look like John, don't you? Pleased to meet you, Mr um-er. Sit down, now. The kettle's boiling. I'll just make a cup of . . .' She bustled away, gasping, 'You'll have scones now, will you? I'll just . . .'

Feeling dazed and sheepish, Owen groped for a chair and sat

down, looking around for something to hold his attention. They were in an ancient conservatory reeking of geraniums, cats' meat and sunbaked newsprint. The air was as warm as Horlicks and as difficult to inhale. Sweat broke on his forehead, tickled his ribs and slithered down his spine.

'*John?*' he hissed.

'Sssh, not now. Too complicated.'

He mopped his brow. 'My God, it's hot.'

'That's your nerves,' Gwen whispered. 'Calm down, will you? I think she's a bit upset.'

'Perhaps we should go.'

'We can't now, can we? She's warming the scones.'

'So how's your mam, Gwen?' Mrs Caldwell dashed in again, bearing a laden tea-tray which she set on the table with a crash. 'You pour, *cariad*. You know how you like it. I'll just . . .'

She went out and in, fetching jam, then butter and at last a plate of scones. 'There, now. Is that all? Help yourself to a scone, Mr um-er. The jam's raspberry, just made, so if you don't like pips . . . Phew, isn't it hot? Like a furnace. I know we shouldn't complain, but . . . On holiday here, then, are you? How do you like it? Where did you meet Gwen? Say if you don't like pips. I made strawberry, too, but it didn't set so well.'

She was talking for the sake of talking and even when she addressed her solicitations to Owen, she directed her gaze elsewhere: at the teapot, the sugar bowl, the plate of scones. She reminded him of a woman who'd come to him with a lump in her breast and spent the first ten minutes telling him about her aerobics class, rattling on just like this, never meeting his eyes. At last, she'd turned away, to stare at the wall. 'It was afterwards, in the shower . . .'

Mrs Caldwell did almost exactly the same thing. She talked herself to silence, reached for the butter, stared at her plate and then swung around to face him.

'Why've you come here?' she snapped. 'What do you want?'

He was certain, then, that she knew something. His heart clenched like a fist and seemed about to burst with the tension of the moment. He couldn't breathe; he couldn't think. He thought – until Gwen laughed – that he was going to faint.

'Hey, hang on, Joyce!' She reached out to grasp Mrs Caldwell's wrist. 'What are you getting so worked up about? Owen doesn't know Glyn—'

'John!' Mrs Caldwell snapped. 'His name's John! Glyn, indeed! Bloody ridiculous—'

'John, then,' Gwen conceded patiently. 'But Owen's never met him, Joyce. He's just reading *Song of the Stars*, and we thought . . .'

Owen couldn't take any more. 'Excuse me—' He pushed back his chair and stumbled into the garden, almost blinded by his own sweat. He stood on the path for a moment, trying to calm himself, trying to fill his lungs. But it was almost as stifling outside as it had been in the conservatory. The bottom of the garden ended at the foot of the cliff he'd seen from the road; Mrs Caldwell had trained fruit trees against it and the rockface was radiating almost as much heat as it was absorbing from the sun. He strolled around, very deliberately inspecting the vegetables: cabbages and spinach, lettuce bolting to seed, a healthy row of runner beans on old-fashioned coppice poles.

'Owen?' It was Mrs Caldwell. 'I'm sorry I was rude to you. It's just . . . You look so like him.' She closed her eyes.

'I'm sorry too, Mrs Caldwell. I didn't mean to—'

'No. Well. Gwen's told me about your – er . . . But I haven't got a sister, you see. I can't help you.'

CHAPTER TWENTY-EIGHT

It was a cold, dry, bright day, with clouds many-layered, the lowest of them sailing like ships on the wind. The landscape was as Rhodri best liked to see it: shaded with blues of so many tints they defied words to describe them. Harebells reflected in a clouded mirror, pale hearts of violets, the shadows under Malen's eyes.

'Oh, I am rich,' the farmer said half-heartedly. 'For on a day like today . . .'

He sighed. This was his wedding day. He'd done nothing to mark it except to get married. It had seemed tactless to make any fuss. He hadn't wanted to feel any different, to think he possessed her. He hadn't wanted her to feel possessed.

'But no one can say I've borrowed her,' he whispered.

Marriage was for ever. He'd known this very well before today but had tried not to think about it. It was like knowing you were going to die: it scarcely bore contemplation. Yet he recognised, in the gloom he felt now, that the two ideas were linked. A man who knows he is going to die is driven by his nature to grasp at immortality. Before Malen, when the idea of marriage had been as remote from him as a cheque for five hundred pounds, Rhodri had made his grasp through poetry, imagining himself a Chaucer whose voice the world might still hear when he was five centuries gone. Since Malen, he'd written scarcely a word. It was as if his nature was saying, 'This way to immortality, *bach*. To hell with poetry. Children are easier to come by.'

Not with Malen they weren't. Malen was a perversion of Nature, one of the Fair Family who, touched by mortal hand, must turn to mist and blow away.

Garth grumbled and spun around suddenly to look up the mountain, his leg-feathers streaming on the wind like weed in deep water. Malen was out, trudging up the lower slopes of the White Seeker with Nessa. To reach them on foot, Rhodri would need to run a mile or more, yet he could hear Nessa's voice in the caution of her step and the way she turned her head, looking back, always looking back, worrying herself silly. *Are you sure about this, Malen? Did he say you could go? When was that, then? I didn't hear him. Out to the sheep, he said, and not a word more. What if you fall? What if you get lost? What if—?*

'What the hell's she up to?' Rhodri muttered. 'Away, Garth! Pen, away! Turn her home.'

Even against the wind they seemed to fly: Pen to the east, Garth to the west, their net flung so wide that even from the corner of her eye Malen would not glimpse it until it fell. She might be grateful for it, too. Rhodri had taken her out as often as the weather allowed during the past few weeks, but she still had no more idea of climbing a mountain than she had of climbing a greased pole. She didn't breathe right. She didn't fill her lungs.

'Your legs are like the pistons of an engine,' he'd told her. 'If you don't give them fuel they won't run. Oxygen, *oxygen*, that's what they need; and there's plenty of it up here, *cariad*. All you have to do is breathe it in.'

But she'd spent too much time hiding in corners, making herself small. Telling her to open her shoulders and breathe with her belly was – he supposed – like telling her to parachute into enemy territory, an exposure of all she wanted to keep hidden: firm little breasts, neat little waist, the curve of—

O, dammo, he mustn't think of that. Think of blizzards, think of ice, think of . . . Think of income tax; that should do it.

The dogs came together on a snowy step of land a hundred feet up from their target and Rhodri set off to meet them, keeping his eye on Malen in case she took fright. It was of no use to call her or whistle to Ness. The wind was in his face, its teeth nipping bruises into his cheekbones that would remain until midsummer.

When Malen saw the dogs, she stopped walking and stood for some time watching them as they ran back and forth across her path, shoulders bracing, haunches twitching, jaws grinning to show the shuddering red straps of their tongues.

She turned. He'd been told by summer hikers that it was as hard coming down as it was going up, but Malen seemed to be finding it easy enough. She'd squared her shoulders for once and didn't seem as worried about her footing as she usually was. With her hair flying and her coat flapping, she looked as if at her next stride she'd launch herself on the wind and fly away.

'It'll be dark soon,' he said as they met. 'It was silly to—'

She walked straight past him, her gaze skimming his face like the wind, with a nip in it cold enough to bruise his bones.

'Malen!' He laughed and caught her elbow, but the move was

born of uncertainty and when she screamed and shook him off he let her go.

She knew about the cheque. John Evans had told her. That nip in her eyes had been contempt – and he deserved it. Tell her later, indeed. Yes, tomorrow, next week, next month or next year. 'Later' could be infinite when it was paying out interest.

He'd tell her now.

Barring the first, it was the longest evening he'd ever spent with her. She only shrugged when he told her about the cheque, shrugged when he asked what he should do with it. He couldn't believe she wasn't interested and, if only to see a spark of greed in her eyes, he said, 'So I'll hang on to it, shall I? It'll get more interest if I put it with my own savings.'

Another shrug. *Do what you like. I don't care.*

Neither did he, now. He felt like tearing the cheque in half and burning the bloody thing. He wouldn't, though. It would be like chewing his own leg off, an act so unnatural it would break his mind.

Since Mr Evans had fetched her things from the manse, Malen had seemed more settled, more content. She didn't do very much. Her stillness, her apparent lack of any physical energy, had worried him at first, but as time went on he'd realised that keeping still was one of her natural defences. As soon as he went outdoors for an hour she'd get up and do something: clean the windows, scrub the floor. When he came home, she'd sit down again. She was like a rabbit, freezing into the background, pretending she wasn't there.

Tonight, though, Malen wasn't still. She went out to the *tŷ bach* more times than he could count. She pulled at her fingers, chewed the ends of her hair, wandered aimlessly around the table or sat on the window-ledge, watching her reflection dissolve into the night.

Every time he looked at her she seemed more beautiful. The soft light of the lamps overlaid her wild, oil-paint colourings with a warm, sepia wash, turning her skin to honey and her hair to bronze. The palms of his hands ached to hold her, to draw her to his knee and bury his lips in her hair. She was his wife, after all. And he, after all, was not John Roberts. He was tall and strong and graceful. His teeth were all his own. His eyes . . . Oh, dear, dear. How had he come to wed the one woman on earth who wouldn't die for them?

By half-past eight he'd had enough.

He went out to the dogs and spent the best part of an hour with them, slowly freezing, thinking of blizzards, thinking of income tax. It wouldn't be forever. Even if it took a year, she would soften, she would come to him. With patience and gentleness enough, a man could tame a wild fox, so why not a woman? She was only seventeen. There was time for her to heal.

She'd married him, after all. It was true she hadn't wanted it except as the lesser of two evils, but she'd been brave and strong, determined to see it through. She'd even managed to sign her name, not just to the register, but to the vows themselves: to love and to cherish him, until death.

Love suffereth long, and is kind . . .

How long, though? And how kind?

Malen had gone to bed when he went back inside and, rather than prolong his agony, he put out the lamps, leaving the one on the dresser to light him to his room. He tamped down the fire, hooked up the guard and bolted the door. As he reached for the last lamp he saw Malen standing like a wraith between the wall and the dresser. She was shivering. She'd crossed her arms over her chest and was staring at him as if at a monstrous reptile still dripping from the lake.

'What's wrong, Malen? Why aren't you in bed?'

She tried to speak: 'Ah-ahh-ah,' but otherwise didn't move, not even to blink.

'What has frightened you? A mouse, is it?'

She was in her nightgown: not the cardboard box he had bought her, but a soft, washed-out thing of pale green wincey that revealed rather more of her shape than he cared to notice. 'Come on,' he said. 'Go to bed before you freeze. You'll tell me better when your feet are warm.'

He took her hand. She screamed and shrank away from him, curling her shoulders to the wall. Only then he understood. This was their wedding night, and he had made her no promises.

He took the lamp. He stood at the end of the settee to light her way, bowing gallantly from left to right, his hand sweeping the air. 'Nothing has changed,' he said. 'I'll sleep in my bed, and you'll sleep in—' His hand, with his gaze, completed the sweep.

But there was nothing behind the settee. Her bed had gone.

149

CHAPTER TWENTY-NINE

Owen didn't want to be with Gwen any more. He didn't like her. She was pitiless, a do-gooder of the worst possible kind, polishing her halo with the rags she'd made of other people's pride. He wished he'd never laid eyes on her. He wished—

'Sorry,' she said. 'I made a complete balls-up of that, didn't I?'

Owen did not reply.

'Tact was never one of my strong points. I haven't wanted it to be. It's only a polite way of telling lies, isn't it? And it gives people time to plan the lies they're going to tell you. I've got this theory, Owen, that if you tell the truth, the truth will come back to you. Even if it's an unpleasant truth, at least you know what you're dealing with.'

He sighed. He knew what she meant and she was probably right. But only half right. 'Tact,' he said, 'is a product of civilisation. Without it we'd be—'

'Pollution's a product of civilisation too. So are a thousand other rotten things. My point is that civilised behaviour can go too far. Up its own backside, in fact. Take politics—'

'I'd rather not, thanks.'

She laughed. 'All right. Take any good thing – and democratic government *is* a good thing – one step too far down the right track and you'll suddenly find yourself on the wrong track. I know. I just did it, didn't I?'

Owen sighed and gave in. She seemed to have as little sympathy with her own failings as she had with anyone else's, so perhaps he'd been wrong. But he still felt as if he'd been pulled through a hedge backwards and he didn't dare think what Mrs Caldwell was feeling now.

'What was that about his name? Is Glyn a pseudonym?'

'No. He changed it. About ten years ago, this was. He put an advert in the paper – here, I mean, in the local rag – to tell everyone he'd be Glyn from now on. Most people laughed. His mother didn't. She can't stand it. As you noticed.'

'Is she always that jittery?'

'I've never seen her like it before. I told her you were the image of him before I took you in and she didn't seem to mind. It was when she saw you she went to pieces.' She sighed. 'My fault. You've gone right off me now, haven't you?'

'No, no. I still like your legs.'

'How about my nose?' (She had a thing about her nose.)

'Your nose is beautiful,' he said, realising with a grin that he was inwardly paraphrasing Rhodri Thomas: *with a blue bloom and a fresh dew, a nose can be beautiful indeed.*

'Right,' she said, all unsuspecting. 'Let's go to bed, then.'

They sat on the peak of Einion Ddu, watching the early stages of the sunset. Even from this high point they would not see it slip behind the world, only behind the furthest mountain, from whose feet the mists were already rising – apricot mists that matched the tangerine sky almost to perfection and transformed the hills into floating islands: a magical, mystical effect that recalled the Arthurian legends and made their creation seem as natural as taking breath.

Owen didn't generally like sunsets. 'Red sky at night' had never, for him, seemed the good omen it was cracked up to be. It made him sad, put him in mind of wars and conflagrations, made him think the end of the world had come. But it was impossible to be sad while Gwen was with him. While Gwen was with him, *everything* was a good omen.

The view stretched for twenty or thirty miles in every direction, and with the breeze in his face Owen might have convinced himself he was flying.

'I never want to go from here,' he said.

'From here, or from down there?'

He wasn't entirely sure. He knew only that it was true, that he belonged and wanted to spend the rest of his life here. Not on the mountain, necessarily, but within sight of it, within reach of it. Within reach of *this* – whatever it was. Peace? Yes, peace. But also . . .

'Do you feel small when you're up here?' he asked

'No. I feel small when I'm in a room full of people. I feel like an ant when someone's kicked the anthill, scurrying around in a panic, trying to rescue the eggs. It's so important to rescue the eggs, isn't it? The work must go on. Life must go on.'

'I don't think I can go back to medicine.'

'No, I didn't think you would. Can you afford to quit?'

He smiled. 'Only if I live like a sheep. But that doesn't matter.

151

I've got no responsibilities now.' For the first time since Alison had left him, he could see that she'd done him a favour. If it hadn't been for the kids he could have thanked her for it. But he felt happier about the kids, too. He felt happier about everything. 'It makes me feel small,' he said. 'Pleasantly so; not so obvious. I suppose I mean "obviously striving".'

'Striving to be big?'

'Yes . . . No. I'm not sure. I think it had something to do with being married, having to meet a certain social standard. The right house, the right car, the right schools for the children. It wasn't something I needed – class is probably the only thing I've never been much bothered about – but it was important to Alison and I thought . . . Well, you know what I thought.'

'Yes, I know what you thought. I think you were very nearly right, too. Marriage *should* be about serving the other person's needs – only not to the point of self-destruction, which was where it nearly took you. No woman wants that from a man. You should have told her to whistle for the right bloody car. She'd have liked you better for it.'

'Hmm. I doubt it. But I don't mean it was a financial struggle; it just seemed . . . It was an enormous *effort*. Medicine is an enormous effort whoever you are, whatever your circumstances, and I'm not the first to snap under the strain; but . . . Well, I don't know. I don't think it was the job so much. I think it was just me. It was unnatural for me; I was just trying to fit, trying to stretch myself to fill too large a space. I think being small will suit me better.'

'How small would you like to be?'

'About as small as David Samlet. I'm not sure I can do it. But I can try, can't I?'

She took his hand. 'What about Joyce? Do you want to leave it now? She does know something, I'm sure, but we can't . . .'

'No, we can't. I'm beginning to think it doesn't matter, anyway. What did Rhodri say? A man is as a man is made? I was made in a certain way, Gwen, and I've been fighting it off for as long as I can . . . for almost as long as I can remember. Trying to be what other people wanted me to be. In Glyn's book . . . the part of Rhodri that hates gossip . . . I think what he means is that other people's talk reinterprets him, changes him, so that he isn't sure who's right – them or him. Did you notice how he anticipates the gossip before it happens? That's what I've always done, but with rejection, not gossip. And where did it get me?'

152

'Here,' Gwen said.

He laughed. 'So it's not all bad.'

They drove north the next day to take a look at Snowdon, but the land was bleak and desolate and Owen was oppressed by a sense of history which nothing Gwen told him of Welsh history, myth and legend could relieve. He felt that something horrible had happened here: worse than Merlin's dragons, far worse than the death of Gelert, worse even than what was known of Edward the First's brutally protracted murder of Welsh sovereignty. Even in the pretty (and tourist-jammed) town, where tea-rooms and souvenir shops came nineteen to the dozen, he felt haunted by something unspeakable.

'What, though?' Gwen asked, bewildered.

'I don't know. A massacre, perhaps. I want to go home.'

'I thought you wanted to climb Snowdon!'

'I don't, now. Sorry. Get me out of here, will you?'

They spent the afternoon strolling the near-deserted beaches of the west coast, dined – very stylishly – in the garden of an ancient abbey-turned-hotel and arrived back at the cottage just as dusk was turning to darkness. The feelings Owen had experienced under Snowdon had disappeared except as a disturbing memory, but he suspected that it had had very little to do with Snowdon. The revulsion he'd felt there had been – he thought now – a kind of valediction: a last touch of loathing for the man he had been and would be no longer.

'I'm going to write to the adoption people,' he said as he unlocked the front door.

'Wow,' Gwen said. 'When?'

'Now. I'll find out their address first thing in the morning.'

Gwen patted his shoulder approvingly. 'Ooh,' she said. 'There's my brave boy. You won't regret it, honest.'

He laughed. 'I know. Crazy, isn't it? All these years it's seemed impossible, and now . . . Easy as falling off a log. Look,' He held out his hands, palms down. 'Not a tremor. Put the kettle on, *cariad*.'

She shook her head, pretending wonderment. 'Bilingual, too. The man's a miracle. *Ydych chi eisiau coffi?*'

He narrowed his eyes and took a risk. 'Yes, please. Black, decaff, no sugar.'

He was not surprised to hear the phone ringing a few minutes later. Jill had rung him every evening since she'd returned to London and was probably worried to have found him out tonight.

'Hi, Jill.'

There was a pause. Then a very Welsh, breathless woman's voice said, 'Owen? Is that Owen?'

'Yes . . .?'

'This is Joyce Caldwell speaking. Gwen's mam gave me your number. Look, can you come up here? I . . . I've got you on my conscience.' She was crying. 'Will you come?'

She showed them into her sitting room and offered sweet sherry which Owen hadn't the heart to decline. Once he'd accepted it, there was nowhere to put the glass; every flat surface was littered with framed photographs of Glyn: naked babe, bundled toddler, boy-on-a-swing, boy-on-a-bike, first day at school. In none of them did Owen recognise himself. Glyn had been a fat little boy (Owen had starved himself until he was six) and didn't begin to look – just vaguely – familiar until he was about twelve. Even then he was a reflection not of Owen so much as of the boy he'd wanted to be – the one who could say 'fuck' without first looking over his shoulder.

Since Owen had last seen her, Mrs Caldwell seemed to have shrunk and shrivelled, aged ten years overnight. He was reminded of the Welsh flag, drooping and shapeless, the dragon's fire burning its own feet. For long minutes she sipped politely at her sherry, asking if Gwen liked it – 'Mm! Lovely!' – if Owen didn't – 'Yes, it's fine!' – saying she'd always preferred Bristol Cream, but had they seen the price? She said she didn't have many vices left. They were all too expensive.

'Even lying,' she said, 'costs.'

She sighed and lifted her chin to speak to the clock on the mantelpiece, her mouth determinedly firm, her voice clear and calm. 'We did adopt John, of course. I had him when he was six months old. I don't know if he had a brother, but you're so like him . . . It was like seeing . . . Your voice is different and I think you're a bit taller. Otherwise you could be twins.'

She bowed her head. 'I never told him, you see. I couldn't.'

'Doesn't he know?' Gwen whispered.

'Oh, yes, yes. That's why he went away! It was my fault. I didn't want to tell him, I didn't want anyone to know. I told so many people I'd had a terrible labour with him, I almost came to believe it myself, but I'd only had miscarriages before.'

She pursed up her mouth and added sullenly, 'No one knows what it's like to have a miscarriage.'

Like dying oneself, Owen had been told, *and living afterwards as a ghost, hung in chains.*

'We lived up near Flint, then. As soon as we got the adoption papers – John was eighteen months by then – we moved here and I started lying about him. I wanted him to be mine, you see, Gwen. I wanted him to be *mine.*'

Gwen knelt on the floor and took her hand. 'It's all right,' she said softly. 'There's no need to say any more if you don't want to.'

Mrs Caldwell smiled tearfully. 'Don't tell your mam, *cariad.* I don't know how many lies I've told her, over the years.'

'I won't tell a soul.'

'It doesn't work, though, does it? The truth always comes out, one way or another. Emlyn kept saying we'd have to tell him before he found out for himself, but I held it off and I held it off . . . Then, about a year after his dada died, John found the adoption papers and that was that. He didn't tell me at first. He went very quiet; I didn't get a word out of him for months and then . . . He just threw it in my face. He said he'd never forgive me; said I'd robbed him of his identity, made him think he was *us* when he was *them.* I didn't understand it. I still don't. What was *wrong* with us? We *loved* him!'

Owen didn't think it the right time to explain it. She was confiding in Gwen, anyway, just letting him listen, but suddenly she turned to look at him and wailed, 'I know I was wrong! I just don't know why . . . Why he . . .'

Owen didn't know, either. Glyn had suffered the exact opposite of his own experience and had reacted to it in the opposite way: rejecting, rather than fearing rejection, breaking away instead of hanging on for grim death.

'I don't know,' he said gently, 'and I can't answer for him, Mrs Caldwell. But it sounds to me as if – er, John – felt he'd been taking the wrong measurements, looking in the wrong places for the clues to his own nature. He'd thought until then that he was a certain person – and then found out that he was someone else.'

'Is that how you felt?'

'In a way. It was different for me because I'd always known I'd been adopted. But because the pattern of my own history – and my genetic mix – was denied me, I felt I had to try to fit the only model I was given, even if it didn't suit me.'

155

Mrs Caldwell stared at him and then, wearily, returned her gaze to the clock on the mantel.

'So I didn't *suit* him,' she said acidly.

Owen wished he hadn't used that word. In repeating it with such bitterness she'd changed its sense, made it small and cheap, a paltry excuse for the waste of her life. Yet Glyn had been gone twenty years, and a man doesn't do that to his mother unless . . . Yes, there was probably more to it than that: previous hurts and resentments, perhaps, which his discovery of the adoption had underlined. But it was useless to ask, and too cruel to suggest that she might have hurt Glyn more than she knew.

'I think it might have been more a case of his not suiting himself, Mrs Caldwell. Being unhappy with himself, I mean, not with you.'

'Oh, it was *me*, all right. He told me he hated me!'

Owen looked at his hands, into the sherry glass which, by courage alone, he had almost emptied. He could feel the sweetness corroding his teeth as surely as Mrs Caldwell's grief was corroding her soul. A toothbrush would solve his problem if he could reach it soon enough. Only Glyn could solve hers and Owen had a feeling he never would. Not soon enough, anyway.

'No, wait,' Gwen said gently. 'Look at it from his point of view for a minute, Joyce. As Owen said, just now, he probably felt he didn't know himself any more and, when you think of it, that must be a terrifying feeling, like going mad, almost. It was *that* he hated, not you. He just needed someone to blame, Joyce – and you were handy.'

Mrs Caldwell nodded, but the expression on her face said, *You don't understand.*

'Owen did the same thing,' Gwen went on gently. 'But he blamed his real parents, not his adopted ones. He said they'd abandoned him, you see, Joyce, as if he was nothing. And he hated them for it, all his life – or thought he did. But really he just hated himself, because he *believed* he was nothing.'

Mrs Caldwell frowned. She blinked and looked into his face as if only then comprehending why he was there.

'Oh,' she murmured. 'But why should you think they abandoned you, Owen? If you *are* John's brother, and I think . . .' She lowered her eyes. 'Well, it's not my place to say.'

Owen's heart was in his mouth. He swallowed it and took a slow, calming breath. 'Do you know what happened to his natural parents, Mrs Caldwell?'

'Yes, they died. Some sort of accident I think it was, though I don't know the details; the adoption people didn't tell us anything. They were Welsh-speaking, I *do* know. Quite bright, too, they must have been.' She sighed. 'John was . . . is . . . a very bright boy.'

Owen squeezed his eyes shut on tears.

They died.

CHAPTER THIRTY

It had been a good winter for the sheep: dry and cold, with very little snow. By the middle of April, with only forty ewes still to lamb, Rhodri calculated that he might increase his flock by as much as ninety per cent. Lowland farmers would sneer at such a boast – in a good year they could approach two hundred per cent and say it was easy. But mountain ewes rarely produced twins. Twins were the result of lush autumn grazing of a sort never found on the high tops; and after a dry, sparse summer when the sheep lived hard and fattened little, many would produce no lambs at all. But ninety per cent was worth crowing about. At least it made a profit.

With the dogs positioned to head off the latecomers, Rhodri stood at the highest point of the pasture, rattling a bucket of feed. The ewes put up a bleat and stampeded towards him. At the bottom of the field they moved in a dense, woolly knot. As the slope steepened, the thin ones rushed out in front and the heaviest fell back. The first dozen to reach him were probably not in lamb. The last dozen would lamb during the next few days and the dogs cut these out and took them to the gate. Rhodri emptied the bucket, jumped over the wall and opened the gate to the lambing fold, where Malen was waiting with more feed.

Even in his wildest dreams Rhodri had never seen Malen as a farmer's wife, a helpmeet, yet she'd adopted that role as if she'd been born to it, cooking and cleaning, fetching and carrying, dropping everything to give him a hand when he needed it. And she seemed happy enough. A hell of a lot happier than he was, although he still had hopes. Of a kind.

Her decision to sleep with him had been the best thing she'd done for herself since she'd come here. He'd thought at the time it was the best thing she'd done for him, too, but nothing's that easy. He still didn't know why she'd done it. Maybe she'd thought it better to volunteer than be forced, although in Malen's case the terms were synonymous; she'd wanted to consummate their marriage as much as he'd wanted to be boiled in oil.

Sometimes, as she slept serenely beside him, he felt that the pot he'd fallen into was already bubbling. Even in darkness he was beguiled by her beauty, which seemed all the greater when he couldn't see it, couldn't touch it. His blood never failed to rise to the occasion; his mind never ceased to tread those paths of seduction his body was denied. Yet he knew now (with gratitude) that he was not capable of rape. Malen knew it too and if the change in her since their wedding night constituted a beginning, rather than the end he too often feared . . .

Yes, too often, for if she was safe from him, she had everything she wanted and might never wish to change it. She was inviolable because she had been violated: he was certain he could not have shown a virgin the same restraint. He almost dreaded the end of lambing, when he'd no longer have an excuse for spending his nights with the sheep, and it seemed bitter indeed that he should find a cold, windswept field more comfortable than a warm feather bed with Malen in it.

With the ewes safely penned, Malen scooped her fingers towards her mouth and presented her palms to him, twice. *Supper'll be ready in twenty minutes.*

He smiled, 'Right you are,' and watched while she made her way back up the mountain, quick and strong, her spine straight, her legs consuming the steep, frozen ground as if it were a flat road. In freeing her from fear it seemed he'd liberated all her energies and confined his own. He'd never felt more weary.

He slept for an hour after supper and then took a lamp for his evening's tour of duty in the lambing fold. A shepherd working alone couldn't hope to help all of his sheep and most could manage pretty well without him, but he still had to go down every few hours to catch the few that couldn't and to match the newborn to their mothers and mark them a pair.

The only gate to the fold faced south. Since Rhodri usually approached from the north (and in any case wanted the gate kept shut) he entered and left the fold across the wall. He'd taken one of the stones from the top to aid his entries and exits and although he'd heard a few ominous clatterings from below, he imagined the stonework would survive the few more weeks that were asked of it.

He was wrong. The wall gave just as his full weight levered into it. Had he not been holding the lamp he might have thrown himself clear, but his fear of being burned was greater than his fear of being crushed, so that, when he landed, he landed flat on his face, with the lamp intact, upright and still brightly burning. His legs were trapped under half a ton of stone wall.

He realised he'd almost lost consciousness only when Garth began licking his face. 'Don't,' he murmured. 'Go and get Malen, will you, *bach*?'

Dogs have no real understanding of human language. They learn through association, habit, routine. Break the routine, say something new and, as far as the dog is concerned, you might as well be reciting Homer in Greek. After waiting a while for Rhodri to right himself, Garth clawed at his arms, trying to dig them into action. Pen thrust her nose under his chin and pushed upwards. *Come on, come on! There's work to be done!*

'Fetch Malen,' he said. 'Fetch Malen. *Fetch Malen*!'

Garth ran around in circles, frantically sniffing the ground: *Tell me when I'm getting warm, will you?*

Rhodri tried to move his legs, and although they wouldn't move he knew they were still there, still attached to his body and his brain, if only because they hurt so much. The temperature was well below freezing and if he was losing blood he might not survive until Malen missed him. And why should she miss him? During the past few weeks he'd often stayed out half the night, going home only when he knew she was asleep. If she hadn't missed him then, why should she miss him now? He could die out here and she wouldn't notice.

The light of the lamp somehow intensified the darkness all around, and the tiny circle of warmth it provided intensified the cold, frightening him almost to tears. He closed his eyes, but that was worse still, giving him nothing to think about but pain and wild terror. If his legs froze . . . Oh, God, if his legs froze, he'd be better off dead!

He turned from the lamp to watch the stars, forcing himself to concentrate, to think of higher things. Cassiopeia, *Draco* the Dragon, *Ursa Major* the Great Bear. As old as God, that one was: known to ancients the world over – Egyptians, Phoenicians, Eskimos and Indians – by the same name: the Bear. Yet it didn't look like a bear. A ladle, a saucepan, a hammer or an axe, but never in a million years a bear. So why had they called it that? Why had they *all* called it that? When did an Egyptian meet an Eskimo and talk to him about the stars?

It was impossible. They couldn't have arrived at the same name independently; nor could they have met to talk it over and agree. No . . . It all pointed to something else, something more ancient than they and even stranger: a memory they all shared of aeons long gone, when they were not separate nations but the shivering, skin-clad primitives of a single tribe. Or Nimrod's ambitious brickies, the architects of Babel, who'd built a tower to heaven against the face of God.

And the whole earth was of one language and one speech . . .

It seemed a terrible irony to him that his most distant ancestors could speak to him across the divide of countless millennia – 'We call it the Great Bear,' – and he be incapable of sending a single word – *Malen* – across a few hundred yards of his own mountainside.

Pen had given up trying to shift him and was lying *couchant* beside him, gazing anxiously into his eyes. 'Fetch Malen,' he said. 'Come on, now, Pen; help me, *cariad*, will you? Fetch Malen!'

Pen quirked her eyebrows at him and a soft little whimper issued from the glistening black ball of her snout. *I don't understand. I don't understand.*

The cold fell out of the sky like stones. It seeped out of the ground, shrouding his heart. A long time passed before the thought at last crossed his mind, not that he could, but that he *would* die. The mountain had killed him after all.

'Bastard,' he whispered.

And the mountain mocked him: *Who built the wall?*

CHAPTER THIRTY-ONE

Owen's letter to the adoption people was brief, businesslike and to the point. His letter to Glyn Caldwell, although not significantly longer, was a miracle of tact and diplomacy. It said everything and nothing at all; and although the 'everything' was easy enough to write, the 'nothing' took five drafts and almost as many hours.

He was addressing the envelopes – Glyn's care of his publisher – when Gwen arrived. He was sick with nerves and at the touch of her hand on his shoulder he turned into her arms and clung to her like a child. The thought crossed his mind that he was clinging to his past, but when he counted the days since he'd met her he let go again, acknowledging that he had nothing to cling to beyond the moment, the 'now', the one day at a time, Mrs Brown.

'It's no good,' he said flatly. 'I can't do it, Gwen. I thought I could—'

'And you were right by the look of things,' she said, brisk as ever. 'All we need now is stamps. Got any?'

'No,' he lied, with relief.

'Come on then. Race you to the Post Office.' She snatched the letters from the desk. 'Last one to the ford's a pillock!'

He shrugged, smiled and fetched his keys, certain she'd wait for him, certain too that she wouldn't wait long enough to let him catch her. Of course he had to post the bloody things. Before he'd written them he'd had no doubts, had known (give or take Glyn's feelings, which he'd done his best to protect) that this was something he had to do; that *must* be done. Like Rhodri, he was taking the first step on a road he had deliberately chosen. All he needed was the nerve – or the Gwen – to give him a shove in the right direction.

He'd had a few fantasies about marrying Gwen, marrying her frankness, marrying her sanity, but he knew it would be like marrying money: a short-cut to a state one should earn for oneself. Or be born to, as Rhodri had been. Owen had read almost to the end of the book now and was having a few thoughts about Rhodri which – so far – Glyn hadn't written. Rhodri's parents had been only hinted at and although the father seemed to have been a weakling, it was the mother Rhodri hated. *He would never have come back, except to her funeral.* Yet it was she, Owen was certain, who had given Rhodri his strength, not just through negative influence of the sort he'd mentioned early on, but through her blood, her genes, her lineage. And Rhodri hadn't yet realised it. Owen wondered if he would before the end of the book. He wondered if Glyn had seen the irony.

He was also beginning to wonder if Glyn had approached the adoption agency too, and created Rhodri from the information he'd gleaned of his parents. The time seemed about right: there'd been enough clues to set the story somewhere in the early fifties. The thought excited him more than he liked to admit. He knew he was being silly. The book was a fiction, not a truth, and even if it contained a few elements of truth, it still wasn't *true*. But it would be wonderful if it was . . .

As he'd predicted, Gwen was waiting for him where the lane turned downhill towards the ford: wheeling her arms so that her breasts, separated by the crossed strap of a leather satchel, bounced in comical independence of each other. He grinned and broke into a sprint and she squealed and cantered off downhill, yelling, 'Cheat! Bloody cheat!' when he took a short-cut through the bracken and headed her off to reach the ford first.

'Pillock!' he roared, and caught her in his arms as she ran out of control on the last, near-vertical, incline.

It might not have been the sexiest moment of his life, but it was certainly the sexiest he could remember. Each of them was wearing shorts and very little else, each hot and sweaty, dusty, panting. His hands moved from her ribcage to the rounded flesh of her behind, lifting her up until she rode on his hips and her mouth met his with a greed which matched his own. Instinct took him ahead of himself to lay her on the riverbank, where tree-dappled sunlight would wash over them like the sea. Reality reminded him that the riverbank was mostly nettles and he set her on her feet again, fighting an overwhelming desire to tell her he loved her.

'Oh, God,' he breathed. 'Oh, God, oh, God, oh, God, you're so beautiful.'

There was a pause before she murmured, 'God gets enough bloody compliments. What about me?'

'Ha.' It was the nearest he could get to laughter. He wanted her so urgently, loved her so completely, it seemed almost worse than sacrilege to make a joke of it.

'Come on.' She took his hand. 'The Post Office'll be shut.'

'I don't care.'

'I do. Come on.'

They walked in silence for the next few minutes. Owen was aching with suppressed lust, dazed by the physical effect she had on him. He'd been celibate for he didn't know how long – the best part of two years, probably – and had scarcely noticed the lack while it had lasted. Now she'd started him off again he felt as randy as a teenager: ever ready and never satisfied, always wanting more.

'Why do you care?' he asked at last, mostly by way of changing the subject, but also fishing for clues to her own feelings.

'Care about what?'

'The Post Office. The letters.'

'Oh, well, I know you. If you don't post them now, you never will. You made the decision before you wrote them. It's only nerves stopping you now, and that's . . . silly.'

'Cowardly, you mean.'

She laughed. 'You said it, not me. It's not something I'd say about anyone; myself included. I sometimes think heroes don't realise their danger. Either that, or they were suicidal to start with. I'm not saying heroism doesn't exist, mind. I just think it's rare. I also think the bravest part of doing anything is actually making the *decision* to do it.' She gave him a little hug. 'So you're brave enough for me, *cariad*. I'm just licking the stamps.'

The Post Office – a sub-branch – was combined with a small general store, just along the road from the Station Arms. As they approached it, a hearse drove by with a plain, unadorned coffin in the back. Owen had seen many such hearses, many such coffins; death, after all, had been as much a part of his professional life as had birth, and he'd ceased long ago to have any sentiments about it except in terms of the worn cliché, 'a blessed release'. Love and lust, ambition and failure, pain, fear, anxiety . . . Death was an escape from all that.

Yet for some reason the sight of this hearse, this coffin, gave him a strange pang of sorrow and he stood for a moment to watch it out of sight, vaguely wondering why he cared.

'Who's died?' he murmured.

'What?'

'The hearse.' He pointed to the bend in the road.

'Dunno. Haven't heard of anyone. Got any change for the stamps? I've only got a tenner.'

Owen smiled sheepishly, took out his wallet and extracted a book of stamps. 'Fool's errand. Sorry.'

'Right,' she grinned. 'That's it. You can lick your own bloody stamps. I wash my hands of you.'

He affected to tremble, but the letters had lost their power to scare him and he posted them without a qualm, seeing them now as an end, not a beginning. A blessed release. It was a release he felt like celebrating.

'Since we're here,' he said, 'let's get some wine.'

Gwen pulled a face. 'Only if you like British sherry. There's an off-licence a bit further down.'

It was a lot further down. Before they arrived Owen had begun to understand how the Station Arms 'village', with its clustering of church, cottages and pub, linked with the rest of the town. The place was shaped like a half moon, with the river running along the straight edge and the Station Arms and the main road bridge at either extreme. Joyce Caldwell and Gwen lived at the top of the curve.

'And Gethin Morgan lives down here,' Gwen said. They were turning a corner as she spoke. She was raising her arm to point out Gethin's cottage. But as her voice trailed away, Owen found himself staring into the open rear door of the hearse. The coffin had gone.

CHAPTER THIRTY-TWO

Rhodri woke, warmly heaped with blankets in a grey dawn, the fire blazing beyond the fender and Malen's arm around his shoulders, lifting him to drink. He had only vague memories of the nightmares of the night and could not have said he hadn't dreamed it until he saw her face, frost-bruised and scalded with tears.

'Malen,' he whispered. 'What—?' But the words left him and he fell back against pillows and slept. He dreamed that Malen lay naked beside him, stroking his body. He struggled to escape, muttering (in Welsh, so that she wouldn't understand), 'No, no. Leave me alone. It's not allowed.' But he couldn't for the life of him think why. Something to do with the chapel, was it? Or with his mother, who had loved him too much?

You can't be loved too much, someone said. *Even when it's the wrong kind of love, love makes you strong.*

In his dreams he wept for his strength, wept for the bitter cold and for the pain in his legs as he crawled up the mountain, with Malen's arms around him and Ness licking his face.

'Stop it,' he said. 'Stop it, will you? I'll have no face left if you carry on.'

He opened his eyes and found Malen kneeling beside him, gently stroking his face with the cold cream he'd bought for her own wind-chapped skin. He blinked and the memories came back: dark, flickering and sinister, like a silent film spliced out of sequence. Malen, heaving rocks from his legs. Malen, all but carrying him home. He had no idea, now, how long he'd waited for her. Ten minutes can seem like so many hours when you think you are dying. But he was alive – just – and his legs were not broken. Gashed, bruised, skinned . . . but not broken.

'Thanks,' he murmured. 'I'd be dead if you hadn't . . . What time was it when you came for me?'

Two hands and an index finger. He'd been lying there the best part of three hours.

'What made you come?'

Malen pointed to Nessa and then at the door. She made scratching motions with her hands. Scowling, she drew whirling little cogs at her temple. *Nessa was going crazy, trying to get out.*

'Good old Ness,' he said.

Dogs don't understand much of human language, but they know others: the language of senses and of soul which men, if they ever knew it, forgot long ago. He was pretty certain that Pen and Garth hadn't left him, yet somehow they'd sent messages of fear and confusion to Nessa. Or perhaps *he* had, for terror has a stink all its own and he had been terrified: not just of death, but of the agony of living – perhaps for many hours – until he died.

Tears seeped from the corners of his eyes and he grabbed Malen's hand and squeezed it. 'Thanks,' he whispered again and she smiled and stooped to kiss his cheek. She knelt beside him and stroked his hair with a firm, gentle hand. Although she had never before touched him like this, it did not seem strange to him. They'd both been scared out of their wits. They both needed comfort. He wrapped his arms around her. He buried his face in the wind-woven silk of her hair and would have slept again had her hand not moved from its resting place on his shoulder. Under the blankets, over his chest. He opened his eyes just as her mouth touched his, soft and warm, sipping rather than kissing, in a manner he found pleasantly irritating, if only because it made him hungry for more. He still didn't expect more. It didn't even cross his mind. But he couldn't help curving his hand to the back of her head to press her lips closer and, when she didn't recoil, closer still.

Habit is a curious thing. In the instant that the warmth in his limbs changed from comfort to desire, his thoughts turned to income tax and he retreated, closing his eyes, averting his face, letting his arms fall limply at his sides.

He had touched Malen a thousand times and in a thousand different ways, yet she'd never failed to stiffen at his touch and find an excuse to move away. Even when he tousled her hair, made her laugh, her very laughter seemed designed to put a few extra inches between them. Now, except for his own reserve – his own fear – there was no space between them.

He turned to look at her and found her watching him with a shy, questioning intensity, her lips softly parted as if to ask, as he had longed to ask her so many times, 'Shall I go further?'

The answer was yes, but also no, because of course the reason he hadn't attempted to force her was that he'd been terrified. Terrified of the stiffening of her body and the dismissive turn of her head, terrified of being deemed contemptible because he was a man, with the same natural needs and functions as the man who had broken her. If, now, she should lead him to the brink of fulfilment and then turn away, she'd break *him*.

He tried to ask, 'Are you sure?' tried to warn, 'Once we begin there'll be no turning back,' but the words wouldn't come. He wanted her too much.

He turned his body towards hers, wincing as his legs collided with each other. He cradled her face in the palm of his hand, catching his breath when, instead of withdrawing, she closed her eyes and nuzzled closer. Her skin, like his, was scorched by the ice of the night, cheeks flushed, lips swollen, eyes shadowed with exhaustion. He had watched her grow stronger and more hardy these past few months, but now she seemed as fragile as a lace moth poised on the heather; only move an inch and she'd be gone.

He stroked the hair back from her face, wondering at the creamy parchment of her brow, the tiny, coppery curls which sprang from her hairline, the misty shadow of her temple.

'You are beautiful,' he whispered, and her fingers strayed to his face to trace the lines of his brow, his nose, his mouth.

You are beautiful, too.

He laughed and took her in his arms to whisper in her ear, to blow warm breath upon her senses. 'Come to me,' he said. 'Don't leave me now, Malen.'

He kissed her, riding a switchback of joy and terror as she drove her body against him like a lamb butting its mother for nourishment, drinking his kiss to its dregs. She *wanted* him!

A tearing pain seared his arm and he yelped and leapt away, dazed and staring, to find Nessa standing over them, her brows quirking with bewilderment, a horny paw poised to give him another dig if he didn't behave. *I don't know the hell what you're up to,* she said. *But whatever it is you can stop it, right now.*

Rhodri groaned. Malen fell away from him. She stood up and walked away and, while the strength drained from his limbs and the hope from his heart, she turned around, tipped her head shyly towards the bedroom and reached out her arms to him.

Come.

CHAPTER THIRTY-THREE

Gethin Morgan had died in his sleep, between a set of clean sheets. He'd always changed the bed on Sundays.

'It was his only day off work,' Gwen sobbed. 'His aunty made him do it: change the beds, do the washing, clean the house. It's true what Rhys said: she drove him like a slave, but it was only – only . . .'

'Ssh, ssh,' Owen plucked a handful of Kleenex from the box on the kitchen table and shoved it under her nose. 'Don't cry any more, Gwen. He died peacefully; he died well. He kept faith, *cariad*, right to the end. His aunty would have been proud of him, wouldn't she?'

But she couldn't stop crying and Owen rather felt like joining her; not for grief, exactly, but for the curious stroke of fate that had kept Gethin alive just long enough for Owen to meet him and hear what he had to say.

It was hard to believe, now, that he'd only screamed.

He met Gwen's mother at the funeral and began to understand what kind of girl Gwen really was. He could see traces of her face in her mother's: the same damson-dark eyes, the same generous mouth. But the resemblance ended there. Mrs Jones was a tangled knot of arthritis, emaciated and pain-ravaged almost to extinction. Her hair was short and iron grey, prettily styled in frond-like waves to disguise the fleshless stalk of her neck and the hollows of her cheeks. Owen heard himself asking, 'What's wrong with hairdressers?' and called himself a self-centred bastard. He'd noticed at the time how Gwen had looked at him. Why hadn't he asked what was wrong? Why hadn't he cared enough? And if he'd wondered at all, he'd only *vaguely* wondered why a girl of Gwen's strength and independence should still be living at home. Well, he knew now. She couldn't get away. Her mother would be helpless without her.

The chapel was packed to the rafters. Afraid of the fine Welsh singing that Gwen had warned him would be an inevitable part of the service, Owen sat near the door, preparing for a quick exit should he burst into tears and shame himself. But he needn't have worried. The only shame at that funeral would have been to remain dry-eyed among a host of weepers as the minister waxed lyrical on the triumph and the tragedy of Gethin's world of silence.

Owen spent the best part of the service with his eyes squeezed shut or directed at his feet. Or at Mrs Jones's hands, her fingers reduced to boneless flaps, her knuckles as shiny and bulbous as rain-soaked shallots. Gwen's sister sat on her other side – a taller, heavier version of Gwen with a pleasantly bland expression which Owen thought indicative not of niceness so much as of a space between her ears. She was bovine; a peaceful grazer. The thought that she might one day be served up in a Big Mac would never enter her head.

These few sideways glances apart, he saw very little of what was going on and didn't notice that Gwen had left her seat until an expectant silence fell. He looked up. She was standing on the podium where the minister had stood a minute before. Her eyes were closed, her shoulders braced, her mouth shaped as if to say, 'Ashes,' although the sound which emerged was without shape: a hum, a soft vibration of the air which set the hairs on Owen's neck erect and brought his arms out in gooseflesh.

> What are words on another's tongue?
> Glimpses through torn curtains,
> Starlight through clouds.
>
> Each of us is a world we travel alone,
> Returning with tales only of moments:
> River in flood,
> Beggar at the door,
> Sunrise over the sea . . .
>
> Like stars clustering the night
> We gather within rooms,
> Spilling our radiance as if to touch,
> To shine my light upon your world,
> Yours upon mine . . .

Owen's eyes flew wide. Until now, he'd thought the star song a poetic version of Gethin's scream: a cry of desolation, of utter loneliness. It had seemed to say, Even if you can speak, no one hears; even in a crowd, you are alone. But it wasn't saying that

170

at all. Or, if it was, it wasn't true. For although Gethin had known no language he had, in effect, written these words through Glyn. And although he'd never heard a note of music, he had sung this song through Gwen. He'd been mad, yet had pulled Owen clear of madness and taught him, in a matter of days, that keeping faith with oneself was all that mattered.

You can't touch the stars. But they touch you.

CHAPTER THIRTY-FOUR

The next house down from the manse – a paddock, an orchard and the river came between – was the doctors': two of them, man and wife, known to no one by their name (which was Davies), but always as the Doctor and the Lady Doctor. Most spoke of the Doctor with a respectful smile and of the Lady Doctor with the blushes and groans indicative of something perverted and shameful. She was English: that was half of it; the other half was mere prejudice. Women were not clever enough to be doctors. It stood to reason, therefore, that she'd kill you as soon as look at you.

Rhodri had never put either doctor – male or female – to the test. The only time he'd needed them he'd been too crippled to get down the mountain and, by the time he was well enough, he hadn't needed a doctor. Love had healed him. It had taken its time, but that was all to the good. Three days in bed with Malen . . . Cure anything, that could.

Yet even two weeks later his left knee was still painful and had a tendency to swell if he walked too far, but since Malen couldn't shop and they were down to their last carrot, he had little choice but to try it. He sang for a while, trying not to notice that at every flexing of his knee someone hammered a six inch nail into it, but long before he reached the manse he could think of nothing else and was wondering how he would get home again.

The Lady Doctor was working in her garden, kneeling to a border of daffodils and chickweed, her narrow hips encased in pepper-and-salt tweed, her hands in thick leather gauntlets. She said good morning, coldly, as to a foreigner. For spite, Rhodri enquired, '*Sut ydych chi*?' and walked on.

He had moved out of her sight when she called out, with dignity, 'Very well, thank you. How are you?'

He laughed. '*Da iawn, diolch.*'

'Liar. What's wrong with your leg?'

He turned on his heel, twisted his knee and jammed his teeth on the pain. The Lady Doctor was out on the pavement now, watching him, one hand stripped of its glove and clenched loosely on her hip. Her colouring – such as it was – put him in mind of driftwood, bleached clean of its nature, translated into something rare and strange which bore little resemblance to the tree it had once been. Pale hair, pale brows, eyes so light one might think they were blind. It wasn't an arrangement he'd ever fancied, yet still, barely conscious that he was doing so, Rhodri peeled off her tweeds and her twinset and saw that her body was as neat and youthful as Malen's, although at least fifteen years came between them.

'Oh,' he said. 'Nothing that won't wear off, given time.'

A man who had not lived with Malen, a man who depended on words to teach him the secrets of a woman's thoughts and feelings, might not have noticed the subtle change in the lady doctor's expression: a flicker of pain so fleeting he would have missed it had he blinked.

'I picked a quarrel with a wall,' he conceded, sighing.

'Oh, dear. How's the wall?'

'Beyond medical aid.' He tapped his leg to oblige her. 'Unlike me.'

Her office was painted green, with fluttering white lace at the window and a nice bit of Axminster underfoot. Afraid to seem afraid, he'd stripped off his trousers before she'd finished soaping her hands. She quirked colourless brows at the twilit shinscape of black, blue and yellow, folded her arms and asked aloofly, 'Didn't you say you won?'

He shrugged. 'I had help. The wall didn't.'

Her hands were cool, firm and gentle. She probed the tendons and bones of his knee, soothing the heat that burned there, and then, without warning, gave the joint a sharp twist, making him gasp at a pain which – afterwards, when it failed to return – he told himself he'd imagined.

'There. I think you'll find it easier now. Keep off it as much as you can for a few days. Call in on your way back and I'll run you home in the car.'

He stared at her. 'No, no, I won't trouble you.'

'Doctor's orders.' She was looking down her nose, writing something. 'How is your wife, Mr Thomas?'

He swallowed a lump of gratitude. No one else had ever spoken of Malen thus; few had spoken of her at all since he'd married her, but perhaps that was only because he'd looked daggers at them when they tried it. For the chapel's sake, John Evans had been discreet about the reasons for Roberts's suicide and even the newspapers had guessed elsewhere for the cause.

Married or not, Rhodri was still under suspicion, and he supposed everyone was still counting months with narrowed eyes, awaiting the babe conceived out of wedlock.

There! Told you, didn't I? Oh, I knew what he was up to, all along!

'My wife,' he said, relishing the word, 'is in good health, thank you.'

'Good. Have you . . .? Did you ever discover . . .?' She stood up, walked briskly to the window and closed it. 'You can get dressed now, Mr Thomas. Does she – does she speak to you at all?'

He dressed slowly and carefully, observing the tautness of her mouth, the tension in her shoulders. He guessed that her interest in Malen was neither gratuitous nor strictly professional and realised that they must have known one another, even if the difference in their ages had made friendship unlikely.

'Oh, yes,' he murmured. 'She speaks to me. Not with words, but I am beginning to wonder how much words really matter. What, for instance, were your motives when you called me a liar?'

'Heavens, I didn't mean—'

'No. But you wanted to ask after Malen. My leg was just an excuse. Am I right?'

She laughed, but there was a hectic light in her eyes which reminded him suddenly of Garth, hoovering the mountain for something he could not find. 'I never hear much about her,' she said. 'People gossip in Welsh, don't they?'

'Learn Welsh,' he said. 'Or learn that gossip is rarely worth hearing, whatever the language.'

'That's true only so far as it goes. Language – if you understand the language – reveals itself as much in its means of expression as in the expression itself. Sometimes you can learn the opposite of the words that are actually spoken. *Da yawn diolk*, for instance—'

Rhodri grinned. '*Iawn*, as if you would yowl, and *diol-ch*, as if you would spit.'

Humour touched her eyes, fleetingly, like a mist. 'Yes, well, however you pronounce it, it means, "very well, thank you". Except that when you said it, it meant, "Mind your own business," and a good many other things beside. Am I right?'

Rhodri smiled at her sideways. 'There, you see. You know the language very well. And do you also know Malen?'

'I knew her before her mother remarried,' she said, turning away, folding her arms. She was shy, afraid of herself and, perhaps, more than a little afraid of him, wild Welshman that he was.

'Go on,' he urged softly. 'I didn't know her then. What was she like?'

'Ohh . . . She was a lovely girl: vivacious and – and rather too full of herself, I suppose, as most girls are at that age. They think they know it all, don't they? They think they have the world . . .' She opened her hand and stared wistfully into the palm of it. 'But she was also very sensible. She thought things through. She told me, just before the wedding – she'd have been thirteen then, I suppose – that she thought it a good thing, because it would mean she could leave home – go to university, she meant – without having to worry about her mother. I took the impression that she thought Mr Roberts rather contemptible. A few months after that . . .' She shrugged.

'You knew what had happened?'

'No. I only guessed. Do you know, Mr Thomas? Or are you guessing, too?'

'I am not guessing.'

'She told you?'

'No. I suppose I just followed a hunch.'

Hunch, he thought, and almost cried out, 'Eureka!' for a hunch was precisely what he'd followed. Not the promptings of the devil, not the errand of the Lord, but the naggings of his own mind, his own decency, his own compassion for a child in torment. So that was a relief.

The Lady Doctor slanted her head to one side. 'What's funny?'

'Words. I've been looking for that one for months. Hunch, *hunch*. It's a funny one, isn't it? You can carry it on your back yet never see it. I've been wondering what took me to the manse that night. Something outside me. Something beyond me. Something beyond my understanding. Yet after all it *was* my understanding. A hunch.'

'About the minister?'

He nodded.

'And now?'

'Now she is loved.' Almost in spite of himself, he heaved a happy sigh. 'And she is loving. I think it will be enough to heal her, Doctor. Don't you?'

She seemed startled. Her eyes darted to his face and then away again before she smiled and agreed. Or did she only smile? Afterwards he couldn't remember and, when she drove him home, little more than an hour later, he couldn't bring himself to repeat the question. He didn't want to know.

175

CHAPTER THIRTY-FIVE

The crematorium was an hour's drive away: too far for Gwen's mother. They waited until the crowds had gone before attempting to leave the chapel. Eluned rushed off to fetch her kids from her mother-in-law; Gwen went to fetch the car; Owen pushed the wheelchair to the gate. Mrs Jones, her voice as powerless as crumpled tissue, scooped one of her useless fists through the air to draw Owen's ear nearer her mouth.

'She's been a new girl since she met you, Owen. You've done her the world of good, taken her out of herself a bit . . . She needed that, you know. I'm a terrible burden to her.'

'I'm sure she doesn't think so.'

'Hmm . . .' She smiled wanly. 'She'd be mad if she didn't, wouldn't she? Anyway, I just wanted to say thanks for—'

'Oh, shut up, Mam.' Gwen grabbed the wheelchair and gentled it over the step, her tight little biceps bulging under the demure black linen of her dress. 'Don't thank him, for God's sake. He's been taking me to bed, not the bloody opera.'

Owen went hot and looked elsewhere.

Mrs Jones rustled a giggle from the bony plate of her chest. 'Just as well, too,' she said. 'They're doing *HMS Pinafore* again. Will you come to lunch, Owen? We're having stuffed aborigines.'

'Aubergines, Mam.'

'Oh, well.' With Gwen's arm around her, she extracted herself from the wheelchair, tottered around to face it and lowered herself, with infinite care, to the front seat of the car. 'I'm not sure I like them, anyway.'

'How can you say that? You've never eaten an aborigine.'

'No, but I saw how much garlic you put on them. He won't like it, I'm warning you. Your father never liked garlic.'

'Owen's different. He's liberated.' She lifted her mother's legs and turned them into the carwell. 'He does his own ironing.'

Wide-eyed and holding his breath on laughter, Owen waited for the next sally, but Mrs Jones had run out of steam and said nothing else until they embarked on the more difficult process of getting her out of the car at the other end. Then, 'What, shirts and all? What's wrong with the man? Is he merry?'

'*Gay*, Mam.'

'No! Is he? Why's he sleeping with you, then?'

It was a game. Owen knew it was a game. But there was something in the way Gwen responded – almost feeding her mother the lines – that made him think the game was rigged to disguise something worse than physical pain.

The interior of their home had a faded, rather battered air that reminded him of his childhood, and, to his amazement, awakened strong feelings of nostalgia for a time he'd convinced himself had been scarcely worth remembering. In Gwen's home, as in his parents', nothing matched, nothing was new (or even valuably old), and if anything had been chosen for its beauty, that beauty had faded long ago and been replaced by another of a different sort. Not love; nothing so high-flown. Just acceptance.

You don't fit, you don't match and we keep tripping over you, but you're here, you belong to us . . . And that's good enough. Not better than love, perhaps, but very much better than breaking faith.

After lunch, when her mother had gone for her nap, Gwen served coffee in the garden at the rear of the house: a series of grassy terraces which plunged off down the mountain, with a dramatic view of Einion Ddu (about ten miles distant from this point) and a less dramatic one – barely visible in fact – of the red brick chimneys of Paul's cottage. Owen would never have thought to look for them and was touched that Gwen had taken the trouble to do so: keeping him in view even when they were apart.

For a while they were quiet. The stuffed aborigines had been served with an appropriate – and very good – Aussie wine. Now Gwen was tired and mildly drunk and, Owen suspected, more grieved about Gethin's death than she'd had time, yet, to express. There was a taste of tears, and of change, in the air. The sun still shone, irradiating the geraniums with such heat it seemed as though their shadows would be forever etched upon the grass. But beyond Einion Ddu storm clouds were building: vast white banks of cumulus: mountains beyond mountains, range beyond range. It was hard to believe they were only vapour and that some tiny, parka-clad hero was not, at this moment, ice-picking his way to peaks which toiled half a mile higher with every step he took.

Paul and Jill were coming down this weekend (separately; Jill was bringing Owen's car) and they'd curse blue flashes if they caught only rain after so many weeks of sunshine. It wasn't going to be easy, telling Paul he wouldn't be going back . . . Paul could

177

be a manipulative bastard when he chose: always finding your weakest point and niggling away at it until he'd won the argument. He wouldn't win this one, but it looked like being a stormy weekend: with thunder or without it.

'Weather's breaking,' he murmured.

'Mm, I know. Sad, isn't it?' Gwen sat up, swallowed the cold dregs of her coffee and demanded brightly, 'So what do you think of my mother?'

'She's very sweet.'

Gwen raised a cynical eyebrow. 'Oh, there's perceptive. You should have been a shrink.'

He grinned. 'Yes, missed my chance, didn't I? All right; she's *complicated*. Trying too hard not to care, perhaps? She gets her tangles worded up a bit, doesn't she?'

For a moment Gwen seemed unamused. Then, 'Don't mick the afflocted,' she said. 'It's not nice.'

'Sorry.' He swallowed another grin. 'What—er? Um . . .' he scratched his head. 'What's it all about, exactly? Shyness?'

'No, not really. She's . . .'

'Hmm?'

'Years ago, when my father was alive, she said something wrong – quite by accident – in the middle of a family squabble.' She smiled wearily. 'I was seventeen – very superior, demanding my rights, making her life a misery – and she called me a boiled sprat. My dad laughed until he cried. He didn't laugh very often and when he did he was almost bearable. So she did it again . . . And again. It was deliberate, then, of course. I don't know what it is now. Habit, I suppose.'

'How old is she?'

'Just turned sixty.' She sighed and stared off down the garden with glazed, sleepy eyes. 'She was beautiful when she married my dad. Men turned to look at her in the street, and he'd hold her hand and say, "She's mine." Ten years after that, he was calling her a cripple, a burden, a disgrace to the great family name. *Jones!*' (She pronounced it '*Chawns!*' which came with its own, quite independent, hiss of contempt.)

'And she hasn't forgiven him?'

'Puh! She won't even admit there's anything to forgive! She thinks he was right, that she cheated him, robbed him of the best days of his life. Can you *believe* that?'

Owen looked thoughtfully at his hands. 'All that matters is that *she* believes it. When everything you stand for is rejected, you have to believe you're wrong, that they're right, that you're every-thing they say you are. It's just a way of preparing yourself for the next rejection, strengthening yourself for it before it can happen.'

'But he's dead!'

'You aren't. The way she sees it, she's taking the best years of your life, too, and it's only a matter of time before you tell her so. Rejection breeds rejection and the subtleties of it . . .'

'Yes?'

'Come from inside, not out. It's not what's said or done to us that causes the damage but how we interpret it. The star song again,' he added softly. 'It's what you said about Gethin, isn't it? Once you start thinking about it, you find yourself thinking about everything.'

'Ohh . . .' Gwen's face crumpled with sudden tears. 'He's *gone*, Owen! I can't believe it! He meant so much to me!'

He knelt at her feet, shoving a clean hanky under her nose. 'And to me. He changed my life. I'll never forget him.'

Gwen blew her nose: an enormous, farting blast which scared all the sparrows from the birdbath. 'It's because he had nothing,' she said. 'That's what it was for me, anyway. He made me look closer at everything I had, even the little things, like blackbirds singing in April, or ordinary bits of knowledge, like where the river comes from and where it's going. He didn't know that, you see, Owen. For him the river ran only as far as he could walk, and he never—' Her voice broke with a sob. 'He never – walked to the sea!'

Owen found himself observing her nose, which was redder and shinier than he'd ever seen it, thinking how genuinely beautiful it was just because it belonged to someone who could see beauty in everything. *Where the river comes from and where it's going* . . . As he knew to his cost, there were few 'ordinary bits of knowledge' more beautiful.

'Go on about my mam,' Gwen said at last. 'What can I do to make her see—?'

'There's nothing you can do. People have to . . . This seems strange: I was going to say that people have to work things out for themselves, but *I* can't claim to have worked anything out. I met Gethin; I met you, and everything just fell into place. It was a gift. I haven't a clue why I was given it. All I know is that it couldn't have been manufactured; it had to happen when I was ready, and

I have a feeling that "ready" is the same as "rock bottom". Maybe our lives are full of gifts we can't even see, let alone accept, until we've got nothing else.'

This was a new thought which reminded him of an older one: his first walk on the mountain, the empty landscape which had gradually filled with colour, shape and line until – then as now – he'd been overwhelmed by its beauty, its clarity. The simplicity of it all.

He sighed and took Gwen's hand between both of his, rubbing it gently. 'What I mean is . . . the things Gethin said to me were there all the time; I'd been hearing them all my life, but not listening. It's the same for your mother. If she's not listening – and she's not, I'm afraid – there's nothing you can do to make her hear.'

Gwen pulled him into her arms and rocked him like a child, yet he knew now that she was seeking comfort, not giving it. He also knew that she'd been seeking it all along and that, perhaps to a lesser degree, she too was failing to listen. All that stuff she'd fed him at their first meeting – *Not married yet, Gwen? They don't fall off trees when you're thirty, you know!* – how much of that was a denial of her own needs? And how could she answer such needs while her mother lived?

He was certain he'd be all right from now on; these past few weeks had brought him back to base in more ways than one. But a base is only a beginning and a beginning is nothing at all: no job, no home and barely enough money to get him started again, even had he known where to start. Yet habits die hard and it had been the habit of his lifetime to put down roots in the most inviting patch of soil, to send clinging tendrils around anything that looked strong enough to support him. It would have been easy to say, 'Marry me. I'll look after your mother, give you the children you want, secure your future. Marry me and I'll stick with you till I die.' But it wouldn't do. He wasn't that kind of bean any more.

'You never told me,' Gwen murmured, 'exactly what Gethin said to you.'

He smiled. 'I can't pronounce it. It was in Welsh.'

'Can't you translate it?'

Each of us is a world we travel alone . . .

'Yes,' he said. 'Maybe I will. One day.'

CHAPTER THIRTY-SIX

Spring came to the mountain only when the bluebells and wind-flowers of the valley were spent. It was a stark and subtle spring, marked only by the greening of the thorns and a flush of pink in the grass where bilberries unfolded new leaf. The wind (which, like the glove factory, took only two weeks off in the year and that mostly for day-trips) still whistled over the rocks and drummed against the ears, but the ice had departed its breath; the last of the snow had gone. If you could find shelter against a sunny slope, you could almost persuade yourself it was summer.

Yet Malen was sad, roaming the high tops with bowed head, searching the remote mysteries that dwelt – beyond Rhodri's reach – inside her mind. Rhodri was puzzled by her sadness which, it seemed, had nothing to do with him. It was nothing he'd done or failed to do, for she seemed to love him more as time went by, and his few months of celibacy now seemed like a distant dream – one of those brief, tormented dreams which, although you wake in a lather, you immediately forget, wondering what the hell it was that had frightened you. Sometimes, when he thought of it, he could despise himself for finding it so hard. Before Malen, three loveless months could go by without his notice; Young Sue Philips was not one to drive a man mad with longing, just a mite tetchy now and then, just a mite lonely. And she'd always been *ready*; that was the thing with Sue. She hadn't kept him waiting, wondering, fearing he'd wait for ever.

Fear, not lust, had made him sad while he'd waited for Malen. He was beginning to realise that fear *was* sadness; that all the miseries on earth arose from that source and no other. He was afraid, now, of Malen's sadness, which he could not understand and she had no means to explain. As many times before, he wished that she could speak and, almost in the same instant, drove the wish from him as he might drive a wasp, aware of the sting in its tail.

He scanned the mountain for a glimpse of her, and found himself, for the first time in half a year, searching for words to describe what he saw. Instead, he found himself translated to a farm in the valley, looking up from a distant place and seeing the mountain as he knew others saw it: a series of humps and bumps in the ground, having rather less significance than a molehill. No malevolent dragon, sleeping off the feast it had made of stolen lambs. No ancient giant, exhaling its wisdom at every breath. Earth and rock were all it was. Sheep and heath and grass and thorn.

'Is it time for me to leave you, then?' he whispered and heard no reply save the buffeting of wind against his ears. But that, too, was an answer.

When at last he found Malen, she was standing in a grove of stunted thorns, her hair whipping the wind. Someone strange to the mountains – a man from London seeing it for the first time – might have thought she stood in a grove of boulders with no more life in them than stone. Yet they were trees: some so old they'd grown pale beards of lichens, and not one of them higher than Rhodri's knee.

'Ahh . . .' Malen wove her hands over a particularly twisted specimen as if trying to untangle it, like a yarn. 'Ah-ahhh . . .' *Poor little thing.*

He put his arm around her shoulder and pointed a little way down the mountain to a tree which had put up a straight trunk and a rounded green canopy, the lowest branches of which were five or six feet off the ground.

'That tree was like this, once,' he said. 'And this—' He indicated the 'boulder' with the toe of his boot, '—was once a tiny seedling, as soft and tender as a flower stalk. Sheep, wind or frost nipped it to the ground, and the following spring it sent up two shoots from the callus of the first. It was cut back again – year after year, callus upon callus. But it has survived, Malen. It has built a little house, you see, to shelter it from harm.'

Malen splayed out her fingers and laid them across one another to make a grid, a cage, a prison.

'No,' he said. 'It is a house, *cariad.* Look.' He squatted to view it more closely, drawing her down beside him. The tree was covered with new green leaves, on stems so short they barely fluttered in the wind. Rhodri eased a little peep-hole to look through. 'It's hollow inside,' he said. 'There's a space there, Malen, where the wind never blows and the sheep can't reach. Inside there, a new shoot will break and grow tall and straight, protected in its house until it's strong enough to stand alone.'

Malen frowned and thought it over until, quite tentatively, she tapped her chest. *I will grow, too?*

182

He laughed and pulled her into his arms. 'Oh, you,' he said. 'You're *twp*, you are.' He kissed her eyes and her nose and then stood back a little, preparing to kiss her mouth. 'You're already growing, aren't you? Perhaps it doesn't seem—'

With an abruptness which both astonished and offended him, she twisted clear of his embrace, walked a little way down the mountain and stood with her back to him, her arms hugging her ribs. He'd got it wrong again . . . Oh, God, if only she would speak!

He joined her, dodged in front of her, tipped his head to see her face and was astonished all over again to see that her eyes were squeezed shut, her teeth bared in an angry grimace and her face the colour of strawberry juice. Blushing? *Blushing*? What the hell did *that* mean?

'Tell me,' he said. 'And no beating about the thorn bush this time. Just tell me. I love you, see, *cariad*. I can't bear to see you sad like this. All I want is to make you happy.'

I did everything I could to make her happy, his father said as he died. *But she was never . . . satisfied.*

He swallowed and turned away. He couldn't cleanse himself of his own blood. He couldn't make himself stone when he was butter. All he wanted – all he'd ever wanted – was to make her happy, pretending his own happiness could be found in that. But it didn't work. It couldn't work. A man must live for himself and give of himself only those things he could spare. His love, yes. His soul, no. Malen had her own soul. She didn't need two.

'Come on,' he said briskly. 'Let's go home.'

No. She shook her head, took a deep, shuddering breath and jabbed her index finger towards his chest. Then her chest.

'You and me?'

Yes. She laid her palm under her breasts, met his eyes and held them. She tilted her hand to stroke it outwards and down in a deep, arching curve which came to rest in the pit of her belly.

Rhodri's mouth dropped open. For a moment he was as dumb-struck as she – or, rather, more. She had said, *I am pregnant*, very clearly, but he could say nothing at all. He was too busy. Selling the farm, buying another, fathering this child and one or two more, educating them (he saw the entire brood traipsing through a leafy farmyard in Grammar School uniforms), seeing their poems reviewed in the *Times*.

When at last his mind and his eyes refocused on Malen, he saw that she was trembling, her face taking the lines of hope and fear he knew so well.

'Oh, *Malen!*' He grabbed her off her feet. He swung her in his arms. He lathered her face with kisses and tasted her tears.

'Why are you crying, *cariad*? Don't you want it?'

For a moment she stared at him with swimming eyes. Then she laughed and flung her arms around his neck, confusing him with a show of relief that made him wonder again how her mind was working.

'You thought *I* wouldn't want it?' he asked. 'Oh, Malen, Malen, how could you think that? Didn't I tell you I love you? Didn't I tell you a thousand times? Haven't I explained—?'

She pushed him away, wrinkled her nose, put her fingers to her mouth and flicked them outwards, shrugging.

Words, words. What are words?

He laughed. He pulled her head to his chest and gently stroked it, overwhelmed with love for her and the first line of a poem.

CHAPTER THIRTY-SEVEN

There were soft rumblings of thunder all night, but no rain. Every time Owen woke (which was often) he felt hotter, more stifled. He dreamed that he was lost on the mountain, terrified and alone. It was dark, yet the sky still burned with the afterlight of sunset, a dense, smoky orange that dimmed the stars. He was aware of something terrible following at his back and he ran from it, into the reach of something yet more terrible from which he turned and ran again – and woke up sweating, his heart racing with panic.

He lay awake a long time after that, pondering the dream and a few dozen other things, the most disturbing of which was Rhodri's 'Lady Doctor'. His mother? Possibly, although Glyn Caldwell's description hadn't come anywhere near; she'd been a large, florid, raw-boned woman, with all the frail vulnerability of a dray horse. The same capacity for gentleness, too, although one was always wary of the reined-in power, the capacity she'd had for mowing one down and ploughing one in.

But his mother had never practised in Wales. His father had, for a year: the year they'd adopted him. Could they have known his real parents, known them without telling him? He hadn't asked, of course. He hadn't wanted to know and it was too late now to change his mind. A man was as a man was made, and however he was made – by birth or by upbringing – *that* was what he must deal with.

He felt cold suddenly. He got up to close the window and, to his amazement, saw nothing beyond it. No stars, no mountain, no trees. A dense, chill fog – perhaps the skirts of the clouds he'd seen earlier – had covered it all.

He woke much later than he'd intended and spent the morning in a panicky rush of housework, hoovering everything not small enough to disappear up the nozzle, dusting everything else.

Jill arrived bang on the dot (he'd hoped the fog would delay her), just as he was stowing the hoover, the Pledge and the Jif back in their appointed places. She kissed him. She said, 'God, you're looking marvellous – so *brown*!' and, 'I need a pee,' in virtually the same breath. Owen laughed and turned away, beaten by his own good intentions: he'd forgotten to clean the downstairs loo.

They made coffee and sandwiches. Jill was brown, too – had probably spent the past few weeks 'gardening' on a sunbed – and was wearing white trousers and a pink silk jacket, which emphasised both the perfection of her figure and the tragedy of her face. Nose too big (Gwen would love it), eyes too small, chin non-existent, the skin around her mouth puckered like huckaback after a twenty-year stint of acne.

'How was the car?'

'Fine. Same as mine.'

'Oh, yes; I keep thinking it's still the Volvo. I can't actually remember buying the Golf, you know. Huge chunks of the past year are still a complete blank.' He frowned. 'And I worked through most of it. Did I kill anyone?'

'No one important. A few old biddies. But they'd have died anyway, Owen. Honest.'

He laughed. 'Well, that's a relief.'

'You look so different. So relaxed, so . . .' She smirked.

'What?'

'Gorgeous. Amazing what a long holiday can do, isn't it?'

'It's not a holiday.' It came tripping off his tongue so easily he could scarcely believe he was saying it. 'I'm not coming back.'

'I know. At least, I was pretty sure you wouldn't. Paul guessed, too. Ages ago, actually.'

He widened his eyes. 'Really? How many ages?'

'As soon as Alison went.'

Owen shrugged. He felt rather hurt. 'That obvious?'

'I think it was more a case of "not obvious enough". He knew how shattered you must be because – well – the children, but you didn't say anything; you just carried on as normal – which *isn't* quite normal, is it? He said he'd give you six months.' She smiled sadly. 'You lasted a bit longer.'

He sighed, feeling some kind of weight lift from his mind. 'I had to,' he said. 'You wouldn't have brought me here in winter, would you? And I had to be here.'

Jill smiled and nodded. 'Home,' she said.

Paul arrived quite late and very tired, but not so tired that he didn't want to sit up talking half the night. Mostly shop. His enthusiasm for medicine had never waned and Owen had always seen him as the ideal GP, a man who kept professional objectivity and human compassion in a state of perfect balance, a brilliant diagnostician, a terrific administrator, an intellectual and a physical athlete who could keep as many balls in the air as were thrown at him and still make time to play tennis.

In the weeks which had passed since Owen's collapse not much could have changed, yet he found himself viewing Paul differently, observing weaknesses where before he'd seen only strengths. His age was showing – he was fifty-four – and in his voice Owen detected a rather tetchy edge, a faint, self-pitying whine reminiscent of Jonty on a bad day, when his every attempt at having fun was doomed to end in tears. Just tiredness? Perhaps. But how much of his tiredness was Owen's responsibility? Owen had been the computer-buff, the trouble-shooter; and although there were four other partners to share the load, Paul must still be picking up most of the pieces – not to mention the time it took to advise (and mop up after) the locum.

The words, *I'll come back,* reached the tip of Owen's tongue more times than he could count, but on each of these occasions a little man in his ear hissed, *Keep your trap shut, stupid.*

In the end, he said, 'For your sake I'd like to say I'll come back, but for my sake I can't. It'll be a long time before I do anything exclusively for someone else, Paul.'

He tensed himself for the arguments, but none were forthcoming. Paul stretched out in his chair, closed his eyes and said wistfully, 'I envy you.' After a while he said, 'You know those films – war films mostly, I suppose – where the hero sets out on a truck journey across the desert and, just when you think he's made it through, his wheels start spinning in the sand. Every time he tries to get clear, he digs in deeper and there's no way out except to spend time shovelling. But he has no time; the enemy is upon him and he's as good as dead. He makes one more attempt: low gear, steady on the throttle . . . And suddenly he's away. It's like a resurrection, a re-birth. You can watch that film – or one like it – time after time and still get a kick out of it. It's not the same when the cavalry turns up to rescue him. The kick comes from seeing him do it on his own, with nothing more to help him than he had before. Same truck, same sand, same man.'

Smiling, Owen shook his head. 'The cavalry came for me.'

'No. I think you went to meet them. But that's by-the-by. The point I'm making is that life is probably meant to be a series of deaths and re-births, not just one birth and one death with a lot of wheel-spinning in between. We're too complex for that. I think there should be a rule . . . No, I don't, of course – I can't afford it – but it's interesting to think about. A rule against doing anything for more than twenty years. Then you have to chuck everything in and start something new.' He struck a pose. 'I'd simply *have* to be an actor, luvvie. No, a *singer*. Pavarotti!'

Although not a vegetarian, Paul lived mostly on fish, fruit and vegetables and had the spareness of figure, rather than the spare tyre, to prove it. Worse yet, he couldn't carry a tune.

Owen grinned. 'I think Fred Astaire might be a better choice.'

'Oh . . . *Mmmm*.' Paul's smile reached his ears. By the time it had faded, he was asleep. Dreaming of Ginger Rogers.

The rain came at last not in a deluge but in a steady, almost silent, downpour, a weeping for things lost that Owen had believed would last for ever – or at least until September. Brilliant colours, sparkling reflections, shadows prostrated at the feet of the sun. It had lasted barely six weeks, yet those weeks had encompassed both the end of his life and the beginning. He knew he'd remember it until he died, much as he remembered the summers of his childhood: sunburn and midge-bites, seaweed and candy-floss.

It had been a busy weekend. They'd visited David Samlet and then, at Jill's suggestion, done some 'fantasy house-hunting', looking for a suitable place for Owen to live and work which (in his fantasies at least) was exactly the same as David's. They hadn't found it. But they'd discovered something Owen hadn't even considered: that for the price he'd get for his London home he could buy three in Wales. So he'd be richer than he'd imagined. There'd been an element of vague desperation in his earlier 'plans', a knowledge that, however ovine his life-style, he could barely afford to support himself long enough to learn anything, let alone earn anything.

Now he wanted nothing more than to get started, get on with it. And there was nothing stopping him except a deep-seated terror of fire. Burning bridges, burning boats. He knew he'd put a brand on his past when he'd told Paul his plans, but the fire was still only smouldering. It could be put out. Pick up the phone, dial 999: 'Er . . . Paul, before we decide anything, could you give me another week to think it over?'

He had a suspicion that if he did that, if he allowed himself the slightest chance of changing his mind, he *would* change it. For sheer cowardice change it. And what the hell would be the point?

What would he gain? Nothing, save a further (and this time life-long) dose of self-hatred. He'd thought it all through; sanely and sensibly thought it through to its most obvious conclusions. And he had no reason to change his mind, unless . . .

Why hadn't Paul argued? How could he have just sat there and accepted that his partner – his friend – was giving up everything to follow a childish dream?

He'd thought it all through . . . Sanely and sensibly . . .

Sprinkle me lightly. Salt's bad for the heart.

Dear God, was he still crazy? He'd been crazy four weeks ago, and no one *he'd* ever heard of had recovered from a breakdown in four weeks flat!

But he wasn't entirely certain he'd had a breakdown. Would Paul have brought him here if he'd been crazy? Would he have left him here, all alone? No. Being stressed out of one's skull wasn't the same as being blown out of one's mind and Paul had known the difference, even if Owen hadn't. So that was all right. It *was* all right. Now all he had to do was to *convince* himself it was all right and get moving. He'd have to go back to London soon, to sort things out, put the house on the market, arrange finances . . . A million little details, each one of which made his heart slam with terror. Burning boats . . .

He wanted Gwen, that was the trouble. He wanted to tell her how scared he was and to have her laugh him out of it. But she'd taken her mother to Hereford to visit a branch-line of the family. They wouldn't be back until Wednesday and he wasn't sure he could wait that long to be laughed at.

'Hey, come on,' he said aloud. 'Be a soldier for me, will you?'

But it wasn't the same. He couldn't pronounce 'soldier' the way she did. Be a soul-dear. Be my soul, dear.

Yes, perhaps. One day. But not yet.

A man must live for himself and give of himself only those things he could spare. His love, yes. His soul, no.

His soul . . . Alison had been right about that, poor girl. He'd given the damn thing away, and only now – by the skin of his teeth – grabbed it back again. It was a slippery little bastard, too; always trying to wriggle away, to Paul, to Gwen. And they didn't need it. *He* did.

CHAPTER THIRTY-EIGHT

Although he'd noticed the changes Malen had wrought on his home, Rhodri didn't fully comprehend them until the lady doctor, newly informed of Malen's condition, came to examine her. He met her at the *carn* and carried her bag while she picked her way over the steep, rocky track which, for want of a better name, he'd always called a path. But no one wearing high-heeled shoes and a tight skirt had ever climbed it before and, when she glared at him and said, 'You might give me your arm,' he was stricken with a shame that scalded his face and a fear that melted his bones. What if she should say the place wasn't fit? What if she should put Malen in the hospital? She'd go crazy; she couldn't bear it, he knew.

By the time he showed her indoors he was trembling (partly with temper), almost blinded by his own sweat and deafened by the thud of blood in his ears; and when he heard her gasp, 'Oh, this is lovely!' he thought for a moment he'd imagined it. Lovely? His little hovel? He blinked, looked again and saw that it was no longer his little hovel. It was Malen's little home. She'd white-washed the walls, sewn tidy green curtains to replace the army blankets he'd had there before and scrubbed and polished everything else until, like a sheep newly shorn, it had revealed its true nature. Even the old settee, which he could have sworn was meant to be grey, now shone reddy-brown, like a conker.

'It's all Malen's doing,' he said humbly. 'She likes things to be nice.'

'Where is she?'

'In the bedroom. A bit nervous, I think.' He led her through, pausing in the passage to add in a whisper, 'Be kind to her, Doctor; she's—'

'Not half as scared as you are, Mr Thomas.'

She was right. Dressed in nothing but her petticoat and the crimson mantle of her hair, Malen received the lady doctor with a smile which rocked Rhodri to his roots, making him realise, for the first time since he'd known her, that she was capable of vanity. And why the hell not? Beside her, the doctor looked like a photograph, taken on the eve of the war and left to bleach between the window and the blackout. Yet when he looked at the doctor's face, he found that her smile was the same: her pale eyes shining as if with forbidden laughter, her mouth proudly pursed upon secrets he could not share.

He had told Malen he would stay to act interpreter to the doctor's unpractised eye, tell her, 'She means, she feels, she wants to know'. But he wasn't needed now. In the meeting of their eyes they'd set him apart like a ram in winter, driven him out to the high tops, his substance spent. For a moment he struggled to keep his place, showing the doctor (as if they were not right under her nose) the washing things and clean towel for her hands, but she thanked him without looking up, and he blundered out, muttering helplessly, 'I'll leave you to it, then.'

He hadn't felt so confused since Malen had first come here. Then, as now, it was as if all his certainties had been tin pots, racketing to the floor from a high shelf. He wanted to walk far and fast, work off the energy of his feelings and, as they flagged, pluck the sense out of them; but he couldn't go now. The bloody woman would probably break her neck on the path if he wasn't here to help her. Stupid madam, coming here in her bloody ridiculous dancing shoes . . . Call herself a doctor? How could *she* be a doctor? She had no sense.

He sat on the front step, his eyes closed, his teeth gritted on rage – and something else, which he took some time to identify.

He – not they – had set himself apart. Even in choosing Malen (and he *had* chosen; his excuses in that department had run out of steam long ago) he'd set himself apart from the common run. He'd thought that Malen was his own, as his dogs were his own, not so much by virtue of her love and loyalty as through her inability (as he'd supposed) to communicate with anyone else or trust anyone else to see her heart. Yet the doctor had seen it in an instant. Malen had trusted her to see it, given it to her on a plate and, in the giving, had told Rhodri very clearly that he was not enough.

He'd had no time to reflect on the significance of this when the inner door opened and the object of his ire came briskly through it, smiling, swinging her bag.

'All's well,' she said. 'Your baby will be born in January, Mr Thomas.' She flicked her brows upwards. 'We'll need to think about that. Could be awkward if you're snowed in, couldn't it?'

He levelled his eyes at her. 'It is already thought of,' he said coldly. 'We'll be away from here before then.'

'Oh?' She seemed more shocked than surprised. 'Where will you go?'

'Where no one knows us.' He realised as he spoke that he was teasing her, lying in a way, for the notion of anonymity had not occurred to him before. But it seemed a good idea now. Where no one knew or guessed at her history, perhaps Malen could put it behind her and learn to speak again. He wanted that now; for his child's sake if not his own. And for the child's sake he must bring himself to ask what hope there was.

'Not a great deal, I'm afraid.'

The doctor was holding his arm again, slowly picking her way back to the car. 'Hysterical muteness isn't a rare condition, Mr Thomas, but I've never heard of a case regaining full speech. A few words perhaps. You shouldn't hope for more.'

'But if the cause of the hysteria is gone—?'

'Gone? Gone where?'

Rhodri scowled. 'To hell, I imagine. Don't you?'

'But *he* didn't make her mute, Mr Thomas.'

'What do you mean? Who else made her mute if he didn't?'

'She did. Not consciously, of course; she has no control over it; but the decision took place in her own mind, and it's probably an irrevocable decision. I could be wrong. I've never seen another case. But I've done plenty of reading since . . . since this happened.' She opened the car door and peered down at her feet in their silly little shoes. 'I'm sorry,' she said quietly. 'I know this wasn't what you wanted to hear, but false hope would be worse for you, wouldn't it?'

She seemed to emphasise 'you' as if she knew him better than she could – except through hearsay – and for a brief, bewildered moment, he wondered just what she had heard, and acknowledged, for the first time in his life, that people might speak good behind his back as well as evil. But the tin pots were still tumbling and from their clatterings and crashings he took only one grain of sense. *Tin-pot*. It meant . . . false.

False hope would be worse for you, wouldn't it?

As the doctor's car disappeared down the mountain, he stood with fists and jaw clenched, knowing that he was false. He had never hoped that Malen would speak again. Save for a few, quite fleeting, moments, he'd never wanted her to speak. And, now that he did want it, it was for the child's sake, not Malen's. As far as he'd cared, she could have been trapped in her silence forever, like a caged bird so sick for freedom it couldn't even tweet. After all, what did a bird matter? It was pretty, wasn't it? Its little hoppings and flutterings were company on cold winter nights. And it could listen, cock its head to one side when you spoke to it and, in reply, say precisely what you wanted to hear and not a word of what it wanted to say. *Let me out. Let me out, you bastard!*

It was one of those rare, crystalline days of early summer which define every detail of the earth with perfect clarity. It would rain tomorrow, but today was pure and clean, the ridges incised upon the sky as if by a surgeon's blade. There were no flaws in it; nothing that was not beautiful save his own soul. He could have wept.

But this is what you wanted, the mountain whispered. *This is what you sought. Did you think I would let you go without finding it?*

Nessa was old and sleepy, too wearied by the rigours of winter to appreciate the balm of the spring. She would not live to see another tupping, to mark with her footprints the peach-bloom of a frosty sunrise. She crept now like a snail, and sipped at each breath as a bird sips at water, but to her last breath she would serve him, if only to listen.

He knelt beside her to stroke her, feeling her age even in the texture of her coat, which had once felt like oiled silk and now felt like ashes. She opened her eyes, lifted her head an inch from the ground and then let it fall again, sighing.

Malen was sitting on the window-ledge with her tongue between her teeth, knitting a tiny white sock for the baby. Rhodri had spent his childhood listening to the click of his mother's knitting needles, watching her fingers worry the work as if to scratch out an itch; but Malen didn't do it the same. Like the giant Bendigeidfran, she went half-way to Ireland at every step, winding the yarn around her ear, around Old Tom, around Bardsey Island and miles out to sea before bringing it back to the needle to make one more stitch.

He sometimes forgot how young she was. The knitting reminded him that she was still very much at the starting post of life, with her race still to be run.

Still stroking Nessa's head, he whispered. 'The fairies will come back for you soon, *cariad*. They will make you new again.'

Without bothering to open her eyes, Nessa banged her tail, just once, on the ground. *Duw, that'll be good.* After a moment she banged it again. *Anything I can do for you before I go?*

'You might have a word with Malen,' he said. 'Teach her to knit a bit faster, will you? It's his other foot I'm worried about, see, Ness. She'll never manage to knit two socks before January, the rate she's going.'

He slanted a covert glance at his wife to make sure she was smiling. 'And,' he went on, 'if it's not too hard for you, Ness, I'd like you to teach her to speak again.' He rolled off his knees to the side of his thigh, settling in for a long chat. 'It's not for my sake, Ness; I love her the way she is. But I am not as important as I thought, *cariad*; not as wise, not as . . . good. I've thought only of myself.'

He stretched out on the mat, turning his back to Malen lest she think he was pushing her down a road she could not take.

'It was an error I walked into with my eyes wide open, Ness, thinking it was right and that there could be no harm in it. If you have nothing to do with other people, how can you hurt them, or they hurt you? The thing I'd forgotten is that people are meant to be sociable: not just to be nice to each other – I don't mean that – but to make comparisons, observations, to measure themselves against each other. I thought I could learn about myself up here, Ness, on my own, with only you and the mountain to advise me. But, in the end, what have you told me? Only what I wanted to hear. And that's wrong, *cariad*. That's very wrong.'

He talked of his mother, who had nagged his poor dada into his grave, calling him a spineless fool, an impractical dreamer, a man with no power, no talent, no hope. Even as a young boy Rhodri had seen truth in it, but he'd thought she'd made him like that: bowed down with words a man who had once been tall and strong.

Strong! He was never strong! Tall, I'll grant you, but what good's that, except to pick apples?

His father had been a poet – a good one, too, when he was drunk enough – but when Rhodri had come to love the written word (deeming it a safe alternative to the spoken one), his mother had turned on him with spite in her eyes and sneered: 'Oh, there's lovely. Just like your da.'

'She scared the life out of me, Ness,' he said. 'I didn't want to be like him; I still don't – I'd rather be dead. But I didn't know it was in his blood. I thought it was all . . . her. And I wouldn't let her do it to me. I wouldn't let anyone do it to me. I was going to be my own man; to live alone and be strong, to evaluate myself for what I truly *was*, not what someone else told me I could be.'

194

He swallowed. 'That's why I chose Malen, Ness. She thinks I came to her by chance, but there was no chance involved. It was choice. My choice. You see what I'm telling you, don't you? What was an affliction for her was a gift for me; what was torment for her was balm to my soul. I chose the one woman on earth who couldn't tell me I was *wrong*. Well, now I've told myself. And I hope you'll tell Malen, before you leave us, Ness. She's only seventeen. Her whole life is before her and she can't live it all in silence with no one to turn to but me. What if I should die? What if I should leave her and the baby all alone?'

He shook his head. 'But it isn't only that, Ness. She's . . . a woman. She needs other women to teach her, to guide her. And she'll soon be a mother. How will she help her child if she can't speak to it, teach it, warn it out of danger when it strays too near the fire?'

He kept meaning to turn to Malen, to see how she was taking all of this, but he'd been scratching Nessa's ear all the while, and every time he stopped she nudged him with her paw: *Keep going, bach. If this is dying, I think I'll do more of it.*

'I haven't realised this all at once,' Rhodri continued gently. 'I thought I had; there was a moment, just after the lady doctor left, when everything fell into place and I understood. But in fact I'd known it all along without *wanting* to know. I'd seen every part of it before, seen it as you see the stars, Ness, without knowing their names, their myths or their seasons, without being able to identify one from another. But there's no getting away from it: I *knew*. And this is what you must try to tell Malen, Nessa. That there is a part of her mind that *knows* how to speak and if she tries . . . If she wants it enough for herself and the baby, she can find it again. Will you tell her that, Ness? Will you tell her?'

Ness opened her eyes, licked his wrist and rolled over on her back with a blissful sigh. *Consider it done*, she said. *Now, do my front, will you?*

CHAPTER THIRTY-NINE

Owen hadn't yet finished Glyn Caldwell's book. He'd been almost there, but just at the part where Rhodri became jealous of the lady doctor, he'd lost heart and become jealous on his own account . . . of Glyn. Glyn had it all worked out. He knew so much about himself. He'd grown up somewhere along the way and left Owen at the starting post: forty years old and still a child. No . . . it wasn't jealousy (not only jealousy) which had stopped him, but fear. Fear of the book, as well as of its author. Fear . . . that his questions would reap the wrong answers.

Yet he'd been given more answers, these past few weeks, than he'd ever thought to ask questions about and they hadn't hurt. They'd closed wounds, not opened new ones. And the odd thing was that while the unasked questions had festered and burned like ulcers on his skin, the answers had settled in the quiet deeps of his unconscious and gone peacefully to sleep there. It was almost as if the answers didn't matter. Only the questions mattered.

'And the next question is,' he murmured. 'Where do I go from here?'

He went house-hunting. The real kind was harder than the fantasy variety. It involved fork-tongued estate agents and their gormless receptionists, road maps and addresses, frustrating hours when you drove around in circles in search of 'Dunroamin', only to be told by the postman that you'd passed it three miles back, but the nameplate had dropped off.

He'd stipulated, 'quiet and rural' and twice found himself looking at properties in the middle of town. He'd stipulated, 'small house, large outbuildings', yet was sent to view places with nine bedrooms and a garden shed.

Gwen accompanied him during the first week of his search and, in spite of the setbacks, made a game of it, made him laugh, made him forget that he was diving into a whirlpool. She also reminded him that, where house-hunting was concerned, men and women had very different standards. He was looking for structural particulars – sound timber and stonework, signs of damp, dry-rot or jerry-building. She was looking for draughts, dirt-traps and storage space – a few dozen things, in fact, that would never have crossed his mind.

Gwen wasn't with him when he found the place he liked, but by that time he'd memorised most of her requirements (back door opposite front door equals wind-tunnel and where do you keep the hoover?) and had almost forgotten his fear of the whirlpool.

He thought at first that in finding the right house he'd also found his third (or was it fourth?) case of Alzheimer's, for the elderly vendor – a Mrs Whittaker – called him 'father' throughout, smiling as if she'd known him all her life and loved him well.

The house was full of mirrors, and he glanced furtively into every one of them, first to check that he wasn't wearing a dog-collar, and then to count his wrinkles and grey hairs. He wouldn't have minded so much if she'd been sixteen, but she was eighty, at least, and built like a sparrow, with a sparrow's mischievous gleam in her eye. He began to wonder if she was winding him up.

But the house was perfect. The date of its building – 1793 – had been carved into the door lintel and since then the place had been modernised only to the extent of acquiring a 1930s bathroom, a few Victorian fireplaces and a lean-to kitchen at the back. Mrs Whittaker had lived there since her marriage, fifty-three years ago, and (if the evidence was to be believed) had never taken a day off polishing it since then. It had been re-roofed in the sixties and re-wired in the eighties. As far as Owen could tell, everything else was original and still as sound as a nut.

After showing him the bathroom and bedrooms, Mrs Whittaker warned him for the second time to be careful on the stairs, which, innocent of carpet, were polished to a dark, oaken glow. It was when she said, 'Mind your step, now, father,' as if he was ninety and stone-blind, that Owen at last plucked up courage to ask gently, 'Why do you call me father?'

She looked up at him, startled, and then quickly turned away, jerking her chin as if he'd insulted her. 'I didn't catch your name,' she said abruptly. 'Hopeless with names, I am.'

'Owen Read,' he said. 'Call me Owen, if you like.'

But she didn't call him anything after that.

Outside, in an acre of neglected ground which had once been a farmyard – 'Just poultry and pigs, you know. My husband was very fond his pigs; like dogs, they are, when you get to know them,' – was a substantial barn, a smaller building which would serve as a garage, and the bramble-grown ruin of the pigsties.

There was also a view which could have illustrated a book of fairytales. A jagged line of blue mountains, a patchwork of wheatfields and pastures and, in the centre of it all, a silver lake that might well have secreted Rhodri's Fairy Bride.

'My God,' he breathed. 'How can you bring yourself to leave all this?'

'Oh,' Mrs Whittaker said. 'It's easy enough when the time comes. We lived here fifty years together, and I miss him as much now as on the day he died. He waits for me around every corner, and when I turn the corner he's not there. Better in a bungalow, I think, don't you?'

It was ridiculous to envy her her grief, and yet he did. He envied, too, the habit of a lifetime that had made her call him 'father,' as if the old man were still there.

'Fifty years,' he echoed wistfully. 'It's a long time to love someone, Mrs Whittaker.'

'Oh, *Duw,*' she said. 'I can't say I really loved him all that much. I just got used to him over the years, knew his ways, his moods, his little habits. He drove me mad, half the time. But you can get used to that, too, and when it's gone you keep looking for it, feeling the tug of it, like a hook. And there's no sense being hooked to something that's gone away, is there? Even at my age, you've got to shake it off and move on.'

Owen smiled. 'I'll buy that.'

'You can have it for nothing,' she said. 'It goes with the house.'

CHAPTER FORTY

Until she ceased to speak to him, Rhodri hadn't known that Malen could speak. He'd known only that he could hear, read, guess at her thoughts and feelings and, like the sun on a rill, turn silent ice to singing water. But when she ceased to speak to him, he learned again that he was not as important as he'd thought.

She'd spoken with her eyes: in the flash of them, the glow of them, in the casting up or the casting down, in sideways glances, in blinking, narrowing, widening, staring, in batting her lashes or quirking her brows. She'd spoken with the turn of her head, with the tilt of her neck, the shrug of her shoulders and the set of her spine. She'd spoken with her mouth as she smiled or pouted, bit her lip, bared her teeth. She'd spoken with her hands.

Yet when he first noticed she'd ceased to speak to him, it was her voice he missed: the thin, wailing cry which had called him to his meals, cutting through the wind like an Alpine yodel so that even when he failed to hear it, Garth would hear and nudge him home.

But on the day of the lady doctor's visit, Malen didn't call and when hunger drove him home to ask what was wrong he found his dinner waiting – stone cold – on the table. Surprised, he looked at Malen, who looked beyond him with a strange, trance-like gaze in which he could read nothing of her thoughts.

'I didn't hear you call, Malen. Malen? Did you call?'

Her gaze slid across him, without seeing him. He could not have believed that a human face could be so quiet, so still, so utterly wiped of feeling. She was like a sucked egg: the same in every particular as the whole, except that it was empty.

'*Be' sy'n bod, cariad?*' He knelt at her feet and took her hand. 'Malen? What's wrong with you? What has happened?'

Then, in the infinitesimal flicker of her eyes, she told him. *Leave me alone. I hate you.*

But he'd been wrong before.

'Malen?' he whispered. 'Are you ill? Do you hurt somewhere?'

She withdrew her hand from his and, gazing steadily at the wall, walked silently away.

He was astonished at the speed with which his fear turned to fury. His heart leapt with it, his throat ached with it, his limbs sizzled with a burning heat that made him want to yell out and break things – beginning with Malen's neck.

He spent the rest of the day walking the mountain and the endless evening sitting, crag-like, on the peak they called the Devil's Horn, watching the sun set beyond the distant sea in a torment of fire and ashes. His rage had not died, only deepened and darkened, as the sky must do when the sun has gone. How could she hate him? How could she *dare* to hate him? And what had he *said* that she should hate him for it? He'd been confessing his wrongs, not boasting of them! How could she not understand that he'd been trying . . . to heal her, to tell her that it was for her sake, not his, that he wanted her to speak. That he loved her as she was . . .

Didn't I tell you I love you? Didn't I tell you a thousand times?

And lied a thousand times, for until today he'd never been certain it was true. Until today he'd loved only the beauty of her, the mystery of her. Loved . . . the *nothing* of her. While he'd thought she could not speak, she'd been an empty page. He could write what he liked there, creating her as he chose. She'd had no power except the power he could allow her. She'd had no voice except the voice he could bear to hear.

The sun had gone and beyond the furthest ridge of the furthest mountain great banks of purple clouds were building, bringing the rain. Above them and a little to the south hung a pale sickle moon. And at its foot a single star.

> *Twinkle, twinkle, little star,*
> *How I wonder what you are.*

But he hadn't wondered. He hadn't wanted to read what was already written. *You think he's defiled her?* Yes. He'd wanted a virgin. He had failed to grasp that violation was at the heart of the person she now was, not the shell, something he could discard as of no account. Her silence was the shell, an armour so tough that nothing could penetrate, nothing ever hurt again the woman she was inside.

Who made her mute?

She had. That was her strength, that was her power. Everything she was flowed through it: cleaner and sweeter for being expressed through her acts, not her words. No pretences, no excuses. No compromises. She was living as he'd always wanted to live: *Take me or leave me. This is all there is.*

'Oh, dear,' he whispered. 'What has she done to me?'

Made a man of you, the mountain said.

She was standing at the sink and did not turn when he spoke to her. He stood close at her back and folded his arms around her. 'I told Ness,' he said softly, 'That I love you as you are, Malen; a bit on the quiet side, yes, but also . . .'

Against her limp resistance, he turned her to face him and, when she failed to meet his eyes, bent his knees to observe the tiny responses she could not hide. But there were tears in her eyes which spoke not of the anger he'd assumed but of a deep, clawing hurt, worse than anything that had hurt her before. So that was his 'shell' theory scuppered and perhaps every other theory, too. The only thing he was certain of now was that *he* had done this to her and the secret of it was . . .

'But you are deep and strong,' he went on hesitantly. 'As I have always wanted to be . . . And failed to be.'

A tear slid from her eye and plopped to the front of her blouse, which gaped between its buttons over the growing swell of her breasts. This observation sneaked into his mind by the back door – only her tears knocked boldly at the front – and long, anxious seconds passed before he heard it hissing, *She's pregnant, you fool. Remember?*

She was pregnant! She was expecting his baby! Six months from now, she would hold the child in her arms without being able to speak its name. Two years from now, she would see it toddle towards the fire and not be able to call it back!

'Oh, Malen,' he groaned. 'What a fool I have been. Listen, my love. Listen to me, now. You are strong and you are capable, you are loving and good. With speech or without it, you will be the finest mother there ever was. For what are words, *cariad*? You will speak to him with your eyes and your hands, you will teach him as you have taught me, with tenderness and patience. And you will sing to him, Malen: songs of the stars and the clouds and the rain. Songs . . . of silence.'

He smiled and kissed her. 'I was wrong to ask you to speak,' he said. 'As wrong as if I'd asked you to be tall, or to change the colour of your eyes. I kept thinking about the girl you used to be, and you are not that girl any more. You have passed through fire

201

and become someone else. Someone finer and stronger. Someone better.'

He led her to a chair and pulled her into his lap. He held her head to his chest, where she could hear the beat of his heart and be comforted.

'You know the story of Branwen,' he said, 'and the Cauldron of Rebirth?'

She frowned. *Remind me.*

'Branwen's brother, the giant Bendigeidfran, gave this cauldron to her husband, Matholwch, as a wedding gift. A magical gift, Malen, for into the cauldron he could lay his slain warriors and have them emerge alive and stronger than before, save only that they could not speak. *Alive*, Malen, and *stronger* than before. Try to think of it like that, *cariad*, not as a curse, but—'

Malen stiffened suddenly and stood up, turning her back to him. Rhodri bit his lip on despair. The story – one of the most ancient of tales – was a tragedy, not a romance, and of course she must know it; no one educated in Wales could fail to know that the magic of the cauldron had been turned against Branwen and that everyone – Branwen included – had died in the end. Even her child had been hurled into the fire.

But he hadn't meant to tell her that!

'Malen,' he sighed. 'Oh, Malen . . .'

He touched her shoulder and she shook him off. *Leave me alone!*

There was nothing more he could do.

He stood at the door with his hands in his pockets, staring out over the mountain. He'd been wrong in his forecast of rain and the wind was no more than a zephyr, lacking breath even to whisper its name. The sun was hot on his face, the air scented with wild thyme and dry earth. The heather was in bloom and the grass at its sweetest, clothing the ground with wine-coloured tweed and green linen. But Rhodri saw none of it. And he heard only silence.

Silence. The very word pained him. It made his heart thump as though with fright, or with a dreadful grief that he must bear all his days without comfort. Strange that it should hurt him so. Stranger still that when he'd lived alone there'd been no such thing as silence. The whole world had spoken to him, had sung to him, if only to echo his own songs, his own thoughts and feelings.

He walked out from the door, for the first time in his life going nowhere, wanting only to put a space between himself and Malen, to be alone again. Even the thought that she might be watching him was an irritation, making him feel as vulnerable as if she'd aimed a gun at his back.

He gained a low ridge and ran down the other side, feeling the mountain rise at his back until it swallowed him and he was free. Free to be himself again: Rhodri Thomas Mountain, hermit, poet, *bachelor*, tenor.

I'll care for nobody, no, not I . . .

But it was no longer true. He cared. And that was why the echoes had gone, because his own voice was no longer enough for him. It had failed him. He was listening for another, now.

And now, for the first time, he began to wonder who Malen really was and what she might have been had Roberts never touched her.

Very tidy; she had ambitions.

What sort of ambitions? Librarian? No. She'd look terrible in Enid Griffiths's glasses. Opera singer: exquisitely dying in *La Traviata*, or dancing the flamenco in *Carmen*? No, no . . . The roles didn't fit; she looked silly, somehow; and silly was the last thing you could say about Malen. Practical, Malen was. Capable. Sensible. Of all the things she'd tried since he'd married her, quick knitting was the only one she still couldn't do.

He walked on, more slowly now, aware of a curious sickness, a crawling dread, which meant, he knew, that he was approaching the truth: a truth he'd known almost from the beginning and rejected out of hand. Malen had no poetry in her. She had no romance. She knew life for what it was – had learned it the hard way – and the first thing she'd learned was that words would never change it.

Her hair was red as blood, her skin as white as milk, and she wore a gown of silver thread, a veil of finest silk.

Damn silly rubbish! He'd married a woman, not a bloody fairy!

A woman. Like his mother. Words had changed nothing for her, either. She'd managed to spit them out well enough – nineteen to the dozen with never a pause for breath – and yet, in her way, she'd been as mute as Malen was, if only because she'd deafened everyone else.

There was no point in saying what nobody heard; no point in writing what nobody read. Better to keep your teeth shut and use your pen to stir your tea. At least then someone might *wonder* what you were thinking.

He'd never wondered what his mother was thinking; it had seemed too obvious at the time. It seemed just as obvious now . . . But the two were different and it was too late to go back and give her a different answer. It was not too late for Malen.

As he'd intended, his walk had put miles between them, but the space had begun to ache a little, as if she'd tied a string to his heart that tugged him home. She needed him. She had no one else . . .

Where the shallow bed of a rill had broken, spilling its waters into shining blue pools, he sat for a while until his mind emptied and filled again with music: trickling water, humming bees, a lark, singing.

> *Dear thoughts are in my mind*
> *And my soul soars enchanted,*
> *As I hear the sweet lark sing . . .*

He sighed.

Malen had enchanted him. The odd thing was that when it had first touched him, her enchantment had been, like the lark's, in her voice. Solid gold. No, fairy gold, for it had turned to dust and blown away. Yet when he counted the times he'd loved her, when his heart had swelled with pride in her and the thought of losing her was madness, she'd been no fairy, but a woman, reaching out from the dark regions of pain to take a fresh grasp on mortality. Cobwebs over the dresser, wet linen, soapy floor. Malen feeding the sheep, Malen calling him home.

She helped him on the farm, kept the house like a shining pin . . . And she had a wonderful touch with pastry. Apple tart, bacon turnovers, cheese and onion pie. The farmer almost forgot what it was like to eat only on Wednesdays.

Rhodri bowed his head, sickness and truth welling up in him so strong he thought he would die of it. Wednesday half-closing. He'd only said it to make her smile, meaning to lose it on the way, yet out of that change had come a dozen others . . .

He jumped to his feet.

O, Duw, Duw . . . He'd told that tale out of his own mouth, without listening to a word of it, neither knowing nor guessing

204

that it was the tale of his own life! Before Malen, he'd been starving! Before Malen, he'd had nothing!

And if he should lose her now . . .?

He turned towards home. He heard the wind, trapped in a hollow of the hills, crying to be let out.

'Rhodri! *Rhodri!*'

But there was no wind . . . He stopped in his tracks and stared wildly into space. His heart slammed against his ribs as if it would burst.

'Malen?' he whispered.

He saw her then – hot, lost and bedraggled in a gully far below – her hands at her mouth, not biting them, but touching them to her lips, wonderingly, as though to trace the taste of blood.

CHAPTER FORTY-ONE

It was easier to 'shake things off and move on' when you knew where you were going. Owen was amazed to find how easy it all was. It was as if past and future were the pans of a simple scale that had tipped out of balance. Too much in the past had meant he'd had no future. Now, too much in the future meant he had no past.

'At least, none worth worrying about,' he told Gwen, who was lying on the bed, watching him pack. 'I know it'll all level out eventually, but at the moment all I can think about is where I'm going, not where I came from. I'm . . .' He uttered an astonished puff of laughter. 'I'm happy! Hey, how about that?'

Gwen affected a sulky pout. 'It's all right for some,' she said. 'What about me? I'm going back to work, you're going back to London—'

'I won't be gone long. Two weeks, thereabouts.'

'And then when you move out to Pen-y-Coed—'

'It's only twelve miles. A half-hour's drive. What's that?'

'It'll feel like fifty in the winter, *bach*. Ice and snow, freezing fog, dark nights. I'll never see you.'

She was probably right, but the thought didn't depress him as he felt it should. The future that was opening up for him – the immediate future, at least – didn't seem to include Gwen, or, for that matter, anyone else. Getting his life in order, putting down new roots – like his first walk on the mountain, it was something he needed to do alone.

No; better to put it the other way around: being alone was something he needed to *do*, if only to prove he could do it. He'd imagined it a thousand times: simple things, like getting up when he liked, eating what he liked, wearing what he liked. (He'd already decided to send his suits to Oxfam.) Deeper things, like learning, working, making decisions by himself, for himself, without having to consider another living soul.

But now he imagined it again and knew that something vital was missing. She was lying on the bed at the moment, looking about as vital as the bed, which he'd stripped to the mattress and covered with a dust-sheet. The future that was opening up for him would be empty if she wasn't in it and he realised now that she'd been there in all his previous imaginings, waiting for him around every corner. Yes, he needed to do it alone. But only as one needs to choose a gift alone, for the purer pleasure of giving it.

'Snow and ice, nothing,' he said. 'I'll dig my way through.'

'Oh, there's heroic.'

'I might even fly.' He laughed and spread out his arms, as if to take wing from a road-side post. 'Like a buzzard.'

Softer and sadder, Gwen's voice joined the echo of his own. 'Free.'

She'd closed her eyes and he stood over her for a moment, watching her, understanding everything she'd said in a single word.

'Free,' he repeated softly. 'But only because of you, Gwenhwyfar Jones. Only because I love you.'

'You said it right,' she whispered. 'Oh, I'll miss you, Owen . . .'

'But not for long. I'm good with a shovel, honest.'

She laughed and was back to normal, brisk and cheerful, folding her arms for a gossip. She asked him his plans for the house at Pen-y-Coed and as they talked he went on packing, barely noticing what he was doing until the suitcase was full.

He smiled and shook his head. 'I used to take three days to pack a suitcase.'

She peered critically at the bundled heap of socks and shirts and shaving tackle. 'What went wrong?'

'Life's too short.' He closed the case and sat on it. 'I've only just discovered that. It seemed long enough before.'

'You wanted to die, you mean?'

'No . . . I just used to gaze longingly at double-decker buses.' He grinned. 'But I've shaken it off, Gwen. I've moved on.'

She said nothing. He thought she was pondering the significance of double-decker buses, or that of his packed suitcase, all zipped and strapped and ready to go. He had to keep reminding himself that she didn't *know* he'd come back, and that this was all grief for her until he did. It was hard to believe she could want him so much. That anyone could want him so much, let alone someone like Gwen.

'Shaken Glyn off, too?' she asked off-handedly.

The question shocked him. He hadn't exactly forgotten Glyn, just put him out of his mind for a while until it became realistic to worry. Three weeks, a month. He probably hadn't had the letter

207

yet, let alone thought to reply. Yet now that he thought of him again, he found him – as he often found Jonty and Em – in a small, aching knot under his heart.

'No,' he said. 'I haven't shaken him off. But I've done all I can. The rest is for him to decide. And if he decides against getting in touch I think I can handle it.' He smiled and shrugged, putting a brave face on it. 'What's a brother, after all? What's your sister, to you?'

Gwen rubbed the end of her nose. 'Like this bloody thing,' she said. 'It's too big, too ugly. It glows in the dark. But I'd be lost without it. Uglier without it, too. There'd just be a great, smelly hole in my face, wouldn't there?'

He flopped down beside her on the bed, knowing that although he wouldn't have a great, smelly hole in his face, he'd still have this ache under his heart, this longing to know. 'That was a bitch of a book,' he said irritably. 'He made you care. He made you care what happened to them. And then he didn't damn well *tell* you! Did she speak or didn't she?'

Gwen opened her mouth and shut it again as he went on angrily, 'I can't see the point of it all! What was it meant to *tell* anyone?'

Gwen bit her lip on a grin. 'I don't think it was meant to *tell* anyone anything, Owen. I think that *was* the point.'

Owen was usually quite good at getting the fictional message, but he hadn't read that book as he'd read any other. He'd been looking for answers. And he'd found . . . Bugger all.

'I don't get it,' he confessed wearily. 'Tell me, will you, Gwen? What happened to them?'

'To your parents, you mean?'

'No! Rhodri and . . .'

But they were the same thing. He'd convinced himself even before he'd read the book that they were the same thing and although reason had popped up at regular intervals to tell him they were different, he'd called it a liar every time.

'I suppose they died,' he said. 'Mrs Caldwell said they died. But how? When? And *why*?'

'Carelessness, p'raps. New baby, nappies put to dry on the fireguard, a flying spark . . .'

Owen's heart leapt. He turned to look at her, his eyes wide and staring. But he didn't see Gwen. He saw a dark sky and a red sunset. A fire beyond the horizon. A *fire*. Oh, of course . . .

'What do you mean?' he breathed.

'Glyn wrote to me.' She lowered her eyes, almost guiltily. 'I had the letter this morning. That's why I came over, actually. I've just been waiting for the right moment.'

'He wrote to *you*? Why you?'

'I suppose because you told him you knew me.'

'But why didn't he write to *me*?'

'He doesn't know you, Owen. He doesn't know what kind of man you are. Just because you look like him doesn't mean you're the same, and for once in his life . . .'

'Yes?'

'He's been sensitive enough to realise it.' She paused. 'Well, to tell the truth, I think he's protecting his own feelings as much as yours. Have you imagined what it'll be like, for instance, meeting him for the first time?'

'Yes, of course . . .' He hesitated, knowing this wasn't, strictly, true. The scene he'd imagined had been their third or, perhaps, twentieth meeting, when all had been said that needed to be said and there was nothing to talk about beyond women, politics and the Triple Crown – things you could discuss without touching too many raw spots. He hadn't imagined the first time because he was certain it would be agony.

'No, I suppose not,' he said.

'No. Neither had I, but now that I do, I think the best it could be is bloody awful. I mean, you're not likely to rush into each other's arms, are you? You'll just stand there, and . . .' She raised her eyes to the ceiling and although Owen followed her gaze, he found nothing there to reassure him. They'd just stand there and blush, mumble things about the weather . . .

'Glyn's had longer to think about it, of course,' Gwen went on. 'And he's had help. He says the adoption people give you counselling before they—'

'I know that! But they haven't answered my letter, yet! Does he expect me to wait, for God's sake? Look, if he *knows*—'

'Now, now. Be patient, *bach*. Let it happen in the right order, will you?' She leaned over him, stroking his hair with a soft, motherly hand. '*I'm* counselling you, so behave yourself and listen. Are you sure you *want* a brother, to start with? He isn't a bit like you, you know, except to look at.'

'I don't want him to be like me. That's the last thing I want.'

'Why not? You're a good man, Owen.'

'And Glyn's not? Is that what you're saying?'

He heard the defensiveness of his tone and knew that he needed all the counselling she could give him. Without saying or thinking a word of it, the message he was conveying – and feeling – was, *Don't wreck my dreams*!

'Sorry,' he said. 'Go on.'

'All I'm saying is he's different from you. You might not like him, Owen . . . And he might not like you. You've got to be prepared for that.'

'I am prepared. You've counselled me already, remember? Through Eluned.'

'Yes, but I forgot to mention something about Eluned. I love her, Owen, and she loves me. The only reason she doesn't give me anything is because she hasn't got it to give. But *if* she had it, Owen, she'd give it a thousand times over. I can't say the same about Glyn: first because he doesn't love you, second because he doesn't know you and third . . .'

'Because he left his mother? That's everything, is it? No fault on her side, for instance?'

Gwen heaved a sigh. 'All right,' she admitted wearily. 'I'm not being fair. And it's *not* all his fault. She spoiled him rotten, made him think he was God Almighty—'

'And then let him find out he was nothing!'

She sighed again. 'Did you notice where Rhodri said his mother had loved him too much?'

'Yes. I also noticed that he added, "You can't be loved too much. Love makes you strong," which sounds to me suspiciously like gratitude. People *change*, Gwen. You haven't seen him for twenty years. He might have changed.'

'Well, no . . .' She stretched it out until Owen glared at her, wanting to shake her, like a salt cellar, to hasten the flow.

'It's eight years,' she said. 'For his mother it's twenty. I shared a flat with him, actually, when I was in college in London. Before my dad died, this was.'

'You *lived* with him?' Owen sat up, snatching himself from her embrace with a violence he regretted when she laughed and sat up, too, resting her cheek in the hollow of his shoulder.

'Shared a flat with him, stupid. There was never any danger of anything else.'

'Why not?'

She shrugged. 'Didn't fancy him.'

Owen suspected sour grapes and, in other circumstances, might have cared enough to mention it; but there was something he cared about more. 'Did he tell you he was adopted? Have you known all along?'

'No. It didn't even cross my mind until you told me about yourself. Even then I had doubts, if only because . . . Well, you do look like him, but it's all on the surface, Owen. You're so different in other ways; the physical resemblance completely fades after a while. Anyway, even if I had known, it wasn't my place to say anything, was it? Only Glyn – or Joyce – had the right to tell you something they'd told no one else.'

Almost in spite of himself, Owen abandoned his sour grapes theory. She was just trying to protect him from his fantasies.

'Okay,' he said. 'We're different. I accept that. But in what *ways* are we different? I want to know what he's *like*, Gwen!'

Gwen shrugged. 'Oh, well that's obvious, isn't it? He's exactly like Rhodri: arrogant, selfish, self-centred—'

Owen struggled to sit up again, but Gwen pinned him down, digging her chin into his chest to look into his face and laugh.

'Oh, you missed all that, did you? What book were you reading, then? *Mary Poppins*?'

He groaned and rolled away from her, but already he felt a kind of relief settling inside him. He wished he knew someone who'd read the book without preconceptions, who could judge it for what it was, without knowing or wanting anything more. He wondered whether an independent reader would have seen Rhodri's faults, or completely overlooked them, as he had, loving him regardless, as if he were a brother. Arrogant, selfish, self-centred? Yes, Rhodri had been all of those things. But he'd known it all along, had struggled with it, *tried* to change it. And that meant—

'But *Glyn* wrote it!' he said. 'Glyn *wrote* it, Gwen.'

'Yes,' she said gently. 'I know.'

'So he *has* changed, hasn't he? *I've* changed.'

'But you're still the same man; that's all I'm trying to tell you. You haven't changed into someone else; you've just accepted the man you are and were and always will be. That man isn't perfect, Owen, and the things that were wrong with him before will be wrong again if he isn't careful. The same is true of Glyn. He may have accepted himself, learned to live with himself, I mean, as you have. But it doesn't mean he'll know how to live with *you*. And

211

then how will you feel? Rejected again? Abandoned? Left out in the cold?'

She was right. In spite of everything she'd said about Eluned, he'd imagined Glyn as one might imagine Paradise, a world apart but still attainable, a world one could inhabit that was better than one's own. And of course it wasn't. He and Glyn were *two* people, not one, their worlds not merely different but separated by light-years. The best they could do was twinkle at each other across the divide – or perhaps wiggle noses, as Gwen and Eluned did. *Come in, come in. Are you receiving me?*

That was the important thing: to keep receiving, keep *trying* to understand. And that was what that sodding book had been about, after all: not the gift of speech but the gift of hearing. Rhodri hadn't had it; he'd been too in love with his own voice to hear anyone else's. He'd even got the town gossips wrong, and the chances were he'd never understood a word Malen had said until she'd 'stopped speaking to him'. Then he'd ceased to hear his own voice and heard hers, at last. Very neat.

'Did Glyn tell you to say all that?' he asked. 'It was good, Gwen. You're wasted on teaching.'

She grinned. 'Good? It was bloody brilliant! And no, he didn't tell me to say it. He couldn't. That's why he wrote to me, because I know you and he doesn't. He just said, "Tell him I'm not Father Christmas. And tell him, if he can get it down the chimney, I want a mountain bike."'

Owen laughed and cried on the same breath, but stopped doing both – stopped breathing, too – as Gwen said briskly, 'I'll tell you about your parents now, shall I?'

He stared at her, suddenly afraid, and she gathered him into her arms and added firmly, 'But first I'll tell you why Glyn wrote the book. When he found out he'd been adopted he was scared, Owen, like you were. He wanted to know, but he didn't want to know. He wrote to the adoption agency a hundred times in his mind, but he didn't actually do it until he was twenty-eight, eleven years later. It was a huge relief, he says. He thought he was going to find out everything about them . . . But he didn't. Just their names, their ages, where they lived . . . He was told he had a brother and that his brother was two when he was six weeks old. His brother was called Owain – not Owen – and he was called Glyn, so that's where that came from. No wonder Joyce hates it. It's the ultimate rejection, isn't it?'

Owen shook his head. She didn't understand. No one could

understand who hadn't felt the same and already he was rehearsing the Welsh version of his name: Owain, O-wine. It was all they'd left him.

'Did he—? Did he try to find me?'

'Yes and no. The agency wouldn't give him any details about your adoption; they had to respect your privacy, they said. Glyn understood that, of course, but he was angry; he felt cheated, even worse than he had before – and that's why he wrote the book. He was reinventing them for himself, he says, drawing pictures of them in his mind: a man he could call his father, a woman he could call his mother. So it was all fiction, *cariad*. The only truth in it – the only truth that would be recognised in a court of law, that is – is that they were hill farmers and that their names were Rhodri and Malen Thomas. He was thirty; she was twenty-four.'

She propped herself on her elbow to look intently into his face. 'How do you feel?'

Everything. Nothing. Too much and too little.

'Okay,' he said.

'You sure?'

He nodded.

'Right. I'm going off on a bit of a tangent, now. Glyn told me to, so you mustn't get impatient. There are two kinds of hill farmers, Owen: the ones you see in the Station Arms and the ones you don't. When Glyn was little – when I was, too, but not so much – you'd sometimes see the second kind doing their bits of shopping in town. You could easily recognise them because they looked so different, like people from another age – thirty or forty years back. Shy, secret people, they were. The bank managers and market auctioneers might have known their names, but no one else did. They seemed to drift in on the wind and drift out again the same way. They don't really exist any more. They've all got Land Rovers and telephones now – and the bloody telly, of course – but in the fifties and sixties and for generations before that, they lived up in the hills all alone and spoke to no one from one week's end to the next. Beautiful they were, Owen; like saints some of them. Look into their eyes . . . I know what Glyn meant when he was describing Rhodri's eyes, but he didn't get it right. They weren't like jewels or forget-me-nots; they weren't even blue, necessarily. Just deep, deep . . . *deep*.' She sighed.

'And my – Glyn's parents were like that?'

'He thinks so. They left no word of themselves, you see, Owen.

213

He found two people who remembered them, who'd actually *met* them, I mean. And the one said, "He was tall; he had a limp . . . I think." And the other said, "No, I don't recollect they ever *said* anything."

'They'd met them, but all they really remembered was the way they died. And Glyn had already found out about that in the newspaper.'

'About the fire?'

'Yes.' She began again to stroke his hair, her hand as gentle as the soft, soothing timbre of her voice. 'The house burned to the ground, you see, Owen. That was the worst of it, Glyn says, that there was nothing left to tell him who they were. Books, photographs, letters, clothes, maybe even the little shaving mirror you remembered . . . All gone. Yet Rhodri – your father, I mean – was a poet . . .'

'He *was*?' Owen rocked up on his knees and spun around around to face her. 'Are there any books, any—?'

'Hush. Don't get excited, now. He wasn't famous; he wasn't even all that good, Glyn says. He had three poems published in the local rag, and that's all Glyn could find, so it's unlikely there were any more.'

'Did he send you any copies? Can I read them?'

Gwen smiled pityingly. 'They're in Welsh, you fool. *He* was Welsh. What's he want to write poems in bloody English for? Welsh *is* poetry!'

'Ah.' He guessed he must look stricken, because Gwen's smile suddenly sweetened and she held his hands and squeezed them, loving him, listening to him, understanding everything.

'It's all right,' she said gently. 'Glyn's doing a translation for you, so he's not so bad, I suppose.'

He curved his body into her arms.

'There was something else they left, *cariad*, better than any number of poems. It said in the newspaper that Rhodri must have brought you and Glyn out and gone back for Malen. They didn't make it, of course. And when it was over there were just two little orphans to prove they'd ever lived. But think, now, Owen. What could they have left that was worth as much? Think of your own life, of all the things you've done, the things you've said, the things you possess that might one day tell a stranger what kind of man you are. Not one of them can be compared with the existence of your children, can it?'

'No.'

214

'And – I'm only theorising, so don't correct me – one of them has your eyes and the other your smile. One has your hands and the other your memory. But where did *your* hands come from? Or Glyn's talent with words? Look into your mind, *cariad*, listen to your voice, look into the mirror and you'll find your parents there. They didn't need to give you anything else. They gave you themselves.'

She went on talking, soothing, comforting, but her voice became a background murmur, still sensible, yet far away, made insignificant by the only words he'd wanted to hear: *Rhodri brought you out. He brought you out.*

'They didn't leave me, then,' he said.

'No. I never believed they did. But I can see why you would have thought it. Your dad put you and Glyn in the *tŷ bach*, down the back, but I suppose you were too frightened to stay there. You ran off down the mountain, all by yourself. Poor little kid. It was hours before they found you.'

His heart thudding, Owen ran through his nightmare again, trying to piece it together, trying to see something beyond the darkness and the lurid sky, the terror. But already it was fading. It was as if it had happened to someone else, some stranger-child of whom he could say, *Poor little kid. It was hours before they found him.*

'Years,' he said. 'I've been running down that bloody mountain all my life.'

Gwen's arms tightened around him. 'Never mind,' she whispered. 'They've found you now.'

They sat in silence for a long time. Owen would have liked the silence to last longer, to carry him, like warm air under the buzzard's wing, on a tireless flight over a perfect world. But Gwen was still rooted to the earth. The silence couldn't carry her.

'So? How d'you feel now?' she asked. 'Better?'

Was that the word for it? He thought it probably was, but it seemed inappropriate, inadequate to describe this peace, this freedom, this . . .

Holy the air, the water and the fire . . .

Poetry again. But then, it ran in his veins. His father had been a poet.

'Or worse?' Gwen added anxiously. 'I suppose you'll see Glyn, will you, when you're in London? I'll give you his letter and the

215

newscuttings he sent me, about the fire and the inquest. Just photocopies they are, of course; he hasn't got the originals . . . Owen? Say something, will you, love?'

He could feel Rhodri's arms around him, his own arms around Jonty and Em – and they were the same thing: a circle, a cycle, Rhodri's first flower of spring, the seed of the seed that renewed itself without end.

'I can't,' he said. 'Words aren't . . .'

What are words on another's tongue?
The night's cry, the star's song,
The moan of the wind on the mountain.

ABOUT HONNO

Honno Welsh Women's Press was set up in 1986 by a group of women who felt strongly that women in Wales needed wider opportunities to see their writing in print and to become involved in the publishing process. Our aim is to publish books by the women of Wales, and our brief encompasses fiction, poetry, children's books, autobiographical writing and reprints of classic titles in English and Welsh.

Honno is registered as a community co-operative and so far we have raised capital by selling shares at £5 a time to over 350 interested women all over the world. Any profit we make goes towards the cost of future publications. We hope that many more women will be able to help us in this way. Shareholders' liability is limited to the amount invested, and each shareholder, regardless of the number of shares held, will have her say in the company and a vote at the AGM. To buy shares or to receive further information about forthcoming publications, please write to:

Honno, 'Ailsa Craig', Heol y Cawl, Dinas Powys,
Bro Morgannwg CF64 4AH.